HEARTS ACROSS FOREVER

MARY MONTAGUE SIKES

HighTide
Publications, Inc.

Deltaville, Virginia

Published by High Tide Publications, Inc.
www.hightidepublications.com

Thank you for purchasing an authorized edition of Hearts Across Forever.

High Tide's mission is to find, encourage, promote, and publish the work of authors. We are a small, woman-owned enterprise that is dedicated to the author over 50. When you buy an authorized copy, you help us to bring their work to you. When you honor copyright law by not reproducing or scanning any part (in any form) without our written permission, you enable us to support authors, publish their work, and bring it to you to enjoy. We thank you for supporting our authors.

Edited by Cindy L. Freeman
Book Design by Jeanne M. Johansen

ISBN: 978-1-945990-25-0
Publisher's Note: This book is a work of fiction. Names, characters, places, and incidents are the product of the author's imagination or used fictitiously. Any resemblence to actual persons (living or dead), businesses, events, or locals is concidential.

Library of Congress Cataloging-in-Publication Data
Sikes, Mary Montague, Hearts Across Forever by Mary Montague Sikes. —2nd edition, revised

1. Americans—Jamaica—Fiction 2. Plantation life—Fiction 3. Reincarnation— Fiction. 4.

Jamaica—Fiction. I. Title

PS3619.I54 H4 2001 813'.6—dc21 2001036452

ACKNOWLEDGMENTS

My appreciation to my daughters, Allison, Alicia, and Amy, who have endured their mother's passion for writing, painting, sculpting, and exploring the paranormal.

My everlasting gratitude to Olen, whom I believe I have known before and that somewhere along the way our hearts have crossed forever.

A Prologue

HOOVES OF TWO powerful horses pounded the rutted roadway leading from Rose Hall Plantation toward Montego Bay. Along one side, the Caribbean Sea lapped against the shore with a soft murmur.

Aunt Annie spurred Raven forward, striking the sleek black stallion with vicious strokes of her riding crop. With each whack, Aimee's heart pounded harder.

"Don't hit him," her heart screamed, but no words came from her mouth. If she said something, anything at all, Annie would turn the full force of the riding crop against her just as she used it to control the plantation slaves.

Aimee's long flaxen hair flew in the wind behind her as her own little mare galloped faster to keep pace with Raven. Soon they passed through the dark and deserted streets of Montego Bay. It was well past midnight, and Aimee was groggy. After all Aunt Annie had dragged her from bed and forced her to dress for the impromptu midnight ride.

"Aimee, tonight you will learn the ways of Jamaica," Annie called back to her. Her eyes were bright and wild, shining like polished ebony in the full moon.

Annie yanked Raven to a sudden halt in a small grove of trees, and Aimee had no choice but to pull up her little mare as well. Aimee stiffened, ever conscious of the dark spell that surrounded her aunt.

As she slid from the saddle, Aimee pressed her hand to her forehead and tried to block the pounding inside her head. Why had she been so foolish? Why had she left England and come to this evil place, far from her family?

Her pulse racing, she watched Annie's eyes flare wide, like a crazed horse and heard her speak in clipped syllables. "In Haiti, I learned much from the priests and priestesses." Her high-pitched laughter echoed against the dark night sky.

"I once knew a high priestess who taught me many secrets." The words hissed through Annie's lips. "She told me, as I am telling you now, dear niece, about the spirits of earth and air that live among us. And, she taught me the secrets of power over the spirits. Perhaps, one day I shall teach you those things as well."

From beneath her dark hood, Annie stared hypnotically toward the hills. "Sometimes in the night, I still hear the Haitian drums tatting in the darkness."

Although the air was not cold, Aimee shivered. Almost as much as the slaves did, she feared the small woman who wore her long dark hair pinned high on her head. The woman claimed to be her aunt, but Aimee was not sure of the exact relationship. She was only certain of Annie's strange ways and her merciless and cruel treatment of the slaves.

Annie's heartless behavior with the slaves was what Aimee hated most about her. Hated.

Yes. That was true.

In the full moonlight, she was more certain than ever. She hated, and feared, Aunt Annie so much, she planned to do something terrible to herself. She would marry a man she did not love.

Aimee set her jaw and followed Aunt Annie. Yes, that is what she must do. She would marry Richard Gordon. Because of his money and position, he would take her away from Aunt Annie and Rose Hall.

Richard owned Gordon Gardens, one of the largest sugar plantations in all of Jamaica. As Richard's wife, she would be beyond the power of Annie Palmer. A knot filled her throat.

Getting away from Aunt Annie was the most important thing in her life. But was it more important than marrying the man she really loved?

Tears slid down Aimee's cheeks. She loved William Hill, loved him more than she could bear to think, but he was only a caretaker who could not take her away from Annie Palmer. Besides, if Annie found out about

William...Aimee choked on the thought. If Annie found out, no place in Jamaica would be safe for either of them.

Aimee straightened her shoulders. She could wait no longer. Tonight's events proved it might already be too late.

"I will show you some fine magic tonight," Annie rasped in a passionate tone. "Follow me and keep still," she ordered.

Leaving their horses tied to a tree, the two women moved like silent shadows toward an ugly little shack at the edge of a clearing. As they reached the unlighted hut, Annie pulled open the creaking door, grabbing Aimee's arm and yanking her inside before she kicked it shut.

"Now you will see," she rasped.

The woman lit a partially burned candle that stood in a holder near the door. She picked up the light and moved it to a small round table—the only other object in the room. Then, she reached into the pocket of her skirt and pulled out a gruesome round object.

Aimee gasped and drew back. She recognized the blood-smeared skull of an animal with a piece of cord attached.

"His cat." Annie laughed. It was a heart-shaking sound.

Moving as if in a trance, the woman groped around the door until she found a wooden projection on which to hang the frightful thing. Then, delving into her other pocket, she drew out a gray clay ball into which bits of broken glass and a large feather from a booby bird were pressed. From the same pocket, she pulled out the doll figure of a man.

Carefully, Annie placed the small figure and the clay ball beneath the cat skull. "He will come here and find this." With a triumphant little laugh that grew to a cackling howl, Annie turned back to face her niece. "Sam will soon regret the moment he thought to defy me. Do not be upset. The power is a good one to have. That you will soon learn."

The shudder that began in Aimee's shoulders reached to the depths of her heart. No. Her mind raced. Annie Palmer must never know about William Hill. She would protect him with her life. She would protect him until the day she died. There was no other way. She would marry Richard as soon as possible.

❀ ❀ ❀

Kathryn Calder sat straight up in her bed. Although the apartment was warm, she shivered as if caught in a snowdrift in the dead of winter.

That dream again. She'd had the same dream almost every night for weeks now.

Kathryn got out of bed and turned on the ceiling light. It was only a dream. But why the same dream? And why did she feel so drained when she awakened?

As she ran the details through her mind, Kathryn sipped a cup of water. Tonight's dream was different. Tonight, Kathryn felt Aimee's anguish as if it were her own. In tonight's dream she was Aimee.

Her face grew cold as ice. Taking a deep breath, Kathryn sat on the edge of her bed. Aimee, the woman in her dream, was so in love with William that she was willing to sacrifice everything—her life, her happiness—for him.

What a wonderful love that would be.

Tears trickled down Kathryn's cheeks. If such a love were possible...

CHAPTER ONE

SEATED BEHIND A wide mahogany desk, Kathryn Calder turned her chair to admire the New York skyline. It felt good to have an office with a dramatic panoramic view of the city.

Her spirits high, Kathryn surveyed the elegant room where polished hardwood floors gleamed beneath accents of expensive Oriental rugs. She enjoyed the light from the wall of windows and admired the three original French Impressionist paintings on the opposite wall that brightened the dark wooden paneling.

She smiled. Triple Gold had rewarded her well with the new office and a new title: Director of Regional Marketing. The nine years she had used her innovative ideas and vast knowledge of computers to expand the company's position in national and international markets led to her promotion. She was proud that now she was on her way toward her goal, a position in upper management.

Kathryn turned back to begin work on a pile of papers on her desk, when her secretary interrupted. "Ms. Calder, Mr. Huntington is here to see you."

She looked up in surprise. "Mr. Huntington?" Bradford Huntington headed the international division. What could he want? "Yes. Please send him in."

Moments later, a tall man with graying hair opened the door. Kathryn stood to welcome him, then offered him a chair across from her.

"I have something important to ask you," he said. "We have what is turning out to be an international emergency in the hotels we operate in Jamaica. Their computer system is in chaos, and I need someone I can count on to straighten it out." Huntington paused and looked her straight in the eye. "I need you, Kathryn."

"Me? I know nothing about Jamaica."

"That doesn't matter. You know plenty about computers and how the system should work. That's what counts."

"I … I don't know what to say." Kathryn knew she was caught in a bind. Whatever Huntington wanted, he would get, and she would have to go along. Still … "I just started my new job with this department."

"Kathryn, the job and this lovely office will wait until you get back. Besides being in Jamaica will be like a vacation for you. You can play during the day and work in the evening."

"Play? That sounds inviting." Kathryn smiled. "Of course, I will go, if that's where you need me."

Huntington smiled. "I knew I could count on you." He stood and reached across the desk to shake her hand. "I'll make arrangements and fill you in on all the details." He started toward the door, then turned back. "And, Kathryn, this will be very good for your career. I can promise you that."

After Huntington disappeared through the doorway, Kathryn's smile broadened. She would be quite happy to go to Jamaica if it would help her career.

❋ ❋ ❋

A few days later Kathryn locked her desk and left everything in the hands of her secretary who had been with Triple Gold for more than twenty years. She would have plenty of time to learn her new job when she got back from Jamaica.

As she left the building, Kathryn decided to do something completely out of character. She would take a walk. In all her years with the company, she had never gone down a tree-lined side street that led toward Madison Avenue.

Once on the side street, Kathryn hurried along until she spotted an old building with an art gallery banner hanging out front. She paused for a moment, then decided to go inside just to see what was there. Because this was so unusual for her, she couldn't help chuckling to herself.

But as soon as she climbed the steps and walked through the door, Kathryn shuddered. A chill filled the dim and empty gallery.

Surprised by the temperature change, Kathryn crossed her arms and moved more quickly. Why had she come into this dingy old building in the first place?

Overhead, a chandelier rattled. Startled, Kathryn looked up at the sparkling glass fixture that was trembling as if caught in the wind.

Then she saw it. A painting. The compelling image drew her toward the far wall. Dazed, Kathryn moved toward it with slow measured steps until she stood only an arm's length away.

Her heart raced as her gaze steadied on the plainly clad woman wearing a dull blue bonnet, its brim tilted in an odd position. What was it about the woman bent at the waist to gather a bouquet of wildflowers from a bright field of red poppies that drew her to this painting?

A frosty chill made its way down Kathryn's spine. Her lips quivered. Then, like the scene from a science fiction movie, to her disbelief, the oil paint started to shimmer and glow in a most unnatural way. The image of the woman faded and vanished into the field of flowers.

Kathryn rubbed her eyes. How strange and disoriented she felt. What was happening to her? A weird sensation overcame her. She was floating, shrinking and dizzy all at once.

Kathryn Calder was no longer in control. As if in a dream she was swirling, lifted from the floor into the painting, stepping inside the scene, moving across the field, drifting weightlessly in a cloudy mist.

Someone was calling. Kathryn heard the voice clearly. A familiar voice. Shivering, she turned her head toward the sound. A massive murky building loomed before her in the mist.

Kathryn felt herself float closer. Suddenly the structure came into focus and she could see archways glimmering, empty windows gleaming and sloping roof tiles glistening before her. All around, the air hung heavy with the scent of sweat and leather. Sweat and leather. She swiped at the perspiration beading on her forehead. An eerie sense of danger permeated the air.

Heart pounding, Kathryn tried to turn and run, but she could not. Instead, she drifted on, beyond her control, toward the building. Wet blades of grass stung her ankles, and the scent of a freshly mowed lawn settled around her. She was there, admist the scene, spellbound by the oddly familiar house and its darkened archways. Familiar? How could that be? Her heart raced faster than before.

It was. Kathryn shivered.

"Do you like the painting?"

A masculine voice broke through the mist and struck Kathryn like a blow, yanking her from the peculiar state. Suddenly she was propelled back into the ordinary Kathryn who stood outside the image, both feet planted firmly on the wooden floor.

A cold, dusty taste filled her mouth. With great effort, she wrenched her gaze from the image and searched the dimly lit chamber for the owner of the voice.

She saw no one else inside the dark gallery.

Kathryn swallowed hard. She was edgy, but who wouldn't be under the circumstances?

With complete certainty, she realized she knew the pink-hued building, knew it from long ago, but she could not remember where or how. Beguiled, she stared at the windows that gaped open on the top floor. Kathryn counted them. Nine. Tears blurred her eyes, brimmed over into hot, wet streams and rolled down her cheeks.

"Miss?"

The man's voice. Again. How real it seemed when nothing else did.

"Miss?" the man repeated. The voice was a pleasant, down-to-earth baritone. "Do you always take art so seriously?"

Someone moved closer, and almost at once, Kathryn was surrounded by a familiar, pleasant scent.

She closed her eyes and inhaled the aroma. "Roses," she whispered.

Behind her, the man spoke again. "I'm sorry the painting makes you sad."

Confused and still disoriented, Kathryn turned and peered up through a dark fringe of wet lashes. When she saw the man's tanned face and distinctive china blue eyes, her breath caught. Their gazes held, and, for a moment, she experienced a flicker of recognition.

Who are you? she thought. I know you from somewhere.

Kathryn shook her head to clear her brain of what had to be gallery cobwebs. She studied the man, wanting to make certain he was real. Little else seemed to be.

Confused, she fought off the impulse to run her hand across the broad shoulders that strained against the man's tweed jacket. Taking a deep breath, she tightened her arms against her sides keeping her hands from the strong, chiseled jaw she longed— unaccountably—to touch.

Her eyes still on his, Kathryn stumbled back a step. Could she be caught in a time warp, lost between fantasy and reality? When she stepped through the doorway of the gallery, had she entered a different world? Nice idea for science fiction, but this was the real world.

Kathryn took another deep breath of the rose scent that lingered all around. Surely, this tall, muscular stranger was not wearing rose-scented cologne. But what else could it be?

"Wh ... Where did you come from?" she asked. "I ... I thought I was alone."

The man shrugged and looked at her with his unearthly blue eyes. His face had a comforting quality, like she had always known and trusted him.

"I came from outside," the man said and frowned. "Did you want to be alone?"

"No ... no ... It is a public gallery." Kathryn fumbled to regain her composure. Realizing a dampness lingered on her skin, she turned away and rummaged in her purse for a tissue.

"Here. Try this." With one smooth motion, the man reached into his jacket pocket, pulled out a large white handkerchief and shook it open.

The sparkle that swam in his vivid eyes jolted Kathryn, dredging up another glimmer of recognition. She knew she had seen him before. But where?

On a crowded New York street? Perhaps one of Triple Gold's receptions or a convention meeting. So many possibilities, even walking from the subway to her office.

Their hands touched as she took the handkerchief from him, and an electrifying heat shot through her fingers. Kathryn took a step backward.

"I come in here sometimes just to look at the exhibits," he explained. "That's my painting," he offered, "the one that made you cry."

"Your painting?" She stared at the man in astonishment.

"Yes. I saw it in an antique shop in England, and I bought it. Very spontaneous and very crazy." He chuckled. "When I got home, I found it was much too large for my apartment walls." He shrugged.

"It's been on loan here ever since."

Why was the gallery so cold? she wondered. Did they keep it that way to protect the artwork? Kathryn shivered. This man owned the bizarre painting. How strange.

Kathryn peered at him from behind his handkerchief. What it was about the thick golden-brown hair falling in waves across his forehead that triggered such an unsettling memory she did not know or understand.

It was unnerving, Kathryn thought, that she couldn't place the man. In her work, she found it necessary to put names and faces together and she prided herself on her proficiency in this area. She turned from the stranger and pulled a mirror from her purse. Noting the dark smudges around her eyes and the smears down both cheeks, she tried to wipe them away.

The stranger was watching her. Kathryn felt the weight of his gaze. She put away the mirror and forced a smile.

"Thanks for your help. I ... I'll wash this and get it back to you," she promised, indicating his handkerchief.

"Don't worry about it." The man moved closer. "I have more." His voice was gentle. "You keep this one in case you need it again."

The light fragrance of aftershave lotion engulfed her, but it did not smell of roses. Instead, it had a spicy masculine scent.

Confusion clouded her brain. She willed herself to regain control of her whirling thoughts as she headed toward the outside entrance. She had to escape the confines of the decrepit old building where a simple painting fogged her thinking.

❋ ❋ ❋

Flynt Kincade gazed in wonder at the pretty young woman with long blonde hair and the bewildered look. She appeared ready to run, but he did not want her to leave. Not yet. "Let me introduce myself," he said.

"My name is Flynt Kincade." He extended his hand, and the woman grasped it without speaking.

Without even smiling.

"And you are...?" Flynt was worried the fragile young woman might be ill or on drugs. Her hand was cold, and it lingered in his grip.

"Sorry." She hesitated.

Her clear gray eyes were large and confused. He had a sudden urge to pull her close and hold her tight until the darkness left her face. "I'm Kathryn, Kathryn Calder."

"Kathryn. I've always liked that name." Flynt squeezed her hand, then released it. "It has a 'strength of the ages' ring to it."

She laughed. "I'd like my colleagues to think so."

"Oh, I'm sure they must."

"I need to get out of here," she said in a voice barely above a whisper.

"Fine," Flynt said. "Come with me to the cafe down the street. We can get a cola or a glass of wine there."

"I really shouldn't..." She checked her watch and seemed ready to bolt.

"A short break. It'll be okay," he assured her, wondering why he felt compelled to know her better. "It's right in the next block. Down a very busy street."

"Well...all right."

This time, when she spoke, the expression in Kathryn's eyes was unreadable. Strange. Over the years he had developed quite a talent for reading people and assessing them.

On impulse, Flynt caught her elbow ready to guide Kathryn through the entrance lobby and outside. But she hung back, taking a last long look at the painting. "Your painting?" she whispered. "Really?"

"I'm sure of it."

Kathryn pulled his crumpled handkerchief from her jacket pocket, folded it into a small square, and then carefully tucked it into the side compartment of her leather shoulder bag. "Please excuse me. I'm not myself today."

"And why is that?"

"I've just found I'm going on a business trip out of the country."

"A trip? Good. You can tell me about it over a glass of wine." As Flynt directed her outside, her arm trembled beneath his hand.

"I ... I don't want to go," she confided. "My boss gave me that 'the company needs you there, and we won't forget to show our appreciation' speech. Still..."

He understood her ambivalence. He was already having second thoughts about his own plans.

Flynt clinched his fist. The choice was made. There was no turning back.

CHAPTER TWO

FLYNT'S EYES WERE BLUE.

Although Kathryn did not consider blue eyes unusual, his were. They were china blue—quite unforgettable, with a kind of magical glow and a clarity she suspected would shimmer even in the dark.

And there was something else...that uncanny familiarity. The longer she looked at Flynt, the more familiar he seemed.

A whirl of cool air struck Kathryn's face, sweeping away what little hesitation remained. She took a deep breath. Even though the city streets looked gray and dismal, the crisp air was refreshing. "A glass of wine would be nice," she said with more conviction than she felt.

"A glass of fine wine it shall be, Kathryn."

When Flynt Kincade said her name, it rolled off his tongue with a touch of magic. She liked the little inflection he put on the first syllable. It sounded dramatic and special.

She watched his eyes, hoping for a sign of recognition from him, and was disappointed when she saw none. For a moment, she thought he might remember where they had met. If they had...

Flynt directed her at a brisk pace down one long block then turned into a small restaurant that had a hand-scrawled menu on a chalkboard by the door. The scent of Italian spices drifted through the partly open door.

Inside the small entrance foyer, Flynt guided her between pots of golden chrysanthemums that lined the way into a dining room jammed with tables and chairs. She glanced up at him, acutely aware of his fingers warming her arm even through the heavy fabric of her jacket.

Moments later, he seated her in a cushioned chair at a cozy little table, then took the chair across from her. "Now tell me about your business venture," he said.

Uncharacteristically, Kathryn was at a loss for words. Sitting across from him, looking into his face was difficult. His hair, his eyes ... So disturbingly familiar.

"I'm with Triple Gold. We specialize in computer systems for the hospitality industry," she said, hoping she was covering her true feelings of disorientation. "I head up the teams which get a new system up and running, with no glitches."

Absently, she let her gaze settle on the table's only decoration, a single yellow rosebud in a plain crystal vase. Kathryn frowned and leaned forward to sniff it. But, the flower, a silk one, had no sweet scent, only a slight dusty aroma. She picked it from the vase and studied it in disappointment.

Then she returned it to its place, glad Flynt appeared not to notice what some people might consider peculiar behavior. Instead, he reached across the table and smoothed her hand lightly with his large fingers. "Where are you going?" he asked.

His slight movement to touch her seemed natural, not threatening, not dangerous. Like she had experienced it all before, and it had been all right then.

"Jamaica," Kathryn told him.

"Jamaica," he repeated, and one eyebrow shot up.

"Every time I think of going, it makes me uneasy," she confided.

"Why?"

When Flynt leaned closer, the top of his shirt gaped open. Kathryn stared at the dark brown hair that coiled like springs of wire above his loose white collar. For some reason, the stray hair made him more real to her than when she first saw him in the gallery.

"I don't know. I'm not a timid person. But ..." She hesitated. "I'm a little uneasy about going to Jamaica."

Flynt seemed about to respond when a waitress with a small tray paused at their table, pulled two menus from her apron and plopped them down. Without a word, the woman bustled away.

Kathryn shifted uneasily in her seat. Until just now, when she confessed her discomfort to Flynt, she hadn't realized her concerns about Jamaica. But why tell Flynt? A total stranger?

Without realizing why, Kathryn scrutinized the yellow silk rose. Even the rose seemed somehow linked with Flynt.

Confused, Kathryn pushed aside the menu and the poor rose that, by now, was looking almost wilted. Could silk flowers wilt?

"So…" Flynt said, "about Jamaica?"

"A couple of weeks ago, my boss called me into his office and surprised me with the Jamaica project. He gave lavish descriptions of waterfalls, exotic plants, perfumed air—and a computer installation that just wasn't coming together." Flynt nodded, but said nothing.

Kathryn shook her head. "I know it's a great assignment, and my boss all but assured me there would be a big promotion waiting for me at the end." She shrugged. "I can't put my finger on why, but I'm worried. I've been having these dreams."

"Dreams?"

"More like nightmares, really, and it's the same one most of the time."

Flynt frowned.

"Right after I got the assignment, the nightmares started waking me in the middle of the night.

"Sometimes the dreams are so real, I actually believe I'm there."

Kathryn felt her face flush. "Of course, later, I realize it's only a dream." Absently, she squared the placemat with the table edge. "That's all it can be."

"Do you think the dreams are about Jamaica?"

Kathryn nodded. "Do you ever have the same dream over and over?" she asked.

Flynt shook his head. "I don't remember my dreams."

When the waitress approached the table, Flynt ordered a glass of Chardonnay for each of them. Moments later she returned with their wine.

"To your trip," Flynt said, and they touched glasses.

Kathryn took a small, tentative sip. Almost immediately the wine sent a rush of warmth through her body. "Why did you buy the painting?"

"I don't know," Flynt said. "I saw it in the shop window and couldn't get it out of my mind. My last day in London, I went back and bought it."

He chuckled. "When the shipment arrived, I discovered how big the painting actually was."

"Big enough for a museum." Kathryn laughed. Already she felt better. Was it Flynt or the wine? He seemed like an old friend. She smiled while they chatted away.

When Kathryn glanced down at her watch, the time surprised her.

"I have to go," she said as she stood.

"I don't want you to leave," Flynt whispered.

Kathryn felt her heart tilt.

"I must." She hesitated, mesmerized by his vivid blue eyes. "Thank you."

"You're welcome."

His gaze held steady on her face until Kathryn's knees went weak and she shifted away from him.

"I'm leaving tomorrow." A nervous tingle played down her spine, and she wished she could change her schedule, wished she were not leaving so soon. "I'm staying at Hibiscus Hall in Ocho Rios." Why had she told him that?

An unreadable smile flickered over Flynt's lips as he lifted her jacket and held it. When she slipped her arms inside, their shoulders touched, sending a splendid surge of warmth careening through her.

"Hibiscus Hall, Jamaica," he whispered. The smile on his face grew.

As they parted, Flynt pressed his business card into her hand. "The address is no good after next week."

When she hurried into the congested New York street to a waiting taxi, a twinge of regret followed her. As the cab sped off toward her apartment, she fingered his handkerchief in her purse, then pulled it out.

What was it about the strange painting? Somehow it seemed to connect to her dreams. And Flynt Kincade owned the painting.

Kathryn pressed the handkerchief to her face and inhaled the faint scent of his after-shave. Then she folded it with care and replaced it in her bag along with his business card.

Aimee. A blurry half-memory tried to come into her head, but quickly diminished. Her face turned cold.

Was there a figure in the window of the house in the painting? From somewhere far away, she remembered a figure standing at a dark upstairs window. A sinister figure.

She shuddered. How could she remember?

❀ ❀ ❀

God, she was beautiful. Twisting in his seat, Flynt Kincade watched Kathryn depart with more interest than he understood. Dark shoulder bag slung over her arm, straight blonde hair shifting in the fall breeze, she rushed from his life into an empty yellow cab.

The moment he found her, standing like a perfect alabaster sculpture, he was tossed off-balance.

He longed to touch her, but, of course, he could not. It certainly made his mistake about buying the too-large painting worthwhile.

Yes. Kathryn Calder made quite an impression on him. A smile flickered over his face as his thoughts lingered on the information he had not shared with Kathryn. By some peculiar throw of the dice, next week he was heading to Jamaica himself. After deciding to exchange his corporate life for something more fulfilling, he had made some far-flung applications. To his surprise, there were several offers and one of the choices South University had given him would make him Professor Flynt Kincade. After much consideration, he chose a position in the Caribbean over the conventional setting of the main campus in Atlanta.

Flynt took a bite of mushroom and another sip of wine. Teaching nine-week courses at colleges scattered throughout the Caribbean islands might be even better than he imagined. Kingston, Jamaica, was the site of one university and the first place he would go.

He was about to tell Kathryn when she began to describe her nightmares. He did not get another chance.

As he finished the mushrooms and took his last sip of wine, Flynt jotted the words, "Hibiscus Hall," on his cocktail napkin. With a smile, he tucked it into the pocket of his jacket.

Yes, Jamaica would be a fine place to begin his teaching career. And he would get to see Kathryn Calder again.

❀ ❀ ❀

The surface of the Olympic-size pool sparkled in the morning sunlight. Exhausted from swimming six laps, Kathryn climbed over the side and collapsed on the lounge chair next to her blue canvas bag.

Kathryn took a deep breath of the sweet, perfumed air. How much she loved Jamaica. From the moment she saw the orange-tiled roofs of the houses from the airplane window, Kathryn was captivated.

The lounge's thick plastic pad felt warm against her body, but even in the heat, she was cold. She pulled a towel over her shoulders. Rolling onto her side, Kathryn peered across the manicured lawn that stretched lush and green beneath the almost cloudless tropical sky.

In the mid-morning light, the exotic grounds of Hibiscus Hall glowed like a magic oasis. Towering palm trees bordered the circular drive, and hibiscus bushes, bright with pink, yellow, and red blossoms, edged the brick walkways, exuding a lushness Kathryn sensed without touching. She took a deep breath, hoping to capture the faint scent of scarlet bougainvillea that grew nearby.

How different Jamaica was from New York. She gazed beyond the tropical foliage to where the blue-green waters of the Caribbean Sea glittered and sparkled. She watched motor boats roar past pulling water-skiers.

Smiling, Kathryn settled back into the cushions. For the past two weeks, the island had enchanted her. The tension that gripped her early on had lessened, but still she could not forget the alarming incident in the gallery.

Sometimes at night, when she looked in her bedroom mirror, her heart pounded. Uneasy, she half-expected to find a face other than her own peering back at her through the glass. A pale, thin face, like that of the woman in her dreams. Not dreams, Kathryn thought, forcing herself to be honest. They weren't dreams; they were nightmares.

Even tropical enchantment could not make her dismiss the effect Flynt Kincade's painting had on her. Nor could she forget the dream about Aimee.

Squirming, Kathryn took a long breath of perfumed tropical air. Why couldn't she just enjoy the resort amenities? After all, they were hers to use as if she were a vacationer. The tedious work with computers and staff was scheduled for evenings.

Rolling onto her stomach, Kathryn gazed across the bright bougainvillea blossoms that sprawled like wild flames in the tropical garden. She marveled at the exotic scenery. The main building of Hibiscus Hall was an Italian Renaissance structure. Its golden-yellow stucco walls glowed in sharp contrast to the vivid blue sky. Nestled between two smaller resorts, the complex fronted a pristine white sand beach. High in the sky above the center tower, scattered cumulus clouds drifted like dabs of whipped cream.

Kathryn sighed. The bright colors and warmth of the day were very different from the afternoon in New York when she met Flynt Kincade.

Flynt Kincade. Kathryn could not believe herself—the way she was obsessed with the memory of him, a stranger she met in a brief encounter. Although it was trauma that brought them together. Not an encounter.

She fluffed her hair with a towel. Now, two weeks after that meeting, Flynt seemed dreamlike and unreal. Her mind drifted to recollection until she heard someone call her name.

"Kathryn. Here I find you. Everywhere I have looked."

Startled from her thoughts, Kathryn lurched from the chair to her feet where she saw Mara Hoffman, the resort's public relations director, striding toward her.

"Mara. Hello." Brushing sticky strands of hair from her face, Kathryn grinned at her new friend, aware of the joyful energy that always surrounded her.

"It is good that I find you." Mara's German accent was thicker than usual. "See what I have to show." She shoved into Kathryn's hands a clipboard with papers and photographs firmly attached. "It is for the new brochure."

When Kathryn sat, Mara sat next to her.

"Look. This I bring for you to see." Purposefully, she flipped through the pictures and pulled out one of the enlargements. "See. Rose Hall Great House is for tourists a good stop. For the brochure I make for Hibiscus Hall, this photograph is very good."

The moment Mara thrust the photograph of a big old building into her hands, Kathryn gasped. Rose Hall. Her fingers shook. She stared with disbelief.

The house looked exactly like the one she had seen in the gallery in New York, the one in the mysterious painting Flynt had on loan there.

"Rose Hall," Kathryn murmured.

"Yes," Mara said. "That is the name."

Kathryn stood, retreated a few steps, then turned back.

"Where is this place, Mara?" she asked in a tight voice. Questions raced in her mind. "Can we walk there?"

Stifling a chuckle, Mara tossed her head, sending short blonde hair in all directions. "So much excitement, I did not expect." She took the photograph from Kathryn. "Rose Hall is near Montego Bay. We cannot walk."

"Oh."

"It is all right. I will take you," Mara offered. She stood up next to Kathryn and put an arm on her shoulder. "Later today," she promised, "if that is what you like."

"Yes. Please." Kathryn's heart pounded at the thought. She did not understand her desperate desire to visit the big old house, but it was there. Nor did she understand the heavy weight that filled her stomach the moment she saw the photograph. No matter.

She must heed the disturbing compulsion to visit Rose Hall. Kathryn felt sure that seeing the old mansion in person would put an end to its mysterious hold on her. Besides, Mara would be there with her.

❊ ❊ ❊

"Thanks for taking time off," Kathryn said that afternoon as she climbed into the passenger side of the red BMW. A wave of hot air struck her face.

Mara grimaced. "A red car is oh so bright in the sun. And hot."

Kathryn smiled as she rolled down the window. Mara's charming accent lessened her tension, if only for a moment.

"Always, I have wished to go to Rose Hall. Always, from the guests, there are too many questions. I cannot get away." She shrugged. "Today, my thanks to you, Kathryn, I now go."

Tilting her chin up, Mara tucked a flyaway section of pale blonde hair behind one ear and carefully turned the car through the brick gateway and out onto the narrow road. When Mara turned on the air conditioner, Kathryn rolled up her window.

As they wound along the rough pavement through the town of St. Ann's Bay, Kathryn's uneasiness about the island returned. Twice when traffic forced Mara to stop the car in the street, small children and adults knocked on the windows, begging for money or offering to sell them sugarcane. The hopeful expressions on their faces brought tears to Kathryn's eyes.

"Doesn't it bother you to see these poor little children?" Kathryn asked. A little girl with large dark eyes was peering through the window.

"No. I cannot let it." Mara stared straight ahead. "If I look, it too much hurt, and I must depart Jamaica. If I do not look, then I can stay."

When the car curved through the last street and entered a long stretch of empty green countryside, Mara sighed and whispered, "It is now much better."

Hungry, crying children. A lump filled Kathryn's throat. A sliver of memory edged into her awareness then vanished. She closed her eyes. What was she trying to recall?

"In all Jamaica, Rose Hall is the most beautiful mansion, but it is the story of Annie Palmer that makes it famous," Mara said in her stilted English, then directed a meaningful glance at Kathryn. "The 'white witch'."

"A white witch?" Kathryn asked, though she had focused on the name 'Annie.' The young girl in my nightmare was trying to escape her Aunt Annie, Kathryn thought.

"Yes, the white witch Annie Palmer. I will give you a book to read," she said. "It tells about Jamaica two hundred years ago."

"Is this the same Annie Palmer who brutalized her plantation slaves?" Kathryn asked. Earlier in the week, her favorite waiter and another new friend, Oswald Smith had mesmerized her with tales of vicious beatings. The story had sickened her.

"You will see," Mara said, then turned her attention back to driving.

As the BMW rounded a bend in the road, off in the distance, a pink-hued building stood tall and stately above the horizon. Kathryn took a deep breath. Like a ghostly specter, the ancient house loomed above the highway to Montego Bay.

"That is Rose Hall," Mara whispered, awe in her voice. "In life, it is more real."

Kathryn stared, spellbound, caught in a dark dream, unable to escape. A house where evil shadows dwelled. She shivered at the thought.

Mara turned up the road and drove toward the Great House. The car bumped along the lane, past a wide, grassy hillside to where entry tickets were sold. Kathryn's heart beat faster when through a screen of trees and plants she caught a glimpse of the imposing old mansion.

Mara flashed a satisfied smile toward Kathryn as she edged the vehicle up the slight incline into a parking space. "Finally. Rose Hall."

Kathryn could not move from her seat. A strange, gray haze fogged her vision until the outline of the pink-hued building wavered.

Love lost.

The words echoed inside her head.

Love lost.

The words floated free through her mind.

Somewhere Mara was chatting. Kathryn could hear her speaking as if through a distant tunnel, but she could not understand her words nor could she see her face. Instead, her total focus was directed toward the mysterious old house that appeared firm and steady once more.

She studied the structure. On the lowest level, a series of graceful archways claimed her attention. The brick portico looked so familiar, it startled her.

A slight motion within the third archway caught her eye; and for a split second, a glimmer of light flickered there revealing a form obscured in the shadows. Kathryn struggled to make out the figure.

With clammy fingers, she grasped the car door handle and pushed it down. Vaguely aware of the murky cloud in which she was encased, she heard a voice from beneath the arch, a shrill, irritable woman's voice.

"Aimee. Aimee."

Instinctively, Kathryn responded. It was the name from her dream.

She stepped from the car, all the while keeping her focus trained on the third arch.

The voice was familiar.

Why should the severe, demanding voice be familiar?

Oblivious to Mara's calls, Kathryn edged away from the vehicle and moved across the grass. Aware of nothing else, she glided toward the arch.

All around, a haze of gray drifted in misty puffs from the earth. She hurried beyond the chirping sounds of songbirds toward the shrill woman's voice. Some internal directive compelled her to run until, breathless, she paused on the lawn and stared at the portico.

"Aimee. Come in now, please. It is time to put on your gown for the ball."

A small dark-haired woman in a long, flowing pink dress, stood in the portico, watching her from beneath the arched colonnades. When the woman moved, her full skirt shifted over a wide crinoline petticoat, and a bright beam of sunlight fell across her face, making every feature clear to Kathryn.

Awestruck, Kathryn stood perfectly still. The woman's dark eyes narrowed to match the frown that dented the ivory white perfection of her forehead. Had her lips not been drawn into a harsh, tense line, Kathryn might consider her beautiful.

The woman looked straight at her. "Aimee!" she called.

Feeling herself shrinking downward, Kathryn tried to turn away, but she could not. The name, that name drew her close to the portico.

Kathryn's ears rang, and her head hurt. To block the sound, she clamped her hands over her ears and then against her forehead. How very much her head hurt—as if a vice held it locked within its grip.

"Come inside, Aimee." Hands on her hips, the woman glared toward the spot in the grass where Kathryn stood. "Why I let you live in this house, I shall never know. Perhaps I should ship you back to England on the next boat."

"No, Aunt Annie! I shall not return to England," Kathryn heard a small voice cry out.

Her voice.

The angry woman maintained a hostile stare that both threatened and taunted her. With an overwhelming urge to run and hide, Kathryn took two steps backward and shrank toward the trees. Like a timid young child, she let her shoulders sag forward and her chin dip against her chest. Why did she feel small, insecure and frightened, not at all like herself?

Suddenly, out of nowhere, a tremendous roar cut the air. It was like giant trains thundering past on mammoth tracks. She clasped her hands tight to her ears to block the terrible clamor, but still it persisted inside her head.

Then, without warning, the bones in Kathryn's legs seemed to disintegrate, and the world darkened into murky blackness.

A vacuum of silence surrounded Kathryn.

Falling. Floating.

Blades of grass tickled her face. When she smelled the damp scent, she tried to open her eyes.

Slowly, a flickering sliver of light played into her awareness. Kathryn blinked and pushed up on her elbow.

She looked around cautiously. The dreadful roar was gone and so was the woman. Frowning, she surveyed the portico. It was vacant! Kathryn shook her head in dismay.

"Ist alles in Ordnung?"

Her mind caught in confusion, Kathryn looked up. Then the jumble of unknown syllables and sounds registered. German, she thought hazily. Mara. Her friend was staring down at her.

"Are you all right, Kathryn? What is the matter?" Mara's concern was obvious. "Is it that you are ill?"

"No ... No ... I don't know." Kathryn sat up on the lawn and stared toward the portico, again searching for the woman who vanished.

"Did you see her?" Kathryn's voice was weak and anxious.

"Who?"

"The woman on the portico. She had on a long dress." Kathryn tried to keep her voice steady.

"Maybe she wore a costume."

Mara gave her a blank look. "I saw no one." She reached for Kathryn's hand to help her up.

"What is it that happened? When I called out to you, you did not answer."

Kathryn stood, trying to regain her composure. "I—I don't know. I must have tripped over a root, or something."

Since Mara saw no one, Kathryn decided to say nothing more, telling herself there must be a logical explanation for what just happened.

"A root?" Puzzled, Mara brushed her sandal across the flat surface where they stood. "I do not see a root."

Kathryn shrugged and avoided Mara's eyes.

"Shall we go into Rose Hall?" Mara asked after she checked Kathryn's arms and legs for cuts.

"You go on without me," Kathryn said. Rose Hall was too foreboding for her right now. "Something's caught in my shoe." She scraped her pump against the grass. "I'll go to the car and get it out."

"Then, I will wait for you."

"No. Please go ahead. You're eager to see the house. I'll catch up later."

"You are sure?" Mara flashed one of the charming smiles that made her a favorite with everyone at the resort. "I will then go." She hurried off, twisting around to wave right before she started up the brick steps that led to the front door of Rose Hall.

When Kathryn reached the car, she collapsed against the side to collect her thoughts. Was her mind playing tricks?

Impossible, she thought. Probably the woman was a tour guide, in costume, one of those Living History things, like she told Mara. Still, she was not up to entering the Great House.

Her gaze shifted to the side lawn and on to the trees beyond. The space, all of it, appeared familiar somehow, as though she had visited the grounds before.

Kathryn's head whirled. Everything around her gave her the sense of deja vu. And the name, Aimee, held some unknown significance.

She knew the name. Knew it well.

When Kathryn pulled open the car door and relaxed into the seat, an unexpected thought popped into her mind. If Flynt Kincade were in Jamaica, she would show him Rose Hall.

Flynt.

A small smile grew on her lips. She reached into the side pocket of her purse and pulled out Flynt's handkerchief. This morning, she had an urge to remove it from her lingerie drawer and bring it with her. As she pressed the cloth against her face, a faint scent of his after-shave still clung to the material. When she breathed in the scent, Kathryn felt better.

CHAPTER THREE

AFTER MARA RETURNED to the car, to Kathryn's relief, her friend did not question her. Instead, she raved at length about the interior of Rose Hall. In a lively voice, she spieled off detailed descriptions of furniture and wall coverings in each room, calming, for the moment, Kathryn's disturbing thoughts and making the return trip to Hibiscus Hall seem shorter.

When Kathryn got back to her room, she tried in vain to piece together a scenario that would make sense of the morning's events. What could be wrong with her? Nothing logical came to mind that would explain what she saw and heard.

By late afternoon, Kathryn felt a little calmer and more like her sensible self. She headed to the pool in hopes swimming laps would help clear away the image of the woman on the portico once and for all.

But as soon as she slipped into the water, she heard Mara call, "Kathryn. Come, please. I have here Flynt for you to meet." Flynt.

Kathryn gripped the pool edge to steady herself. A tall man with wavy golden-brown hair and a pleasant tan stood chatting with Mara and Fritz. Dark sunglasses hid his eyes, but a strong Nordic jawline was evident.

She waded through the water toward them. Flynt was no ordinary name, but this man could not be Flynt Kincade, could he? Finding him in Jamaica was too unlikely. If he were bound for Jamaica, he would have told her that day in New York, wouldn't he?

But when the man turned toward her and removed his glasses, Kathryn gulped. Flynt Kincade.

Speechless, Kathryn stared.

Flynt smiled at her in the same pleasant way she remembered. He stood almost a foot taller than square-shouldered, solidly built Fritz Hoffman. When he moved, his bare chest gleamed, and his muscles rippled in the Jamaican sunshine.

"You really are here," Flynt's voice was husky.

To Kathryn's surprise, seeing Flynt again was like finding a dear, long-lost friend.

"I worried your plans might have changed," he said. "I'm glad they didn't."

"But ... You didn't tell me."

For a prolonged moment, Flynt surveyed her face. Kathryn felt an incredible warmth rise in her cheeks. As their gazes held, she was intensely aware of the chemistry that pulsed between them. "The two of you—you know each other?" Mara giggled.

Mara and Fritz were a study in contrast. Kathryn had decided that the day she first met them. Mara always had something pleasant to say; Fritz was normally gruff and seldom smiled.

"Kathryn and I met in New York a couple of weeks back," Flynt said. "I hoped to find her here."

"You met in New York? And you both now are here?" Her silver-blue eyes sparkling, Mara glanced between them. "Then, it was meant to be," she declared. "Fated, as you Americans might say." Beaming, Mara grabbed Fritz's hand and pulled him into deeper water where she started a conversation with a group of new arrivals.

Her mind full of unspoken questions, Kathryn turned to face Flynt alone.

"I'm really glad to see you," he whispered finally. He traced his fingers over her cheek to smooth back a strand of wet hair. "Can we go somewhere to talk?"

She nodded, keenly aware of the heat that flushed her cheek where he had touched her.

With one quick motion, Flynt sprang from the pool, then pulled Kathryn up to stand beside him. He handed her a dry towel and swung another towel over his own shoulders.

How comfortable it felt to be with him again, Kathryn thought. It was as if she had known him forever.

His hand tight on hers, Flynt directed Kathryn beneath a long row of coconut palms that edged the white sand beach. Her pulse pounded almost in rhythm with reggae music from a nearby resort. As they approached the thatched-roof beach bar, the sounds grew louder.

Laughing and chatting like old friends, they hardly noticed the other guests who conversed near the sprawling mahogany service bar. The pungent scent of late afternoon waves, mingling with the fragrance of fresh pineapple, wafted around them.

Kathryn was nervously aware of Flynt's warm breath in her hair as he boosted her onto a high stool. She was also aware of his serious, intense gaze that never left her all the while he settled on the adjacent seat and tucked his feet between the stool's rungs.

"Would you like a drink?" Flynt asked.

"Plain fruit punch, please," she said. "I go to work soon." She watched his eyes, marveling at the sunset colors reflected in the china blue irises, admiring the glossy overlay that reminded her of polished glass.

"Thanks," she said when he passed her a drink with a ripe pineapple slice perched on the edge of the glass. She smiled and took a long swallow, then placed the glass on the bar in front of her. "You didn't tell me you were coming to Jamaica. Why not?" The words tumbled out, softly, with a hint of accusation she could not manage to suppress.

"I planned to tell you. But you left the restaurant too quickly ... before we had time to talk about my plans. Remember?"

Kathryn shrugged. "I told you about my nightmares." She had almost forgotten.

"Are you still having them?"

"Sometimes." She shrugged, needing to change the subject. "I'm glad you're here."

And she was. She thought of Rose Hall and how for no apparent reason she wished for Flynt when she was there earlier in the day.

❖ ❖ ❖

Even though he was in Jamaica for his new job, coming to Hibiscus Hall looking for Kathryn Calder seemed frivolous and terribly foolish, Flynt thought.

It was certainly out of character for a man who once prided himself on being in control and able to make sensible, executive decisions on all levels of his life. Following this woman—any woman—to a resort was far from sensible.

But Kathryn's gray eyes haunted him. Ever since he saw her in New York, he had been unable to get those eyes out of his thoughts. So much sadness and confusion seemed to lie behind them.

From the serious expression still on her face, it was clear Kathryn Calder was a woman with a lot on her mind.

Flynt watched Kathryn. She seemed to be debating what to say next, so he waited.

"You remind me of someone I used to know," she said at last.

"Do I?" Flynt wrapped his large hand around the glass of fruit punch and held tight. Her words made him uneasy. After all, he had learned the hard way that relationships with women could be very tricky and deceptive.

Kathryn stared at him as if she were unable to come to grips with something she saw in his face.

"I'm sure I know you," she whispered, and the way she said it added to Flynt's uneasy feelings.

He would remember if they had met, wouldn't he? He shook his head, and she looked beyond him toward the sea.

"Please tell me why you're in Jamaica."

He was reluctant to tell her. It was like confessing to a crime, he thought. A lot of his colleagues acted as if what he was doing were a kind of betrayal. You don't leave the top job in this company unless you're fired, a friend told him. Still others were glad to see him go, hoping they would move up on the company ladder because of the vacancy at the top.

"I'm changing careers," Flynt said in a quiet voice. As he propped his elbows on the counter and rested his chin on his hands, he let his gaze once more linger on hers. "I'm going into a different profession. Here in Jamaica."

There it was. The look of bewilderment he expected. It always came, especially from colleagues who knew the importance of the prestigious job he had held until a week ago. Flynt wished it didn't make him question his decision.

"Changing jobs? A new profession?" Her dismay was plain in her voice. "But your card said, 'president.'"

"It was time for a change," Flynt said. "Being president of a large company is not without stress."

"But ... but some people work for years to be successful, to reach the top. They give up everything," she said.

Flynt narrowed his eyes and lifted his chin from his hands. "What is success? Emptiness. Regret. Not caring about the effect what you do has on others." A bitter taste rose from his stomach and filled his mouth.

"But..."

"Besides that, for as long as I can remember, I've had a yearning to come to Jamaica," Flynt confided.

"A yearning for Jamaica?" Curiosity on her face, Kathryn lifted her glass and took a long drink. "You have?"

Flynt nodded.

He turned to watch a bright red sail that propelled a lone wind-surfer over the waters near shore. "For as long as I can remember, I've wanted to teach," he said, "so that's what I'm set to do. After a couple of days here, I'm off to Kingston to start my teaching career."

"Teaching? You're going to be a teacher?" Kathryn's disapproval was obvious.

"I'm going to fulfill my dream," he said, still tracking the wind-surfer's path along the darkening horizon. "Fifteen years in a meaningless job is enough."

Memories of the emptiness he felt all those years filled his thoughts. He shifted his feet on the rungs of the barstool and turned to look into her eyes. "My job is all I've had for a long time," he whispered. "I want something more." His hand closed over hers.

❋ ❋ ❋

Kathryn's heart beat a little faster.

Flynt's warm fingers filled her body with excitement. A numbing charge of electricity shot through her. Against her hand, she could feel the blood pulsing through his fingers, could sense his excitement in return. He smiled and pulled his hand away.

They were chatting when suddenly Kathryn was drawn to the way he pushed his wavy hair off his forehead.

"I'm still struck with how familiar you seem. You remind me of ... of someone..."

Flynt chuckled. "Of course, I remind you of a man who found you hanging out in a lonely gallery. Under that unfortunate painting."

Kathryn laughed, too, but it was false mirth. Nothing he could say would explain away the strange feelings he dredged up in her.

As she watched him, a vision of the menacing old house appearing through the fog invaded her thoughts. Rose Hall and Flynt. The connection flashed through her mind along with new glimmers of recognition and more fragments of near-memory.

Or did she have some distant memory?

Years ago, she read a fascinating little book—she couldn't recall its title—but it was a book about far memory.

Far memory. The heroine stepped through a glitch in time and reentered the past. Why did Flynt make her think of far memory?

❖ ❖ ❖

"Water Aerobics!"

The announcement blasted from a giant loudspeaker with a disruptive echo that resounded across the pool. A half-dozen fitness fanatics, shapely arms crossed, stepped silently into the water and swam to where the instructor was starting warm-up exercises. Kathryn followed them into the cool deep water.

"Left leg up ... to the side ... down." A statuesque Jamaican woman, her long legs glistening in the crystal-clear water, chanted instructions to the group.

What had drawn her to the seven-a.m. class? Kathryn wondered. She seldom did aerobics, yet today she felt a nagging compulsion to come to the pool.

Yesterday, she and Flynt talked until early evening—an exhilarating yet confusing experience. When he left her at the door to the resort offices, she was still pondering the underlying connection she felt with him. It was not until she began to struggle with yet another computer program malfunction that she put it aside and concentrated on her work.

Later, back in her room, Kathryn had trouble falling asleep. She kept thinking of Flynt, her odd experience in New York, and the woman who appeared, then vanished, at Rose Hall—the woman Mara did not see.

And Aimee. Even now, that name sent shivers riveting through her. Who was Aimee?

Kathryn took a deep breath and ducked under water. When she straightened up, the chilled morning air left goose bumps on her skin.

Cold and generally miserable, she did her best to fall in step with the others, in hopes bobbing up and down to taped music would warm her body and lift her spirits. "One ... two ... three ... four," the group chanted together.

All except Kathryn.

As she bounced, bits of sunlight played across her face, then danced in abstract patterns on the water's surface. Distracted, she stopped moving, her attention captured by the spinning light that glittered on the pool.

"One ... two ... three ... four," she heard the instructor say.

"One ... two ... three ... four," she whispered absently.

Clutching the side, Kathryn followed the pulsating light. Although she heard the count, she did not move. Her gaze remained locked on the bright surface where sparkles glittered, and pinpoints of blue flew up like frantic butterflies.

"One ... two ..." The voice faded.

Kathryn's fingers slid from the pool's edge and fell limply into the water. The undulating water fascinated her. It glistened, then spun like a carnival friction top, hurling spits of colored fire to all sides.

Motion and light blended with her thoughts. Her mind floated, caught in a mist that drifted vapor-like from the water, obscuring the surface.

A sudden murkiness darkened the pool. Groggy, Kathryn watched a shoreline appear behind it. Along the water's edge, two women strolled, their long skirts sweeping the ground. Both were dressed like the woman she saw at Rose Hall.

Then, a tall man stepped beside them and took one woman's arm. When she saw his face, Kathryn's heart almost stopped. She knew this man, recognized his straight, tall carriage and confident gait. And the cold, dark eyes. Who was he?

Unexpectedly, she felt her knees weaken and buckle beneath her weight. Then she was drifting, floating, flying aimlessly away.

Falling ... unable to breathe ... falling...

A blanket of darkness swept around her. Darkness and water. From a distance, Kathryn heard voices—confused, excited voices, closing in.

Out of control, her thoughts swirled, as if caught in a dark vacuum. A tinkling bell rang out, and a muddle of confusion and commotion followed.

"Help her! She's drowning!"

Hands like iron claws tugged at her arms, pulled on her shoulders, dragged her from the water.

Sputtering ... struggling...

She was tired, very tired.

Chill slithered like a frozen fish down her spine, then traveled to her fingertips and toes. Although she struggled hard, her arms and legs did not respond.

"Kathryn! Say something!"

A stranger's voice thundered loud enough to hurt her ears. Why was someone yelling at her, someone she did not know?

With concentrated effort, she struggled to open her eyes until gradually a small stream of light crept between the lashes. Then she saw the blurred forms of strangers leaning over her.

Dear God. Had she fainted in the water? No wonder her body was icy cold, and people were hovering all around.

Coughing, Kathryn tried to sit up, but a leaden weight filled her chest, pressing her beneath it to the ground.

"Please now, Kathryn. Stay still. You need rest."

Mara's voice. As she recognized her friend's accent, then picked out her face from among the strangers, a wave of relief rushed through Kathryn.

She opened her eyes wider, then squinted until she saw Mara more clearly.

"Kathryn, it will now be all right."

Against her damp skin, Mara's hands were cool and competent. She covered Kathryn with fluffy beach towels that were warm and comforting.

Stifling a new round of coughing, Kathryn sat up and stared at the pool's surface. It shone bright and clear in the early morning sunshine. Lounge chairs and umbrella tables lined the tiled deck. The murkiness, grassy knoll, people wearing clothes from Old Jamaica and shifting light were gone. She twisted around, searching for a remnant of the strange vision that drew her beneath the water.

"What really happened?" Mara whispered. She had brought Kathryn into the hotel lobby and sequestered her in a far, out-of-the-way corner. "I am so much worried." Wiping water from Kathryn's face, she wrapped a small towel around her dripping hair.

"I ... I'm not sure." Kathryn shivered. "I'm not sure at all. Jamaica is beginning to seem a little spooky to me."

"Last night, you worked hard, late into the night." Mara stepped back and studied her with intense eyes. "But there is something more. We did not talk yesterday ... We did not talk about what happened at Rose Hall ..."

Kathryn stared blankly at Mara. She could not talk about it—the imposing old house that seemed to hold strange secrets. And she could not confide in her about the man she saw in her vision. The man she recognized. Who was he?

CHAPTER FOUR

AS SOON AS he heard what happened, Flynt dropped what he was doing and rushed to the lobby in search of Kathryn, his mind a mixture of concern and confusion. How could a woman about whom he knew nothing create such a stir in his heart?

It was damn confusing at best. Ever since his marriage ended, he had been careful to avoid relationships. That was six years ago, and no woman had tempted him. Until now.

When he saw her with Mara at the end of the lobby, his stomach clenched. Kathryn's cheeks, pale as white porcelain, and the purplish cast that tarnished her lips worried him.

There was something special about Kathryn Calder. Something unique that attracted him to her. Something he couldn't quite put his finger on. He frowned, remembering the queer feeling that settled over him in the New York gallery, the feeling that something beyond him had compelled him to come inside to look at his painting that day.

Mara turned when she heard him approach and smiled at him. "Do not worry, Flynt," she whispered. "It is now all right."

Flynt wondered if that were true, especially when he saw the dazed look that remained on Kathryn's face. Mara appeared not to notice. She busied herself straightening up the cozy corner of the hotel lobby where she met with guests frequently.

"Kathryn, take please something to read." She motioned toward scattered books and magazines, dropped in her rush to the pool emergency.

Flynt stooped to gather them from the floor.

"What's that?" Kathryn asked, her voice flat.

Flynt followed her gaze to the cover of the book he held. She reached out and took it from him.

"Rose Hall," she murmured.

❊ ❊ ❊

Rose Hall. For a moment, a glimmer of recollection teetered near the surface of Flynt's mind; then a shade slammed down on the memory, and he could not recover the thought.

Kathryn stared without speaking at the glossy photo of the stately mansion. The title "Rose Hall" gleamed in bold, dark letters across the top of the book. Her fingers trembling, Kathryn traced the outline of each letter.

Flynt watched with growing unease. Kathryn had hardly noticed his presence in the lobby.

"That is about the famous plantation," Mara explained. "It is the one I promised to lend you. This morning I found it in my library." Kathryn said nothing.

Obviously perplexed, Mara glanced at Flynt, then turned to Kathryn and asked, "You want to read it, yes?"

"Yes." Kathryn took the book, studied the photograph, and then laid it on the chair next to Mara. "I'll read it later," she whispered. She continued to stare at the cover. "The arches are empty," she mumbled. "Rose Hall. Love lost."

For a long while, Flynt stood silent in the shadows, observing Kathryn's unsteady reactions. Her unexpected vulnerability, the strained look on her face made him want to draw her close against his chest. For unknown reasons, she seemed different from other women, different in a way he could not explain to himself nor to anyone else.

Absently, Flynt watched Mara pack a half dozen women's magazines into Kathryn's blue canvas bag. The girl on the cover of Cosmo reminded him of his ex-wife.

His marriage had been eight long years of hell on earth. Those years taught him a lesson. Or had they?

He glanced back at Kathryn and felt his heart twist. Her fair hair, delicate features, and thin build were captivating.

Taking a long breath, Flynt looked beyond the lobby to the drive where a young couple—probably newlyweds—descended from a taxi. Bright-eyed and full of hope, they wandered into the lobby holding hands.

Flynt smiled ruefully. He and his ex had been that way once—happy. But he always thought there was something else ... Always hoped. And always, there had been a distant longing that he never understood.

Flynt turned back to where Kathryn sat and studied her face. Smooth skin, far too pale, wide gray eyes filled with confusion. He frowned. This morning, little about Kathryn resembled the self-assured woman he watched get in the cab in New York. He found her vulnerability appealing.

A little unsteady, Kathryn got up. "Come on," she said, glancing at him with uncertain eyes.

Smiling, he picked up the canvas bag and followed her outside onto the walkway that led to the beach. For a moment, he sensed he was following someone else. Someone from the past. Someone he knew quite well.

Puzzled, Flynt rubbed his hand across his eyes and felt his smile diminish. It might take a while to get used to this Jamaican heat.

Three gulls swooped low over the water, then settled lightly on the sand and waddled along the beach. A hundred yards off shore, a small fishing boat buzzed by, held low in the water by the weight of an early morning catch.

Reclining on a rope hammock, stretched between palm trees on the edge of the beach, Kathryn watched the gulls scavenge for food. Nearby, Flynt lay on his stomach on a beach towel with his elbows propped, hands supporting his chin. He gazed toward the sea.

❊ ❊ ❊

Kathryn's stomach tightened when she looked at him. A bar of sunlight glowed golden on the top lock of his hair and glistened like crystal on his tanned shoulder muscles. A damp matting of dark hair swept over his legs from the bottom of his blue bathing trunks to his ankles. His back was smooth and tan, tempting her to reach over and touch it. She did not.

"This is your last day here," Kathryn whispered, a small lump forming in her throat.

She was feeling better now; the sensation of swimming in murky bleakness had left her. She did not want Flynt to leave.

A thrill of excitement swept over her when his gaze left the sea and came back to rest on her face.

Although Kathryn could not see his eyes, she was very aware of them even through his dark glasses.

"I'll be back," he said. "First chance I get. I promise."

"You will?" Her heart fluttered at his solemn oath.

Flynt smiled. "I promise."

One corner of his mouth twisted up when he smiled. Kathryn first noticed it the day they met. Now, it was even more apparent, and it sparked another ember of recognition, another bit of mystery for the growing puzzle. Where had she seen that smile?

Kathryn swiveled her body to a sitting position on the unsteady hammock ropes. Her thoughts meandered in a disturbing circle, past to present and back.

She replayed the early morning events. Could she have fallen asleep in the pool? The strange visions flickered like recurring shadows in her mind.

Her lips quivered.

"Did something happen at work last night?" Flynt's voice rocked through her surreal thoughts.

As though to dust away the ghosts hidden in her head, Kathryn fanned her fingers through her hair. "Last night ..." She paused and took in a deep breath. "Last night, someone deleted an essential program from the hard drive."

"By mistake?"

"Yes. Now, the resort can't tie in with its reservations network, and the names of paid guests can't be located."

"Where is the back-up?" Flynt removed his sunglasses, stood and came toward her.

"No one knows," she murmured.

His intense eyes unsettled her. They made the computer problems seem unimportant.

The force of his gaze sent blood rushing to her cheeks. She turned her shoulder to hide the blush, but he stopped her and pulled her to face him, all the while studying her with his china blue eyes. Without a word, he took her hand, opened the palm to examine the lines there.

Her heart quivered. "What do you see?"

"Nothing. I just wanted to touch you," he confessed.

Flynt traced his fingers down her palm and over her wrist. His touch was warm, seductive. She closed her eyes, recalling another time, another man's touch.

A man with dark hair and strong, calloused hands.

Cold settled over her. Was the memory from the same dark abyss that held the Rose Hall secret? "How do I know you?" Kathryn asked. Her voice quivered like her heart.

"We met in New York."

"That's not what I meant," she said. "I know you from before ..."

"Before? What do you mean?"

Kathryn bit back a lump that leaped into her throat. What before? She did not know.

Suddenly, loud shouting from the beach grabbed their attention. Kathryn looked up to see a large woman flailing her arms in the air. "Get away from me!"

A flurry of commotion and high-pitched chatter followed. Flynt and Kathryn both turned toward the sounds.

"The beach is public. You can't block it off with no guard, and you got no right to build a fence across it, man." The woman's shrill voice surged with anger that echoed through the long row of palm trees lining the beach.

Kathryn and Flynt stared at each other, then hurried along the sand strip by water's edge. The uniformed guard stood outside a narrow wooden house by a fence at the far end of the beach. A fat chunk of wood clutched in his hand, he confronted a large Jamaican woman.

"No way. You don't belong here no way." His heavy voice bristled with anger.

Legs apart in a wide bullying stance, the guard pressed the stick close to the woman's face. With brazen defiance, she stood her ground, raised both fists high and shook them at him. On her right arm, a wide, silver bracelet glittered in the sunlight.

Nearby, at the point where Hibiscus Hall property joined that of the Edgewater Inn, a crowd of angry people gathered. Their presence threatened to heighten the agitation.

With a protective arm, Flynt pulled Kathryn close to his side. "I don't like the looks of this," he whispered. His eyes darted from the crowd to the guard with his wooden weapon raised high.

As the shouts grew louder, Kathryn's heart thundered against her ribs. She glanced up at dark clouds gathered overhead, sensing the danger that hovered over the mob of frantic Jamaican people.

Confrontation in Jamaica was familiar.

She snuggled unsteadily against Flynt's arm, cradled about her. His embrace held her safe as the scene unfolded like a movie before their eyes.

More people migrated from the adjacent beach. Loud, agitated people. The mood of the crowd grew uglier. The guard yanked a radio from his belt to summon the hotel's base station. Right away, a half-dozen hefty, uniformed men marched down a side path and formed a barrier in front of the milling group.

Immediately, the crowd started to disperse, many vanishing like shadows among the palm trees.

The woman who started the trouble held her ground. "What's the matter with you people?" she called after the others. "Ain't you got no guts? Somebody's got to stand up for our beaches. They don't belong to no hotel. They are free spaces."

In a frenzied motion, she waved her arm with the silver bracelet in front of the security force. As the gate guard tried to catch hold of her, the woman spun deftly beyond his grasp and disappeared into the heavy jungle foliage that edged the beach.

Bracelets. Silver bracelets.

Kathryn never liked them much. Not wide ones.

A few years back, a friend gave her a wide silver bracelet, but she never wore it. In fact, it made her so uneasy, she refused to put it in her jewelry box. When her mother found it lying loose in a kitchen drawer and admired it, Kathryn gave it to her gladly.

Now Kathryn stared at the stretch of thick trees and bushes where the woman disappeared. "I wonder," she mused softly. "Could that be Oswald's mother?"

"Oswald's mother? Who's Oswald?" Lips tense, Flynt frowned at her.

"It must be," Kathryn persisted, unaware of Flynt's question. "Oswald worries about her confrontational tendencies."

In her head the shouts and cries of frustrated, frightened people continued, and Kathryn was shocked to see that the crowd was gone. She blinked hard.

"There's trouble brewing, and Oswald Smith's mother is a part of it."

"Kathryn, who is Oswald?"

"Oh, I'm sorry. He's one of our waiters. Since I got to Jamaica, he's looked out for me." Kathryn leaned against Flynt's chest, so close she could feel his heart beat.

Didn't Flynt sense something? Didn't he feel it, too? If he did, he gave no indication. Like an elusive dream, small memories drifted into her mind, then slipped away as though they never existed at all.

"Kathryn, will you be safe after I leave?" Flynt whispered.

He bent closer. So close, Kathryn felt his warm breath graze her cheek. She stiffened, vividly aware of the heated presence of his mouth moving nearer. Her lips trembled; her heart raced. His lips brushed hers, then settled on them with a hot harshness that startled her.

From all around, a sweet fragrance drifted. Kathryn saw the mist as it gathered over them and recognized the subtle perfumed scent of roses—hundreds of roses in full bloom.

Flynt deepened his kiss, thrusting open her mouth with his tongue, sending intense heat rays careening through her. Her body curved against his, and she returned his kiss, dangerously aware of her unexplained response to a man who should be a stranger but was not.

He held her closer, tighter and she did not pull away. Moments later, it was Flynt who drew back. "Next time," he whispered.

Kathryn shuddered. A haunting sense of recollection lingered ... This man had kissed her before.

She had no doubt.

She stifled a sigh. All around, the scent of roses grew stronger until the fragrance saturated the air.

Love lost.

Her head began to throb. She must return to Rose Hall, the sooner the better. The sturdy old mansion held the key.

And she must take Flynt with her. If he would go...

Kathryn heard the gate in the nearby fence swing open and turned to see Mara hurry toward them. "Did you hear so much shouting?"

"Yes."

"It was the mother of Oswald Smith. Now it is much trouble for him," Mara explained breathlessly.

Kathryn looked at Flynt and shook her head.

"For more trouble, Oswald's mother is into Obeah as well."

"Obeah?" Flynt stared at her blankly.

"That's right," Mara said. "Obeah—Jamaican voodoo."

Obeah. Even in the sunlight, the name chilled Kathryn. She had heard more than one of the employees mention it. Obeah. The name went with rose scents, old gray buildings and Flynt. Her face and hands numb, she stared at him, then at Mara. What were the memories that lay hidden just below the surface? What was Obeah?

Flynt's hand closed over hers, and Kathryn wondered if she was caught between two worlds—the present and the dark one where Obeah and superstition ruled.

CHAPTER FIVE

FROM HER ROOM'S balcony, Kathryn stared across the swaying green sea. The waves rolled in hypnotic rhythm along the white sand. Lately, Kathryn felt like a boat tossed out of control in the waves. Coming to Jamaica had thrown her orderly life into disarray. Now, unrecognizable pieces of an unknown puzzle appeared to lay scattered in every direction she moved.

Perhaps, but not quite. There were qualities—bits and pieces that seemed familiar, that she could almost remember...

Obeah. She hadn't heard the word until she got to Jamaica. Why should Obeah concern her? There was no reason.

But it did. Somewhere, someplace in the past, she'd known about Obeah. From some remote point, beyond herself, she knew she'd been hurt by it. But that couldn't be. If she had, she would remember, wouldn't she? But she didn't.

Yesterday she'd listened spellbound to Mara's story of the practice of Obeah in Jamaica for over three hundred years.

"They still have secret meetings in the hills north of Montego Bay." Mara had thrown up her hands. "That is where Oswald's mother is going. It is true in that family it is the mother that is the problem. Her son is concerned, but what can he do? She is too much caught up in the magic."

Oswald can't do much, Kathryn decided. Not once the magic takes hold. As the thought drifted through her mind, she shivered. Magic. What did she know about the magic?

Pressing her hand to her fluttering stomach, she stood and leaned against the wooden railing. Her gaze crisscrossed the wide stretch of beach before it settled on the bright red hibiscus that glowed like crimson fire near the main dining room. She loved the hibiscus blossoms—always had. But today she somehow connected the flowers with Obeah, and that connection made them dangerous in ways she couldn't understand.

Her forehead knitted in a frown, Kathryn collapsed in a deck chair. Where did Flynt fit in? Why had he come to teach in Jamaica on impulse?

Flynt was gone. He left on an early morning bus bound for Kingston, but, to her surprise, he promised to return to Hibiscus Hall once he got ready for his classes.

"You're not going to get rid of me, not yet," Flynt had said. Then he'd kissed her, leaving an odd sensation in the pit of her stomach. And the smell of roses.

She'd gone to work after that, a bit shaken and unsteady, but she worked well into the morning hours and was pleased with the progress. As yet, no one had found a backup program, but some of the office workers had uncovered support materials and guest lists and had begun the tedious task of replacing the lost information in the computer files. All of them had learned a valuable lesson, and this time they were making more than one duplicate copy.

As she pondered the situation, Kathryn smiled.

Things had gone well last night, quite well. Maybe her suspicions had been unfounded. Maybe no one was trying to sabotage the reservations files after all.

Her mind still on her job, Kathryn got up, opened the sliding glass door and slipped through into the jungle motif that dominated her room. On every side, parrots, their feathers glowing red and blue, sat perched, appearing ready to cry out. They gawked at her from the bedspread, draperies, wallpaper and even from two bright watercolor paintings. For a moment, she felt dominated and intimidated by them. Perhaps she should have refused the assignment and stayed in New York.

Pulling on a yellow cotton dress, Kathryn tied a bright blue sash around her narrow waist, then stood in front of a mirror to check her appearance. The dress looked fine, but the pale, somber face staring back at her did not.

She had come to Jamaica to do a job, but Obeah and a disturbing fascination with Rose Hall Plantation had caught hold of her. Standing amid jungle parrots, Kathryn thought about Rose Hall and Obeah. In some way, they seemed connected. She took a deep breath and vowed to learn everything possible about them both.

With that in mind, she stopped by Mara's office and borrowed her copy of the book about Rose Hall.

❋ ❋ ❋

"Did I catch you by surprise?" Flynt watched Kathryn's pale eyes brighten as they picked up glimmers of light from the candles. The glowing tapers cast a kaleidoscope of colored shadows throughout the Kasbah, the hotel's award-winning theme restaurant.

"I like surprises," she told him, but her voice held little of the vitality he'd expected.

She shifted in her seat and glanced around the exotic restaurant, decorated with North African relics and artifacts. "I'm glad you caught the afternoon bus from Kingston."

"So am I." Flynt reached across the table and closed his hand over hers. "Most of the class paperwork was done already, so I had time on my hands." He leaned forward. "And, of course, I wanted to be in Ocho Rios."

He eyed her warily, wondering why she appeared distant. Her warm response to his kiss the previous evening had led him to believe Kathryn would be glad to see him. Instead, her thoughts seemed to be elsewhere, and she looked unhappy, like she had appeared the first day they met.

Flynt grimaced and lifted his hand from Kathryn's. The long, rough bus ride from Kingston was hard on his knees. He stretched his legs to one side and crossed his ankles. Kathryn remained engrossed in her own thoughts. Why had he bothered to rush through scheduling and rearranging student enrollment data to get back to Hibiscus Hall early? As he studied her pale, tense face, he thought it hardly seemed worth the effort, especially since she seemed unaware that he was with her at the table. What could occupy her thoughts so completely?

Kathryn straightened in her seat. Her lips relaxed and a smile softened her fixtures. "You got through early, so tell me about your day." She leaned toward Flynt, inviting him to talk.

"My predecessor already had my classes organized. Guess he planned to work the entire term." He shrugged. "No one will say for sure what happened to him. I heard that he rented a boat and is taking fishing charters out from Ocho Rios."

"Now that's a career change." Kathryn's face brightened. "So, how did you manage to clear your desk?"

"All I needed to do was go over rosters and review a half dozen pieces of course material, which didn't take much time." He was downplaying, but he didn't want Kathryn to know how much special effort he'd undertaken to get back.

Grasping the handle of her china cup as though it might leap from her fingers, Kathryn slowly sipped the spiced tea the waiter had brought. "I am glad to see you."

Flynt smiled. He watched the tuxedo-clad waiter cross the dark wooden floor. "Oswald Smith is one of the people enrolled in my island economy course."

"He is?"

Flynt nodded.

"I ... I hope Oswald does well," she said. "He's ... he's so intense ... And ... and his mother is an embarrassment." She cleared her throat. "You saw what happened yesterday."

"Yes. It's hard to forget that beach scene." He watched another waiter—this one in Moroccan-style clothing—set down a tray of vegetables and two entree dishes. Flynt served both their plates from gold-trimmed bowls that held chicken, herb-flavored rice, and a medley of vegetables.

"Hello, Kathryn." Brimming with enthusiasm, Mara's accented voice broke into Flynt's thoughts.

"Look Kathryn, Flynt. I have someone you will want to meet." Mara's eyes sparkled with excitement. "Here is Carole Brown. Carole works in our hotel. She is office manager to our executive chef."

The Jamaican woman with Mara stood tall and statuesque, and her dark, creamy complexion glowed in the candlelight. She regarded them with serious liquid-brown eyes and a far-off expression. Flynt suspected Carole Brown could enter a room and, with a glance, be aware of everyone in it.

"You will want to talk with Carole." Mara looped her arm around the taller woman. "She knows much that is interesting ... and more that is unusual ... about Jamaica ... and other things as well." The last words were a whisper in Kathryn's ear, but Flynt overheard them.

While he shook Carole's hand, Flynt heard Mara tell Kathryn, "Ask about Obeah. She knows much, and she has been to Haiti." Mara squeezed Kathryn's arm before she walked away.

Full lips drawn tight and lacking any sign of a smile, Carole sat next to Flynt on the cushioned bench. With stately poise, she arranged the wide skirt of her dress, allowing, as if by design, the brilliant red and blue floral pattern to form color accents against the muted browns and beiges of the room's décor. The wide silver bracelet she wore on her right arm reflected candlelight and glittered like a band of stars in the dimness.

For a moment, Kathryn stared at the bracelet—and at Carole.

"Mara tells me you wish to know about Obeah," Carole began, her deep-set eyes taking on a limpid glow.

"Yes." Kathryn leaned forward in anticipation. The waiter returned with flatware and china for Carole and a fresh pot of spiced tea. Before continuing, Kathryn waited until he had disappeared into the shadowy hall. "I've overheard women in the business office talking about it, but they shift subjects whenever I come up or ask questions."

Carole nodded, and the corners of her lips curled upward, giving the first hint of a smile. "For some, it is a part of their religion; for others, there is fear." Her smile disappeared. "And those who know much, speak little. It is part of their way."

An attractive woman, Carole hardly gave the appearance of an Obeah practitioner, Flynt thought. Although he really knew little about black magic and wasn't sure what a practitioner should look like, his gut told him Obeah was not something to mess with. He scowled at them.

"What's wrong?" Kathryn's eyes darkened.

"Obeah." He said firmly. "Stay away from Obeah." His gaze knifed into Kathryn. "Stay away before someone gets hurt."

"What do you know about Obeah?" Kathryn asked.

"Not much, except that secret rituals and black magic can be dangerous."

"The name Obeah does relate to black magic." Carole took a sip of her tea. "Even today, it remains a secret practice.

"Two forms of Obeah are on our island. One is the bush doctor tradition handed down from our African roots; the other is a newer 'science' and uses manufactured objects and medicines made up by druggists."

The frown lines in Flynt's forehead grew into sharp crevices. "Some things are best left secret. This is one of them."

Both Obeah and this woman made him uncomfortable. Obeah was

locked in a shadowy veil of secrecy. Carole Brown acted like a regal sorcerer about to cast a spell. Flynt saw how vulnerable Kathryn was, saw she was in danger and knew he must try to keep her safe.

Obeah had stirred something in his memory, something he couldn't quite articulate. Yet, he knew instinctively that the stirring connected Obeah with Kathryn in a most unpleasant way. He felt weighted down by a great heaviness.

Kathryn stared at him vacantly. In that instant, Flynt knew that no matter what he said to her, she would seek out Obeah and its secret rituals. To warn her against it was useless.

❊ ❊ ❊

Much as she was attracted to Flynt, Kathryn didn't like his bossiness. Carole Brown was giving a perfectly reasonable explanation of Jamaican folklore, and all Flynt wanted to do was dissuade her from finding out more about it.

"Secret rituals have long been part of the lifestyle of the poor, working class. More and more people recognize the value of preserving the folk religions and activities of Jamaica." Carole Brown waved her hand to a small stage at the far end of the room. "These days, Obeah practices and related revivalism inspire dance choreography." She opened her lips in a broad smile that revealed sparkling white teeth. When Carole gestured with her hand, the silver bracelet slid from mid-arm to her wrist, clanking against the tabletop.

Although the bracelet made her uneasy, Kathryn leaned closer. "Please, I want to go to a service. Can you take me?" From across the table, she felt the force of Flynt's frown.

"Perhaps. There's no regular schedule, but I know where a special ritual is set for the end of the week."

"You do?" Kathryn watched spellbound as the shiny bracelet moved again.

"Yes. In the Blue Mountains at the home of one of the 'band' leaders. I'll be glad to take you."

"Good." Kathryn was convinced that if she could learn about Obeah, it would help explain some of the bizarre happenings she'd been experiencing.

As if looking into her mind, Carole studied Kathryn's eyes. "Yes. I will take you. The services are likely to last all day. Perhaps longer. It is necessary that we leave early in the morning on Friday.

Even so, I do not know if they will permit you to see any possession ..."

Flynt glowered at them, seemingly about to protest.

"Possession? In Jamaica? I read an article once about possession in Haiti ..." Kathryn chewed on her bottom lip.

Was Flynt Kincade right? Was she putting herself in danger? She took a deep, steadying breath. It didn't matter; there were answers she had to have. Perhaps through Obeah she would be able to find some of those answers.

Carole stood. "I will tell you all about the folk religions of old Jamaica on our drive into the hills. It will be a long ride, so there will be much time for talking." With that, she gathered up a large straw handbag, and said, "I must go now. Seven o'clock Friday." She clasped Kathryn's hand.

"Do not worry." Carole turned her tall, commanding frame to assure Flynt. "Kathryn will be fine. I will take care of her. Any trouble, we leave right away. Not to worry. I give you my true promise."

As he walked her to the main office where her evening work with the desk clerks was about to commence, Kathryn felt the cool distance Flynt had put between them. Despite her elation over the trip with Carole, she was disappointed by his negativity and missed holding his hand. He didn't touch her until they reached the entrance.

When Flynt caught her hand and pulled her away from the light, onto the garden walkway, tension filled the air.

"For God's sake, Kathryn." His voice was low, but his irritation with Carole's plans rang loudly. "You're naive to tear into the hills with a woman you don't know. If you won't reconsider, then promise me you'll be careful."

"I'm sure it will be okay. Mara knows Carole."

Almost automatically, she placed her hands against his chest. "Flynt, you remember that day in the gallery?"

"Yes."

"Because of that day, I need to know more." Her voice was soft. "Please understand," she said.

"I'd go with you, but Friday's the day I have to be in Kingston." His sturdy fingers settled roughly over her shoulders, then he turned her to face him.

He looked like he wanted to shake her, and Kathryn braced for it. Instead he said, "I want to understand." Muscles tensed beneath his tanned skin. Then, like an artist studying the elegant bone structure of her face, he held Kathryn at arm's length. "I do want to understand," he repeated.

At the sound of his words, her heart pounded so violently, it shook her body. Her gaze locked with his, and her stomach tightened into a knot. His china blue eyes were so like those of someone else, they made her ever more uneasy.

Bending his head down, Flynt moved his lips toward hers in what seemed slow motion. When he finally touched her mouth, it was with a gentleness too sweet for the urgency growing inside her. In an automatic response, Kathryn tilted her hips forward against his lean body. When he pulled her closer, his kiss deepened until she felt drawn to him like a wild animal. His lips smothered the whimper that curled from her throat. His hands curved beneath her and cupped her buttocks, thrusting her against him harder than before.

Even if she'd wanted to, she couldn't pull back from him. It was as if she'd known him always. Except for the crush of body against body, breath against breath, Kathryn was aware of little else. Until she inhaled deeply. Then, close to her nostrils, the scent of roses drifted, and like a whisper in the night, his hand touched her face. At that moment, she sensed that only she could smell the fragrance. "I have to go," she said, still shaken from their embrace.

"Yes, I know." He kissed her once more, longer, gentler until her knees grew weak and she sank into his body.

"Goodnight," he said. "And stay safe."

❋ ❋ ❋

"You look so—how you say it? 'uptight,' Miss Kathryn." From behind the wheel of the ancient, but well-maintained Plymouth, Carole Brown observed her passenger.

The automobile rumbled like a pair of clumsy oxen over the coarsely paved Jamaican roadway.

"Do I?"

Flynt's opposition to her attending the Obeah ceremony bothered her—especially after the prolonged goodnight kiss. She was foolish to trust a stranger, he'd said. Yet, she'd trusted him that day in New York, she thought whimsically, and he wasn't complaining about that.

Despite Flynt's admonishments, she felt safe with Carole. She eased in her seat and rested her head against the cushion.

Last night's brief scene in the hotel garden replayed in Kathryn's memory. The sweet pressure of his long kiss. Hypnotically, she traced the top edge of her mouth. All during the late evening while working with the computer system, she had relived the vivid sensation of the kiss that left her vulnerable in his arms.

"Your friend—he did not like that you go with me. Why is that? Did I not tell him it would be safe enough?" Carole stared straight ahead.

In the early morning mist, dew-coated ferns gleamed eerily. Kathryn peered through the side window beyond the foliage to where the mysterious blue mountain peaks reached toward the brightening sky. Already the road had narrowed, and the surface worsened noticeably. A chilled breeze blew into the car. Kathryn pulled her white cardigan over her bare shoulders.

"Maybe Flynt has heard tales of the African origin of Obeah," Carole said. "The charms and the magic power go back far. They go into the spirit time of West Africa." In an instant, Carole's forehead filled with deeply furrowed lines. Her eyes glistening like pools of hot tar, the woman turned toward Kathryn and spoke in a forceful voice. "That is our true home."

The sharpness in Carole's voice unnerved Kathryn. If the woman's face was any indication, there could be an emotional explosion at any moment. Kathryn was unprepared for that. Perhaps Flynt had been right after all.

As she studied the driver, a flash of light rippled across the car. She blinked and moved her head to avoid the glare. Then, she realized that, like a mirror, Carole's wide silver bracelet reflected rays of sunlight.

Kathryn slipped sideways in her seat toward the door. Of course, Flynt was right. She recognized that now. She should have investigated before heading off alone with Carole Brown.

How did she know where the woman might take her? Already she suspected that Hibiscus Hall had a spy or two on staff working to sabotage the data system. And she had no idea who they might be. Could this woman be one of them?

Deciding it was best to keep the conversation going, Kathryn said, "West Africa is your true home?"

"Yes. That is what I believe. Hundreds of years ago, our ancestors were crowded onto slave ships and forced to come to Jamaica." Her voice bitter, Carole gazed straight ahead down the uneven roadway. "Once they landed, more than anything else, they wanted to return home to Africa. But, since they had no way to get there, the people believed only death would free them to go back."

"Death? What do you mean?" Kathryn could see the tension in Carole's jaw.

"Some believe there exists an ancestor spirit that leaves when the body dies. That is the spirit the old ones thought would return to Africa."

"An ancestor spirit?" Kathryn lifted an eyebrow at the troubling concept. "Have you been to Africa?" she asked, hoping to redirect the conversation away from the mystic. This woman was as mysterious as the mountains toward which they were headed, Kathryn thought.

"No." The volume of Carole's voice rose with passion. "You don't have to go there to know it. Besides, much of Africa lives on in the people of the islands. That is why Obeah still exists." Carole glanced at Kathryn. "To survive on the plantations, the slaves needed something from their homeland. So, in secret, they practiced the Obeah magic."

"In secret? What would they do?"

Carole's hands gripped the steering wheel as she continued to speak. "Sometimes an evil plantation master would be put under a spell and become ill, even die. It was not unusual for an Obeahman to use poisons to harm the cruel owners."

"Poisons?" She was going into the mountains to learn more about people who used poisons?

Carole maneuvered the Plymouth around a slow-moving dilapidated truck. "Poisons are not used so much these days."

"They aren't?" Kathryn struggled to keep her tone even and conversational. "Tell me about the Obeah service we're going to attend."

"Part of what you will see, Miss Kathryn, is Nine Night."

"Nine Night?"

"Yes. It is an old folk custom. On the ninth night following a death, a special ceremony is held at the home of the deceased. We must give a good ... How you say it? ... vibration to the departed one. We do not wish his duppy—"

"Duppy?"

"That is what we call the spirit ... to stay and haunt any of us."

Strange words and customs. Kathryn had to admit that, if only Flynt were seated beside her, or even Mara, she would feel less anxious.

"The Obeah service today will make ready for the ceremony tonight."

"Tonight? I can't stay into the night. I have to go to work."

"It is fine. We will not go to Nine Night." Braking the car to a slow roll, Carole turned to face Kathryn. "There is much to believe and not to believe in Obeah." She seemed to be measuring her next words. "I do not mean to frighten you, Miss, but for some there is a great evil. The Obeahman comes to catch the spirit, or duppy, in a bowl of water and uses his power to destroy it." Kathryn felt the prolonged stare of Carole's dark eyes.

"Then, there is the opposite called the myal man ..."

"Myal man? What is his role?"

"The myal man uses good medicine to release the captured duppies." The Plymouth slowed almost to a standstill. "I do not know or understand it all, but I do fear some of these people."

"Maybe it isn't a good idea to go to the service after all." Anxious as she had been to learn more about native ways, Kathryn now perceived them in a different light. The things Carole described sounded as dangerous as Flynt had warned they might be—and far more bizarre.

An inner voice nagged at her, urged her to take care. Obeah. A memory lingering from the past struggled to enter her consciousness, but it could not. What was it that called to her, that warned her of the danger?

"Do not worry. It will be safe today. You will see." A faint smile flared up the corners of Carole's lips. "Most of these people are good ones. They are friends. It is not like Haiti."

Haiti. The name careened roller-coaster style through Kathryn's mind, revealing a bit of some ancient cloud hidden there. Unknown symbols and visions flashed through her head, causing her blood to pump like the thundering of a herd of African elephants. She had never been to Haiti, so why would the mere mention of the name strike fear in her heart? Good heavens, she must be losing her sanity. Kathryn Calder didn't see symbols or have visions. She was a no-nonsense woman on a career track at Triple Gold, the computer conglomerate.

Last night, when Kathryn read the book about the legend of the white witch at Rose Hall, she discovered the infamous Annie Palmer was said to have learned voodoo magic spells while in Haiti. The whole subject of voodoo made the tiny hairs on her arms and legs stand up as if lifted by an electrical current.

Throughout it all, Kathryn felt a stunning and frightening connection to the past.

And she remembered her dreams ...

CHAPTER SIX

CAROLE SWERVED THE rickety old Plymouth into the yard of a tiny, ramshackle dwelling. The one-room hut, its bare unpainted wood, darkened by the weather, tilted slightly to one side. A half dozen old cars and one rusty truck sat parked in random disarray around the house. In stark contrast, yellow and red hibiscus bloomed like bright jewels along the sides of the building and among the shabby vehicles.

Kathryn shaded her eyes with one hand. Far to one side, out of sight of the road, a group of twenty or so people was assembled. Some stood in a circle chanting; others sang folk tunes, unfamiliar to Kathryn.

"They are singing a Nine Night song." Carole gathered up her bag and a notebook from the car seat and gestured for Kathryn to follow her.

Adjusting her rumpled skirt, Kathryn trailed a few paces behind the tall, dark-skinned woman who was dressed in all black, feeling so much like an intruder that she wished she could become invisible.

"That is the Obeahman." Carole gestured toward a tall Jamaican, dressed in gray trousers and a long gray shirt who stood to one side of the crowd.

At the fringe of the group, Carole halted, placed a finger over her lips and motioned for Kathryn to listen. But, despite her concentrated efforts, understanding proved impossible. Each speaker chanted in the Jamaican dialect the workers used when they talked among themselves.

It didn't matter that she couldn't understand, for the bizarre scene around Kathryn held her mesmerized. Wild body contortions and guttural chants trapped her. She became the motionless audience of five women who danced in the center of a circle. As if in trance, they rocked forward with measured, jerky gestures, eventually settling their bodies on the ground near a small clay ball embedded with feathers.

For a moment, the unlikely object, with the strange gray feathers fluttering in the breeze, struck a familiar chord in Kathryn's mind.

What was it about the clay? And the feathers? Unsettled, yet fixed, her eyes riveted like a magnet on the eerie procedures. Caught up in the action, she lost sight of Carole Brown.

Droning in a high-pitched monotone, a gaunt woman in a faded red dress fell forward on her knees until her face almost touched the strange, feathered ball. Was that Oswald's mother? she wondered. She looked a great deal like the woman on the beach, and she wore a wide silver bracelet on her right arm. While Kathryn pondered the woman's identity, a man moved forward, his body tilted backward like a boneless limbo dancer.

Captivated, Kathryn watched more and more people converge on the center of the circle. Chanting in unison, some brought chicken feathers and placed them around the clay ball. Finally, the man who Carole indicated earlier was the leader—the Obeahman—brought a live chicken into the middle of the circle. When it became evident the Obeahman intended to kill the squawking bird in some type of ritualistic sacrifice, Kathryn became nauseous. But, although she tried with all her might, she couldn't turn away.

Instead, she became fascinated with the bracelet that the woman, who looked like Oswald's mother, wore. Like a shimmering moon shadow, it glistened with a satin sheen in the brilliant sunlight.

She couldn't pull her gaze away. Silver ... Glimmering ... Sparkling ... Blurring... Shifting into slow motion ... Like a fast train flying past, the scene faded.

In a whirling mist of mysterious quiet, a cloud-like shroud swept in to encompass Kathryn. From high in the nearby hills, an electrifying sound rang out—the loud clamor of ringing bells, followed by the shrill voice of a woman calling, "Aimee."

Kathryn swayed and her knees grew rubbery as another vision came. Five wispy male forms stood not far away, and each, in turn, drank from a vessel passed among them. Without seeing its color, Kathryn knew the liquid in the cup was blood.

Haiti ... Annie Palmer ... The words stood out as if written in the air.

Her face icy cold, Kathryn felt her body spinning until, mindlessly, she sank to the ground into a dark oblivion where only blackness, ringing bells, and vast emptiness existed. Then, her awareness slipped away ... For how long, she did not know.

Someone gripped her by the shoulders, half-dragging, half-carrying her. When Kathryn blinked open her eyes, she found Carole propping her against the car and pulling open the door.

"I am so sorry, Miss Kathryn. I did not expect an animal sacrifice. That is not the way we do. The Obeahman is a stranger and has brought foreign ways from another place. I am so much sorry." With gentleness, Carole stretched Kathryn across the seat of her car and placed a pillow beneath her head, leaving her legs to dangle through the car door opening. "One moment. I will be back."

Slightly nauseous and trembling, Kathryn lay alone and listened to the chanting and singing that continued unchecked. She tried to block from her mind the harsh vision of men and blood, but the image persisted. She wished Carole would hurry back, but time dragged on with no sign of her.

When a car door slammed, Kathryn lifted her drooping eyelids and pushed up on her elbow, hoping to see Carole coming. Instead, she found a tall man wearing a patchwork jacket leaning on the car, staring through the door at her. A mass of long dreadlocks covered his head.

Her heart lurched; she opened her mouth to call out, but no sound came. Nearby, she glimpsed two similar strangers ready to pounce toward her. All three men slipped closer, their long, bony frames stretching near the open car door.

Drawing her legs inside the car, Kathryn maneuvered to the far corner of the front seat and pulled her body into a tight protective ball.

The men made a bizarre sight. Dressed in loose, brightly colored shirts, they stared at her with dark unblinking eyes. The stares of the three men intensified, and one man leaned through the doorway. Now she worried that his harsh glare might burn through her clothing and set it afire.

Rastafarians! She thought they must be members of that cult because each man wore a heavy mane of braided dreadlocks. She could almost touch the narrow braids of the man hovering nearest her.

Perspiration beaded on her forehead. Her breath caught in her throat, Kathryn reached behind her, searching in vain for the door handle. Her hand skimmed the vacant side of the door and dropped to the floor.

Suddenly, one of the men waggled a small, stuffed animal against the windshield near her face. A realistic stuffed African lion glowered savagely through the glass.

Breathing raggedly, Kathryn retreated as far away from the windshield as she could. But, with unflinching gazes, the three men edged closer, their eyes gleaming like hot coal fires.

"What can I do for you?" The steady voice belonged to Carole Brown. Carrying a paper cup filled with water, she calmly approached the car.

For the first time, the men released Kathryn from their scrutiny and turned their scourging stares on Carole. But she refused to be intimidated and stepped toward them instead. When she did, without a word, the men retreated, climbed into a faded blue truck and disappeared down the road on the other side of the crowd.

But, as they were leaving, the tallest man held the stuffed lion high and shook it at them with a menacing growl. A small silver bell, attached to the animal's neck, jangled rancorously.

"Here. Drink this." Carole pressed the cup into Kathryn's fingers. She slid into the car beside Kathryn. "I am sorry this has happened. Are you all right?"

"Yes." Her voice sounded stronger, but inside she quivered. Sipping the water, she looked around her, not knowing what she expected to find.

"Have you seen those men before?" Frowning, Carole twisted the silver bracelet on her arm.

Kathryn shook her head. "No, not at Hibiscus Hall."

"I do not know them either." Carole cast a glance to each side of the car. "They are not from here. They are not part of this Obeah group."

The men. A sacrifice. The odd ball of clay. And that voice. That ghostly voice careened like an echo in her mind. Kathryn knew that voice and that name, but she couldn't remember from where. She'd heard the same voice and name at Rose Hall. And in her dreams.

Aimee. Who was Aimee? The thought gnawed at her heart. Why did she care so much? Why did the name keep revolving in her mind?

"Miss Kathryn, please finish your water. We will leave right away. We have been here for long enough."

Kathryn looked at Carole uncertainly. She needed to remain strong.

"Please. Don't leave because of me. I'm quite all right. I could lock the car and wait for you."

"No. I promised to Flynt you would be fine, and I will keep my promise. I cannot have you here fainting." Without another word, she shut the car door and started the engine.

But Kathryn didn't believe she'd fainted. She believed something else had happened, something more trance-like.

"Carole?"

"Yes."

Kathryn hesitated. "Carole . . . Did you hear someone calling? ... Did you hear a woman calling a ... a girl's name? ... Did you hear her calling from the hills?"

Carole blinked her eyes hard. Then she opened them wide and turned to study Kathryn. "No, I did not." But that is not to say a woman was not calling. Much unseen and unheard by others goes on here in Jamaica just as it does in Haiti."

Kathryn sank back in silence, remembering something she'd read in Mara's book about a girl being haunted to death. She had begun to feel haunted herself. Haunted by voices and visions unseen by those around her. Yet, she didn't believe in anything supernatural.

Thankfully, Carole said nothing more about Kathryn's lapse of consciousness or whatever it had been. Perhaps the Jamaican woman thought she had fallen into a trance like some of the other people at the event.

Although Carole reacted calmly and firmly, the incident with the Rastafarians obviously had disturbed her. Then, there was the stuffed lion. What did that animal with the silver bell mean? Kathryn felt certain it meant something. Perhaps Flynt could do some research for her at the university library.

Closing her eyes, she rested her shoulders against the car seat. How her head hurt. How she wished Flynt had come with her. Jamaica's people were complex, and there was much to learn about them—too much for the little time she had. She had added more puzzles to her list of bizarre unknowns. The Rastafarians were now part of that list.

❈ ❈ ❈

Already darkness obscured the blue-green colors of the Caribbean Sea. Only a vague flicker of pink remained in the evening sky as a reminder of the spectacular Jamaican sunset that had faded into the horizon.

Flynt and Kathryn sat at a narrow table for two along the walled edge of a balcony. The exotic view encompassed a broad expanse of water that sprawled directly beneath the outdoor dining room.

Pensively, Kathryn watched Flynt, wanting to tell him what had happened. Yet, she was uncertain how to go about it. Just having him near made what happened in the mountains diminish in importance.

In the twilight, a hint of color glowed in her cheeks, reflecting the cherry red hue of the peasant-style dress she wore.

"You look beautiful tonight, Kathryn." Flynt's voice blended into the velvet luxury of the candle flame flickering between them. "Was the trip to the mountains a good idea after all?"

"I'm not sure." Kathryn wanted to smile at him, but she couldn't. He had been right to be concerned. Both the mountains and Obeah were dangerous for her. More dangerous than she'd ever dreamed. But did she dare let him know?

With a flick of her fingers, she checked to make certain the bright red hibiscus blossom still clung to her hair. The hairpin she'd searched frantically to find was holding the flower securely in place.

"Roses, Kathryn," he whispered, looking at her hair. "You should wear roses, not hibiscus blossoms." The sparkle was in his eyes, the smile still on his lips.

A small knot began in her throat. "Roses?" Why had he mentioned roses? When they kissed, had he smelled them, too? She'd thought it only her imagination. "Yes. In fact, you remind me of my rose garden."

"You have a rose garden?" Kathryn said in surprise.

"I did when I lived in New York City." He shrugged and reached for her hand. "It was a small garden—only seven bushes—but each was a prize-winner with exquisite blooms."

Beside them, the sea grayed as the final remnant of daylight vanished, but Flynt didn't take his eyes from her face. "I especially miss the talisman roses."

"Talisman roses. I've always loved them..." Her voice trailed away.

"I had to have that garden, and to this day I don't know why. Particularly since mine was a roof garden apartment, and space for the roses was at a premium." He continued to stare at her. "God, Kathryn. You make me think of those roses..."

"I'll take that as a compliment."

"I hadn't thought of them since I got to Jamaica. Strange." Flynt dismissed the subject with another shrug.

Strange, indeed, Kathryn thought. The roses shifted like a fragrant breeze through her mind.

"Enough about that. Tell me about your day with Carole and the trip into the mountains."

"I'm glad I went," she said. And she was. Then Kathryn lowered her voice to almost a whisper. "Flynt, I think Oswald's mother was there. It's hard to tell when you don't know someone well, but one of the women looked like the woman we saw arguing with the guards."

From the corner of her eye, Kathryn detected movement. She concentrated on the shadowy bushes beneath the ledge. The movement ceased. She saw nothing except the leafy outline of tropical plants. Her imagination. Nothing more, she decided.

Flynt shrugged. "That shouldn't surprise you. Mara Hoffman told us Oswald's mother was involved with Obeah."

A waiter appeared with a bottle of dark red wine. Blood red. Kathryn's stomach knotted at the sight of it, and her once ravenous appetite diminished. After the man finished pouring each of them a glass, he hovered in the nearby shadows, remaining within easy earshot of the couple. "Flynt, without checking, tell me if you still see our waiter," Kathryn said quietly.

"Yes, he's there. Why?"

"In the three weeks I've been at Hibiscus Hall, I've never seen this man before. And he seems to be hanging about."

Flynt glanced at the nosy waiter. "That will be all," he said, curtly dismissing the man. Then he waited for the man to leave before continuing their conversation.

Kathryn's eyes remained focused on the wineglass, but she hadn't taken even a sip.

Flynt frowned. "Is something wrong with the wine?"

She hesitated. "No. Nothing ... I'm just not used to drinking." How could she explain her response without revealing her vision? In an attempt to change the subject, she asked, "Was Oswald in your class today?" Still, Kathryn didn't touch the wine.

"Yes, he was. Oswald's an amazing young man." Flynt's voice rose with enthusiasm. "He's bright and eager to learn everything he can." Flynt sipped from his glass. "Not so he can go to the States, but so he can improve his status here in Jamaica."

Flynt brushed aside a lock of wavy brown hair that had fallen across his forehead. Kathryn liked the slightly disheveled appearance the fallen strand gave him and resisted the urge to reach across the table and disturb a few more waves.

"He wants to stay in Jamaica?"

"Yes. That's a refreshing idea, don't you think? Too many people here hope to leave." Grimly, Flynt tightened the set of his chin. "They're setting themselves up for disappointment, I'm afraid."

"Oh? How so?"

"Jamaicans go to New York or Miami and find it difficult to live in a big city. They are used to warm weather and a slower pace of living. Still, they yearn for a new opportunity—one that often doesn't come and then…" Flynt let his voice trail off.

Kathryn watched him in silence. Flynt cared about the people. He really cared, like another man she'd once known…

"Flynt…"

"Yes?"

"Do you know anything about the Rastafarians?"

"Not much. Why?"

"I've been wondering about them." How could she share her fear without telling him what had happened in the Blue Mountains? Maybe they hadn't been menacing at all. Maybe she was simply overreacting. No. Not true. One of them had leaned inside the car. She definitely considered that threatening. But, regardless, she wanted to know more about the cult group with the dreadlocks.

"Rastafarians. I'm certain I can find out quite a bit at the University."

"Would you?" She had planned to ask Flynt to do some research on them in the college library. Now, he was volunteering to do just that.

"Of course."

She was vaguely aware of the waiter's return, but hardly noticed when the man lingered nearby.

"What was that?" Kathryn saw a dark form slip from behind three large potted plants and disappear toward the beach.

"I didn't see anything," Flynt said.

Kathryn brushed it off, telling herself she was just jumpy from her day with Carole. As they began their caramel ice cream, Oswald Smith rushed like a flying shadow up the steps from the beach.

"Mr. Kincade! Miss Kathryn! Please. Can I talk with you?" Out of breath and obviously upset, he surveyed the dark crevices behind and around the bushes.

"Of course. What is it?" Flynt stood and motioned toward an empty seat nearby. "Pull up that chair and sit with us."

"No. No." He indicated his head waiter uniform. "As you can see, I am on duty. It is not proper for a waiter." Once again, he regarded the dining room nervously.

"Go on, Oswald. What's the problem?" Flynt said.

"Perhaps you have heard about my mother. She is a bit of a radical."

Flynt and Kathryn nodded in unison.

Agitated, Oswald shifted his weight from side to side. "She got in trouble on the beach the other day. After that my boss warned that if she caused any more trouble, he would dismiss me."

"Yes. We heard that." Flynt glanced at Kathryn before he continued. "What's the matter?"

"Mr. Kincade. There is another problem now." Oswald paused, craning his neck to survey the beach before continuing in a very low voice. "My mother did not come home this evening. By five o'clock, she is always there for the younger children. Already it is dark and after eight o'clock, and she is not there. My sisters are very worried. I fear someone has brought harm to her."

"Could she be stranded somewhere?" Kathryn didn't know whether to mention the Obeah meeting where she believed she'd seen her.

"No. I do not believe so." Again, Oswald took a sidelong look about. "My sister saw her late this afternoon when she returned from the Blue Mountains."

So, she had been in the mountains. His mother had been at the Obeah meeting. She must have been the woman wearing the wide silver bracelet.

"Mr. Kincade. Miss Kathryn. If I go to search for her now, I will lose my job. I cannot even mention my mother to anyone here. That is because she has caused so much trouble already."

"What about your sisters? Can't they help?"

"My oldest sister is only twelve. The other three are little more than babies. My sister cannot leave them alone. She left them for a few minutes to come and tell me. I do not know what to do."

Flynt and Kathryn looked at each other. "Maybe we can help."

"I would be most grateful if you could." Oswald stiffened to a straight, formal posture.

"Do you have any idea where she might be?" Kathryn knew so little about the area it seemed almost ludicrous to offer help. Still...

"I do not know, but she works near here sometimes."

"In another resort?" Kathryn's gray eyes widened. She couldn't imagine Oswald's mother working for a resort.

"Oh no, Miss Kathryn. My mother resents the resorts. She would not work in any of them."

"Then what does she do?" Flynt broke in.

"She's a guide."

"A guide?"

"Yes. She offers to take vacationers around in the town. At the end of the tour, they pay her something."

"You mean they give her a tip." Kathryn realized his mother was like some of the women who had approached her to take a tour of the area. There were so many of them that often it was a nuisance to leave the resort even for a few minutes.

"That's right. Sometimes she makes as much as twenty American dollars in one afternoon. It is a good job for her."

"Where near here does she work?" Flynt persisted.

Oswald's nervous twitching increased. "Workers are building a new luxury resort nearby. Recently, Mother has taken people through the grounds to show off the progress. She may have gone there." He tightened the muscles of his face. "Someone at the construction site may have tried to harm her. She is not much liked around here."

"All right, Oswald. I've noticed the construction from the bus. We'll start where the new buildings are going up. If she's there, we'll find her." Flynt stood, shook the waiter's hand, then caught hold of Kathryn's arm and guided her to the door.

"Turn left outside the front entrance. You can't miss it."

Oswald whispered from behind them. "Thank you for looking. Please find her," he pleaded.

"We'll do what we can," Flynt promised.

As they left the hotel and turned toward the construction site, Kathryn clung to Flynt. She wondered what possible chance they had of finding

Oswald's mother in the darkness.

The people who ran the resort disliked her, but would they do something to hurt Mrs. Smith? Kathryn hoped not, but there were people in Jamaica with strange, dedicated ways, ways that related to Haitian voodoo, so she'd learned today. And there were other things, too, like the Rastas and the stuffed lion. Could Oswald's mother be involved in those things, too? Did she dare mention them to Flynt?

Bright pinpoints of starlight glittered in the velvet blackness overhead. Darkness closed around Flynt and Kathryn, cloaking and caressing them. No streetlights, no sounds other than the steady churning of waves against the shoreline broke the solitude of the night.

"If we had a full moon, it would help." Flynt's warmth edged near her. She felt the heat of him in the darkness, and, even in their search, it caused her blood to surge and rush to her head. When he placed his arm around her shoulders, she grew dangerously aware of every sturdy muscle that rippled to touch her from beneath his clothing.

Inside and out, Kathryn shivered. Alone with him in the dark, she wanted to snuggle closer, but she feared the electrical charges that cut the air between them. She felt them reach, like a threatening hand, through the heavy night air.

"We have to hurry," Kathryn whispered and pulled away from Flynt's warmth. "We have to find Oswald's mother before it's too late."

"She might not be here."

In the darkness, Flynt's voice sounded far off, slightly unreal. It touched Kathryn's ears like a ghost from the past ... Like the eerie voice of the woman calling "Aimee."

"Flynt. I'm afraid something has happened ... Something related to this morning." For a moment, Kathryn hesitated, unsure whether to reveal more. "I told you I thought she was at the Obeah gathering in the mountains. After what Oswald said, I'm certain I saw her."

Nervously, she tugged at the edge of her dress sleeve. Her eyes focused on the darkened earth by her feet. "The dancing and the chants weren't what I expected ... Th ... They were frightening, and..." She breathed deeply. "Oswald's mother was involved in the most gruesome part." In the dark, Kathryn covered her eyes with her hands. "I don't want to think about it."

"You don't have to." Flynt's arms encircled her shoulders with comforting warmth. A rugged, protective heat emanated from all around him, and, just for a moment, she wished she could sink into his arms and never leave.

In her subconscious mind, she heard the name, Aimee. Something unexplained wanted to draw her far back into a forgotten past, something connected to both Flynt and Aimee. What could it be?

Kathryn sank down on a low fence that edged a portion of the construction project. It was one of the few things she could make out in the darkness. "Rastafarians with long dreadlocks came up during the service," she whispered. "Could they have something to do with Mrs. Smith's disappearance?"

In the faint light, Kathryn could barely make out the scowl that emerged on Flynt's face. "At this point, I'm beginning to think anything's possible." His voice was a growl that reverberated into the night. "Come on."

"If only it weren't so dark." Kathryn stumbled over a rise in the bare, rocky ground, then tried to regain her bearings.

"Here. Hold onto my arm." Flynt halted next to a pile of debris and waited for Kathryn to grab the crook of his bent arm.

"Where are we?" she whispered.

"Moving toward the middle of the grounds. When we're more centered, we'll start calling her name."

Cautiously, they made their way toward a central building that looked nearly completed on the exterior. She glanced around uneasily. Here and there in the night, Kathryn thought she discerned shadows—shadows of humans.

"Mrs. Smith. Mrs. Smith." Flynt leading, Kathryn holding onto his hand, they circled the tightly closed building, both calling her name. But they heard nothing, only the resounding splatter of sea water that surged into the deserted sand beach.

"Let's walk along the beachfront," she suggested. Kathryn needed space to breathe. Besides, she hoped reflections on the water might help them see better. Where they now stood, she felt helpless and in danger of falling. And her imagination kept playing tricks, making her see fleeting shadows that looked like they belonged to real people. Even though she was certain they did not, she regarded the shadows uneasily.

"All right." Flynt tightened his grip on her hand and directed her toward the sound of water. When they reached the shore, they turned up the beach, away from town. "Let's try this way first. Damn. I hope she's out here. It's like looking for a lost key in the sand."

"Mrs. Smith!" All along the way, they kept stopping and calling her name. Still, they got no answer.

"What was that?" Flynt slowed his pace and listened.

Kathryn paused. "I didn't hear anything."

"Listen."

"Do you think you heard Mrs. Smith?"

"I don't know." He whispered harshly, pulled her to a halt and turned to look behind them.

Not far away, in the low-lying brush, Kathryn glimpsed a moving shadow. She opened her mouth to warn Flynt, but it was too late.

The shadow flew like a cat through the air. With claw-like appendages, it grasped Flynt.

"What the hell?" Flynt cried out and tried to leap aside, but he didn't make it.

The thrashing shadow fell heavily against Flynt.

Kathryn caught her breath. Flynt plummeted to the ground with a dull thud.

CHAPTER SEVEN

KATHRYN WATCHED HUNKS of sand and shadows rise and fall against the murky sky. Low yelps and grunts punctuated the thrashing, jolting forms.

Then, she saw something else. Long thin braids. A whole mane of them wriggled in disarray like flaring vipers in midst of struggle. A Rastafarian. But what did he want with Flynt? He must be after her, not him.

Kathryn searched for some way to stop the attacker. Finally, she got her hands on a piece of two-by-four. She raced toward the struggling men. Just as she raised the board to swing, the man slipped from Flynt's grip and vaulted away. A springing acrobat, the tall, lean man catapulted in giant steps toward the trees. Braids swinging behind him, he disappeared like dust into the shadows.

Kathryn rushed to Flynt's side. His eyes glassy, a cut bleeding by his mouth, he sat propped against a rocky bank that bordered the sand.

"What ... What was that all about?" Dazed, he raked his fingers through his hair.

"Are you hurt?" Anxiously, Kathryn leaned over him.

Flattening the palms of his hands against the beach, Flynt pushed to a standing position and wriggled his shoulders. "No. I don't think so. Sand on my clothes and a big dose of indignity. That's all." He chuckled, but the sound was forced.

Her hands shaking, Kathryn brushed small granules from the back of Flynt's shirt.

"Where did that guy come from?" Flynt asked. He tucked the tail of his shirt back inside his trousers.

"From the shadows," Kathryn mumbled. "I thought it was my imagination, but he must have been there all along."

"He never tried to hit me. Strange fellow. All arms and legs."

"And braids."

"Yes. Those, too." He grimaced and gingerly touched his cheek. "Must have cut my face when I hit the sand."

Although Flynt was making light of the harrowing event, Kathryn could tell the surprise attack had left him uneasy. She watched him loosen his muscles, then move to stand against a nearby palm tree.

When Kathryn started toward him, a faint glimmer in the sand caught her attention and stopped her. Without a word, she reached down into the darkness and closed her fingers around the cool satin surface of a small piece of metal. Groping, she discovered it was attached to a soft fabric object. She lifted the mystery item from the beach and brushed the sand from it.

"This is hardly the time to go shell-hunting." Flynt's voice teased yet edged on seriousness.

But Kathryn barely heard him speak. She knelt in the sand, holding her find at arm's length. As she came to realize what she had found, cold chills rippled through her body. "It's not a shell."

Clutching the object, she straightened her shoulders and stood up. Although something inside Kathryn urged her to throw it back onto the beach, she could not.

"What is it then?" By now, Flynt's voice hinted irritation.

"Th ... This." Her legs shaky, Kathryn moved beside him and held the article in the light of the moon now rising above the water.

"It's a stuffed animal of some sort." Flynt leaned closer, trying to see more details in the darkness.

"It's a lion with a bell attached to its neck."

"So? Some child lost it."

"Some child didn't lose it. It belongs to that man—the one you were fighting with."

"Of course, it doesn't. It doesn't belong to him." Flynt's response was emphatic. "Carrying around a stuffed animal is a rather wimpy pastime for a man, don't you think? Especially one who jumps people on the beach."

"N ... No." She dreaded telling him but knew she must. "One of the Rastas I saw today had a little stuffed lion with him. Like this one." She held it up. "I think it's a symbol or icon of some sort." Kathryn forced her voice to stay level. "And, Flynt, he was threatening Carole and me by shaking the lion at us when he left."

He chuckled. "Threatening? Come now, are you certain?"

"Yes." Kathryn was disappointed, but she couldn't blame him for not believing her.

"I don't think you need to worry over a silly stuffed animal." His voice gentle, Flynt threaded his fingers through Kathryn's hair that was now damp, sticky and tangled by the wind.

His touch sent a sudden rush flying through her. She looked into his face but said nothing. He must think her reaction to the lion a bit strange. But he hadn't seen those three men glaring down at her in the car; he hadn't heard the voices at Rose Hall; nor, did he know about the ones today. He didn't know, and she couldn't tell him.

"Let's go." He caught her hand in his. "If we're going to find Mrs. Smith tonight, we must keep looking."

"What about that man?" Trudging unprotected along the dark beach seemed to be asking for more trouble, Kathryn thought.

"We'll keep a sharp lookout for him," Flynt assured her, "but, remember, if he'd wanted to hurt me, he would have done more than scuffle. After all, he had the advantage of surprise attack." She had to agree.

As the moon rose higher, the beach and construction site took on a silver sheen; and, for the first time, they could make out their surroundings. Searching the low-lying brush, they crossed the length and breadth of the beach, calling softly, but with no luck.

Kathryn kept the funny little lion tight against her, not wanting to chance losing it in the sand. After all, the lion was the only clue they had to the attack and why it happened. A link had to exist between the beach assault and the three men in the Blue Mountains. She was certain of it.

Flynt stopped and took a long breath. "There's no place else to look except around the unfinished buildings." He stared back toward the new resort. "She's not in the beach area. If she were, she should have heard us calling."

"Unless..." Kathryn hesitated to say what she didn't want to think.

"Unless something terrible has happened to her..."

They turned and hurried toward the buildings. Then a small noise brought Kathryn to an abrupt halt. "Do you hear something?"

"Only the sound of leaves rustling. Is that what you mean?"

"No. I thought I heard something else. Come on." Grabbing Flynt's hand, Kathryn pulled him in the direction of a half-finished building, located a short distance from the beach.

As they neared the rambling, pale gray structure, both Kathryn and Flynt heard muffled cries that sounded more like the whimpers of a hurt animal than human sounds. Together, they wound through discarded boards and jagged pieces of metal. Peering into the building's interior, they noticed the foremost room had been tiled to accommodate a sunken bathtub. Now, the moaning sounds cut abrasively across the tiles from what looked like a rear-bedroom area. Two wooden steps led up to the unfinished room.

"Kathryn, wait here while I check out the noise." Flynt spoke in a commanding whisper.

"No. I am coming with you." She was too curious to wait outside and didn't care how determined he sounded. "Besides, you might need help."

Hand-in-hand, Flynt and Kathryn crossed the ceramic floor, uneven with missing tile sections. Avoiding a pile of sawdust, they clattered noisily across the higher-level wooden floor. If they had tried to remain unnoticed, it wouldn't have worked for the floor creaked with every step.

"I thought the sounds came from this side, but I don't hear them now."

"Here, Missy. Help! Help!" The sound was low and guttural, but it was a woman's voice.

Simultaneously, Flynt and Kathryn moved to the darkest corner of the room. Groping about, Kathryn's hand touched and caught hold of a wrist with a cold circle of metal around it. Without light, it proved impossible to see the person who was lodged inside a crevice in the wall.

"Missy. Thank the good spirits." The voice rasped each word, but the sound was firm and strong.

"Are you Mrs. Smith? Oswald's mother?" Her question seemed a bit callous, as if she wouldn't help someone else.

"That I am, Missy. Colette Smith. But I am hung tight as a stuffed chicken in this hole."

"You're caught on something?" Flynt broke in. He leaned over Kathryn's shoulder, trying to see.

"My leg—it went down between the walls. I cannot make it come out. Thank the good spirits that you came along."

"Are you hurt?" Kathryn asked.

"No. I am hung. That is all. I am afraid an old Obeahman has caught me up in a spell. That is where the hurt is."

As the full impact of the woman's words hit Kathryn, she loosened her grip on the metal bracelet that clung to Colette Smith's wrist. Obeahman? Spell? What did she mean?

"Damn! We need a light." Flynt felt his way around Mrs. Smith, attempting to determine the position of her trapped leg. "Kathryn, try to find a power cord. Maybe the workmen have one around somewhere with a light attached."

"Oh, yes. There is a light," Mrs. Smith offered. "I saw it near the place where the jacuzzi soon will be."

With careful maneuvering, Kathryn made her way back toward the opening and into the moonlight. "Wait. Here's something." She pulled a thick, heavy cord free from a pile of discarded ceramic tiles. At the end of the line dangled a dingy construction lamp. A flick of the switch illuminated a dim bulb.

"It works."

Soon, with the aid of the feeble electric light, she and Flynt were busy extricating the woman's leg that was wedged tight between two sections of wall.

"How the hell did you get caught this way?" Flynt demanded in frustration. "There should be no reason for anyone to walk along the edge of this outside wall.

Mrs. Smith's head drooped. "It is for an American coin. I saw it lying down there, but I could not touch it with my hand. Then I tried to reach it with my slampata."

"Slampata? What's that?" Kathryn stopped pulling and waited.

"So sorry, Missy. Slampata—that is Jamaican. It means shoe."

"Oh."

As the two women talked, Kathryn used her knowledge of first aid to check the trapped leg. "I don't think it's broken," she whispered to Flynt. He prodded and shoved Mrs. Smith's bare leg until, at last, he could pull it, and her, free.

"Thank you, sir, and you, Missy."

"I'm Kathryn Calder. I'm working with the computers at Hibiscus

Hall. This is Flynt Kincade.

Oswald is in one of the classes Flynt's teaching at the university in Kingston."

"That is a good place for Oswald to be. I am glad for him to be at the university. He should get his degree and become a big, important man one day."

Flynt smiled. "Yes, Oswald is going to be one of my best students. I can tell that already." As Flynt chatted with the woman, Kathryn watched the sparkle return to his eyes.

In the dim light, she observed the scratch on the side of his cheek. "It's still bleeding," she declared in a low voice only he could hear.

With her fingertips, she gently touched the side of his face.

"It's okay." Silently, his hand brushed a kiss from his lips to hers.

Flynt's gesture went unnoticed by Mrs. Smith. Her black eyes held a stony stare, and her gaze shot past Kathryn, down at something on the floor.

"No. No." The woman shrieked, suddenly jumping in a hysterical frenzy amidst the rubble.

"Take it away. Take away the bad spirit. A jinnal has touched it." She hopped from one foot to the other, dancing backward away from Kathryn and Flynt. Moving with the agility of a young teenager, Mrs. Smith edged out of the building toward the beach. "I must go now. I must hurry home to see my children. Thank you for my leg." Never once stopping her movement backward, Mrs. Smith disappeared into the darkness along the beach.

"What was that all about?" Flynt's gaze followed the woman's path through the building rubble. "Oswald may have more to overcome than we suspected." A half-grin appeared on his face.

"I have no idea what she was talking about." Kathryn stared after Mrs. Smith in wonder. Could the woman's actions relate to her comments about a spell and an Obeahman? Immediately, as if an unseen force drew her gaze, Kathryn looked down at her side and saw what had caused the woman's flight. The small stuffed lion, with the silver bell around its neck, sat beside her on the floor. In the dimness, it was lifelike.

The iridescent green eyes glowed in the dark. When she picked up the small golden form on the beach, she hadn't noticed the round glass eyes shimmering as they were now. Perhaps the change resulted from the light of the rising moon.

Instead of confiding in Flynt, Kathryn kept her thoughts to herself. She couldn't tell him about the weird notions that started to flood her mind. Flynt had disapproved of her getting involved in Obeah to begin with. Certainly, he wouldn't think kindly of the latest twist in events. Because of Mrs. Smith's intense reaction, she feared the lion had more meaning than she originally suspected. That was an unsettling thought.

"Do you think she'll be all right by herself?" Kathryn asked.

Flynt chuckled bitterly. "That woman could slip unscathed from most anything. Did you see her leg? Not even a scratch. Not a limp."

Kathryn took hold of Flynt's arm when he offered it. He squeezed her hand. "I'm sorry, but Mrs. Smith's attitude bothers me. We spend all evening looking for her; we find her and free her pinned up leg. All she says is 'thank you,' and vanishes into the night. At least, she could have stayed and talked for a few minutes and let us see to it she got back okay."

"Don't be too hard on Colette Smith, Flynt. Something frightened her, something we may not understand."

Flynt said nothing, but his eyes were suddenly serious and dark.

"We'll have to let Oswald know his mother's all right. She can't go to Hibiscus Hall herself."

"We will. Later," he said, his voice low.

In an unexpected motion, Flynt caught hold of her hand and tightened his grip on it. His heated fingers curled around hers, then pressed against her thigh. She took a deep breath and stiffened, knowing it was his touch that warmed her blood. Then, uneasily, she stole a glance at him. He was leading her back toward the beach. Her heart pounded.

Like a vigilant overseer, the moon hung above the rippling Caribbean Sea. Magic shimmers of butter-soft light sparkled in flecks of silver dust over the black waters.

As they strolled along the beach, Flynt's hand against her thigh grew hot. In the darkness, he strained to see Kathryn's face, but her features lay hidden in the shadows. When even the moonlight refused to reveal them, he took a deep breath, then brushed aside a strand of her hair rumpled by the subtle breeze.

"I knew that first day that you were special," Flynt told her. He stopped and his hands on her shoulders whirled her to face him. "I had this remarkable feeling then that I can't explain," he said.

"What kind of feeling?"

"One I truly cannot explain." He tightened his grip on her shoulders.

❀ ❀ ❀

They stood so near the water that waves bathed their feet, but Flynt paid little attention. In the moonlight, her golden hair glimmered like spun silk, and the strands fell in sculptured smoothness to caress her shoulder tops. Wilted and closed, the red hibiscus blossom he'd found for her still clung stubbornly to the silken tresses.

His hand fanned out against her cheek. Soft, Flynt thought, like touching a fresh blossom. Captivated, he pressed his face against her hair and breathed in its scent. Roses and lost battles. Why did she remind him of both those things? He didn't know why, but she did.

Flynt had an urgent need to hold her close, a longing, in fact. With one hand, he cupped Kathryn's chin and tilted her head upward. In the moonlight, the world moved in slow motion. He sensed her eyes closing, her lips parting to receive his kiss. Silver light shimmered on her hair, and, mesmerized by it, he drew back and watched it shift across her head. Then, with a slow deliberation, he plucked out the dead flower.

"You deserve fresh flowers," he whispered. "Rosebuds dappled with the morning dew." Flynt leaned forward and met her warm, sweet lips with his.

❀ ❀ ❀

Kathryn's head reeled. Rosebuds. His words vibrated inside her ears. Rosebuds. Her heart pounded against the suffocating fullness inside her chest. She fought back hot tears that welled up in her eyes and threatened to overflow. But it was no use, for like the day in the museum, the tears fell out of control. Flynt's words had caused her to cry, or was it his kiss? For a moment, she stared at him in confusion, stared through a veil of tears. Then, embarrassed, she pulled away and tried to turn where he couldn't see her face.

"You need another handkerchief," he said in a low voice turned husky. With gentle fingers, he reached out and brushed aside her tears. In the moonlight, she could barely make out Flynt's gaze darkening, then somberly lingering on her face. He took a step forward and again drew her close against his stiffening body.

"Thank you," she said. Her voice was a soft breath against his cheek.

Mesmerized by him, Kathryn fitted her body to his. She enjoyed the power evident in the taut muscles of his chest. Leaning into him seemed as natural as breathing.

A faint breeze rippled over them. Kathryn did not resist when Flynt lifted her skirt and placed his hands on her bare thighs.

"I've dreamed of making love to you," he whispered in her hair.

Dreamed, she thought in wonder. She had more than dreamed. It was as if he had held her in his arms and made love to her before. Was that possible?

Her knees grew weak as his lips grazed her face, touched her ear and trailed deliberately, slowly to her lips. Kathryn stroked his hair and pulled him closer—so close she felt the sturdy beat of his heart.

Behind them, the sea roared, and her heart thundered a thousand times louder. Their kisses deepened, grew more probing, more compelling, more charged with need.

But there was something else, something to which she'd almost become accustomed. With each kiss, the scent of roses increased until the fragrance billowed all around, and through closed eyes, she saw dozens of rose bushes alive with pink, white and yellow blossoms, dancing in the breeze everywhere around them. The vision was like a memory—an enchanting memory filled with its own perfume.

Flynt's soft kisses touched her eyelids and cheeks. "So soft," he whispered, stroking her face with one hand. "Your skin's soft as flower petals, smooth as velvet. Rose petals," he murmured against her neck.

Rose petals. Like in her vision, she thought. She swallowed back the memory and drifted against the hardness of his body, drifted back into the present.

She felt his hands slide below the neckline of her dress. The bare skin of her chest tingled beneath his touch, her breath came in ragged spurts. In another moment, his fingers moved down to loosen her bra. Then her breasts fell free.

Common sense told her to grab her clothes and run away from him. She hadn't known him long. Common sense said leave before she made a mistake, but right now she didn't care much for common sense.

Instead she took a deep breath and waited for his hands to cup her bare, firm breasts. When he did, her breathing almost stopped.

Flynt moved more quickly now. With his hand, he slipped her dress far off the shoulder, exposing one breast to the night air. Satisfied, he bent his head and brought his mouth against the smooth, warm flesh. She moaned softly and let her dress fall to her waist.

"I've never seen a more beautiful woman," Flynt told her. His hoarse voice lingered low in the night air. Brazenly, he stood back and watched the moonlight play across her breasts, then reached to let his fingers trace their smoothness.

A crackling voice broke the spell. "Missy!"

CHAPTER EIGHT

CAUGHT BY SURPRISE, Flynt lurched closer to shield Kathryn from the voice. Kathryn pulled up her dress, thankful for the elastic neckline. Flynt squeezed her hands.

A figure stepped from the shadows a few yards down the beach. It was Oswald Smith's mother.

"Missy. Mr. Kincade." The woman sprinted along the sandy strip, her arms splaying the air, silver bracelet flashing ominously in the moonlight.

When Colette Smith reached them, she spoke in rushed bursts. "I have talked with Oswald. He told me that he was worried and that you offered to look for me. Now, he is angry with his old mother for going off and leaving you here." She hung her head in remorse and studied the ground. "I am truly sorry."

Kathryn's face burned a cherry red almost the color of her dress. She regretted the woman's return, regretted the interruption, regretted the coolness that suddenly filled the air, dissolving the magic.

She hoped Colette Smith had failed to see their passionate encounter. Flustered, Kathryn flattened the palm of her left hand against the fiery surface of one cheek. When she glanced down, she saw the plush golden lion and covertly retrieved it from the sand. With a quick motion of her hands, she managed to hide it in the folds of her skirt.

When she looked at Flynt, Kathryn found it impossible to separate her gaze from his vivid blue eyes. The pupils glowed in the night with a luminescence that sent warmth careening through her.

Moments later, Colette Smith talked non-stop as she hurried along the beach with Flynt and Kathryn. "I would like to explain to you about the Rastas and the lions." She waved both arms in the air. "I have seen before the symbol of the lion." She halted her frenzied pace and turned to Kathryn. "Missy, would you like to know more?"

Kathryn hesitated then glanced at Flynt. "Would you?" she asked, a hopeful inflection in her voice. Again, she was aware of an unseen force that urged her to learn all she could about the Rastas, Obeah and Haitian voodoo.

Flynt shrugged. "Is there somewhere we can go?" he asked. "A secluded spot?"

"Yes. Let's find a place to talk," Kathryn said. They couldn't return to Hibiscus Hall. Not with Colette Smith.

"There is a place at the end of the beach, beyond the last gate." Colette extended her arm in that direction. "It is a Jamaican bar."

"All right," Flynt agreed. "Lead the way." Although he gave no overt indication, Kathryn sensed that Colette's high-handed ways caused him not to trust her.

Following Colette, Kathryn and Flynt wound past a remote, tree-lined section of beach. When flickering gray shadows began to dance across their path, Kathryn tightened her grip on Flynt's hand. She half-expected the man with dreadlocks to swing Tarzan-style from the trees. As if to reassure her, Flynt pulled Kathryn closer to his side.

Eventually, they reached a tiny building that, from the shabby exterior, looked little more than a shack. But, a string of electric lights shimmered in the trees above an open dining area, casting an atmosphere of coziness. Three couples sat on stools around a bar at the far end, smoking cigarettes and chatting. The night air carried the smoke and the sound of voices down the beach in the opposite direction.

"Bamboo By The Sea," Colette Smith announced smugly. "It is the place my friend bought with her tour money. Here, I am welcome."

Kathryn raised one eyebrow. The "tour" business must be better than she would have guessed. She supposed "tour" meant, as Oswald had explained, showing vacationers around the town and new building projects.

They sat down at a small wooden table, away from the other customers.

Their seats overlooked the beach. Kathryn cast a glance of approval at the lights that brightened the area.

"Would you both like hamburgers?" Flynt pointed out a menu board that hung behind the bar.

"Yes, that sounds good." Kathryn kept her gaze on the beach so she could avoid Flynt's eyes.

"Thank you, Mr. Kincade. This day, I did not have dinner. Hamburgers would be most good of you." Colette's dark eyes gleamed like jet black buttons. In the dim light, the lines in her face diminished, giving her a more youthful appearance.

The full red skirt of a young Jamaican waitress swayed, and her white, off-shoulder blouse dropped lower on her arms as she flounced toward their table. After she took their orders and disappeared, Kathryn leaned forward on her elbows. "Please tell us about the Rastafarians."

"To tell everything would take many days and many hamburgers. The Rastas I know are good, kind people. Because their ways are different, much has been blamed on them." She scrunched her forehead in a frown. "Much blamed on the Rastas is untrue."

With the fingers of her left hand, Colette guided the broad silver band up and down her right arm. Apprehension and wonder intermingled, Kathryn watched the movements of the bracelet. "The Rastas want peace and love. And always they have wanted black people to be free."

The three men who hovered over her in the car appeared anything but peaceable, Kathryn recalled. And the man on the beach had attacked Flynt. She had seen his dreadlocks. Dreadlocks like the Rastas wore.

"Like Obeah, the Rasta history goes back to Africa. They put much faith in the king of Ethiopia as their spiritual leader. Years ago, Jamaicans felt strong emotional ties to Africa." The woman's eyes darkened to coal-black spots. "They wanted to go there to help save Africa from the Italians during the fascist invasion."

"Really?" Kathryn marveled that Colette Smith, whom she thought lacked education, was well versed in Jamaica's history. She glanced at Flynt. Even he, who at first appeared impatient with the outrageous woman, now listened attentively.

"It is the dreadlocks that frighten people." Colette frowned. "Dreadlocks are like the mane of the lion."

"The lion. I want to know more about the lion." Kathryn slid to the edge of her chair and clutched the hidden lion with one hand.

"Oh yes, Missy. The lion. Rastas desire the strength and confidence of the lion. It is their symbol. They want to be like their symbol—proud and free. Even the roar of the lion is part of it." Her voice thickening, the dark woman turned her liquid eyes on Kathryn. "Many great kings have the lion for their strength. The emperor of Ethiopia had tame lions living in his house. For some, the emperor lives as the 'conquering lion.'"

Their food arrived—ample servings, complete with French fries. Colette continued to talk, even while ravenously consuming her hamburger in a swift series of big bites.

"What about the little stuffed animal?" Kathryn kept her voice low.

"That is not a Rasta symbol. The Rastas have a picture on paper. Even there is a painting—one with dreadlocks and five lions. That is the symbol. It is not the stuffed animal," she concluded in a voice that had grown louder with each word.

"Then what does the stuffed animal mean?" Kathryn persisted.

Suddenly, Colette spoke in a whisper. "That is something else. It is carried by the bad men—men who claim they are Rastas, but who are not. For the real Rastas, they make the way hard. Many people fear the bad men; they rattle bells to show power. They are from the dark side." Colette peered straight at Kathryn; then, she wagged a crooked forefinger in her face. "Stay away from those men, Missy."

Kathryn shivered. "I ... I intend to."

Flynt broke his silence. "I've heard negative reports about the Rastafarians." He glanced at Kathryn. "About the protests and the problems they've caused."

"Sometimes they have caused problems, but usually they have been right." Colette dropped the palms of her hands to the edge of the table, now filled with empty plates. "The Rastas have not liked the people from your country who have brought the money and bought the land. They buy land for bauxite. And some people from America even bought Rose Hall."

"Rose Hall?"

"Yes. Rose Hall Plantation." With a sudden shove, Colette thrust her chair away from the table and studied the two people in her audience before continuing her story. "In 1963, the Rastas got in big trouble there. Some of them walked across the grounds to get to other property nearby. Then, a fire and fighting brought in the police. That was big trouble for the Rastas."

Kathryn's face grew cold. Rose Hall. She wouldn't soon forget the day she had gone there. And, she knew she'd have to return. She'd have to go back and, this time, enter the building. Something about that old house wouldn't let her forget it. That day she'd gone there with Mara, the building itself seemed to beckon her inside. She had to go back, perhaps with Flynt. Somehow, she would feel safer with him.

"Police troubles hurt the Rastas." Colette was speaking, and Kathryn hadn't been listening. Mindful of the lapse, the woman paused and glared at her. "When there is trouble, many times the Rastas catch the blame. But, like I told you, the people I know are good. They believe in the spirit world."

"Do you believe in the spirit world?" Kathryn asked. So much about Jamaica confused her. She'd overheard the workers conversing, discussing what she had always considered foolish superstitions. Until today.

Without looking at Flynt, Kathryn knew his gaze was on her and that it was disapproving. Like his opposition to her going to the Obeah ceremony, Flynt didn't like her discussing the spirit world with Colette.

"Of course, I believe it." The older Jamaican woman took a deep breath and puffed out her chest.

"Don't you?"

"I ... I don't know ..." She was certain the furrow in Flynt's brow had deepened. Apparently, his patience with Colette's long-winded accounts had waned.

"Okay. It's been a long day for us all. Time to get you back to the hotel, Kathryn." He stood and with large, powerful hands nearly lifted Kathryn from the seat.

"It has been a long day," she whispered. "I have to work for a while with the computers tonight."

When she looked at her wristwatch, Kathryn stood immediately. "I'm already late."

Colette Smith had told them a lot. But she hadn't disclosed as much as Kathryn wanted to know about the meaning of the stuffed lion. She'd told them only that in some way it related to the "bad men." Kathryn wanted to stay longer to find out what that connection might be, but Flynt was eager to leave, and she didn't dare be any later for her job. After all, despite the many diversions she'd found, her only reason for being in Jamaica was the job. She couldn't lose sight of that fact, especially if she wanted to gain company recognition and capture that promotion when she returned to New York City.

On the way back, Kathryn had little time to talk with Flynt because the strange little restaurant was closer to Hibiscus Hall than she'd realized. So many things confused her—things she'd like to discuss with him. She didn't understand the Rastafarians, Obeah or Jamaica itself. But most of all, she didn't understand Flynt, and she didn't understand herself. Her mind overflowed with questions she might never dare to ask him.

"Guess Oswald's mother came along at the right time." Kathryn glanced sideways at Flynt.

"She came at the wrong time." Above the sound of the rolling surf, Flynt's husky voice was barely audible.

Of course, the woman had arrived at the wrong moment, but she'd saved Kathryn from her new feelings, feelings she couldn't dismiss, yet had no idea how to handle.

How she longed to stop in her tracks and once again slip into his warm embrace. That she'd enjoyed his kisses and his touch was undeniable. That she didn't understand her own feelings was frightening. Since she was already late, she had to avoid contact with his wonderful blue eyes. They filled her with a memory that remained a breath beyond reach, a memory that teased and tantalized her. Purposely, Kathryn turned her attention to the moonlit sea and the fresh shells that washed ashore with the evening tide

But, how could she be interested in a man like Flynt— someone who'd given up so much in exchange for so little? That simply didn't make sense. No matter what he did to her heart, Flynt wasn't her kind of man and never could be. Not after he'd changed jobs. Obviously, he didn't care about the same things she did.

Was he a quitter? Flynt had quit the big city for small rewards he believed life as a teacher offered him. She wanted the big things he'd put aside.

Kathryn stole another glance at Flynt. He didn't look like a quitter. Besides that, why did the vision of a field full of roses keep creeping into her mind when she was with Flynt? If she wasn't interested in him, why couldn't she control the peculiar feelings he stirred up?

"Colette Smith surprised me with her knowledge," Flynt confessed suddenly. "I'm not sure what to think about her."

Flynt's voice filtered through Kathryn's deepening thoughts. "Colette told us a little about the way the Rastafarians fit into Jamaican history.

From the few facts I've gleaned already, I gather there's more involved than one cult group." Flynt stopped and gazed across the water now gleaming with brilliant reflections. "I expect these few weeks at the university will teach me as well as my students."

He scuffed his shoe through the sand. "There're no easy solutions to the hurts of history."

"Flynt, I need to go to Rose Hall. Would you mind taking me?"

For a moment, Flynt hesitated. A sudden flash of moonlight settled on his face, brightening his eyes. "All right, Kathryn, but I can't go tomorrow. That's when I've scheduled student interviews."

"Sunday, then? If it's all right with Mara and Fritz," she added. "She said I could borrow their car." A surge of expectancy shot through her.

"Sunday, it is," he said as they turned up the walkway toward the office.

"Good. I'll talk with Mara first thing tomorrow, then we can schedule the details."

Near the entrance, Flynt stopped and pulled her to him for a brief kiss. "Good night, dear Kathryn," he whispered, and once again warmth surged through her.

In a blur, Kathryn edged between the arriving guests who stood, eyes glazed, amidst a muddle of luggage that trailed from lobby to curb. Thankful the strange, frightening day was almost over, she hurried inside. She had lived through a day like nothing she'd experienced in the past. Nothing she could recall.

❉ ❉ ❉

On Sunday morning, when Kathryn handed Flynt the keys, he looked at the BMW. "I wonder if they had a choice of color."

"Fritz and Mara both love red," she told him.

"Flashy," Flynt said, and opened the door for Kathryn. Soon they were driving along the main road that led to Montego Bay.

Just as he'd been on Friday evening, Flynt was so tantalized by Kathryn's presence that he longed to reach across the seat and touch the bare knee that peeked from beneath the folds of her skirt. The sweet scent of strawberry shampoo drifted from her hair to tempt him even more.

Flynt shifted in his seat and looked at her, noticing her stylish hair, cut to barely skim the tops of her shoulders. The white dress she wore was especially becoming. He shifted again as the peculiar fevered need for her grew more intense. His need was becoming obvious and he felt unaccustomed embarrassment, as if he'd reverted to his teenage years.

What was this powerful attraction? Was his acute interest because he hadn't been with a woman for a long time? A very long time? But even as he thought it, he knew it wasn't so.

"You've already been to Rose Hall, Kathryn. What did you and Mara see when you went there together?"

"I didn't go inside the house," she admitted.

❊ ❊ ❊

She'd stretched the truth a bit with Mara, but she found she couldn't lie to Flynt. It might be better if she could, for sometimes a lie tasted better than the truth.

"You didn't go in? Is that why you wanted to come back so soon?"

"I walked on the grounds, but something happened, and I didn't get inside." Flynt waited for an explanation, but Kathryn said nothing more.

Although much of what had happened the past few days puzzled and confused her, Kathryn knew she had to learn what it all meant. No matter where she was, anytime someone spoke of Rose Hall, she grew tense and her stomach churned. For her own peace of mind, she had to learn the reason for her visions and her obsession with the foreboding old mansion.

Aimee. How unsettling that name was. For some reason, the name seemed ready to burst from her memory, but the harder she tried to grasp the connection the more the thought eluded her.

"Here we are." Flynt pulled the car into a parking area near the Great House.

Kathryn sat still in the car. She made no motion to get out.

"Aren't you going in?" Flynt asked. He'd gotten out and now held the door open for her.

After climbing from the vehicle, Kathryn stood for a moment by the car. Fearing what she might see, she kept her gaze directed away from the house.

Then, pressing her lips tight together, she turned toward the pale exterior of the restored mansion, hoping to see nothing of what she'd seen before.

"Why does this old sugar plantation fascinate you, Kathryn?"

Kathryn debated her answer, but found she wasn't ready to explain herself, so she said, "The people I work with talk about it a lot. That's all." Perhaps her imagination had run away with her the day she came with Mara, she thought. Today, Rose Hall didn't appear as foreboding. "Come on." She motioned for him to walk with her up to the building.

"I found a brochure," Flynt told her. "The Americans who bought Rose Hall spent over two and a half million dollars restoring it."

"No wonder the house looks bright and pure." Before, it hadn't been bright, or pure. Her chin jerked up. How did she know that? Once again, an uneasiness blanketed Kathryn.

Walking toward the Great House, they came to a sign that edged above a heavy blanket of orange flowers. The dark stained board with gold letters reminded her of a church sign. A church sign wasn't appropriate here.

"Look at this, Kathryn." Flynt pointed to the words. "It's being restored as 'a historical monument and cultural centre for Jamaicans and all peoples of the world.' A nice sentiment, don't you think?"

Kathryn made no comment. A tight, straight line replaced the smile on her face. The closer they drew to the house, the heavier her steps became. Dark vibrations cluttered the air, and she was aware of them all. Whether real or imagined, she couldn't be sure, but they were there. And, so was the distant sound of a ringing bell. With considerable effort, she blocked the bell from her mind.

As they neared the mansion, Kathryn squinted, trying to pick a form out of the darkness of the portico arches. Thankfully, she saw nothing. But, when they reached the dual staircases leading to the porch balcony, the fragrance of roses surrounded and overwhelmed her.

Mystified, she asked, "Where are the roses?"

"Roses?" Flynt looked from side to side. "I don't see any, but there might be some in the garden. Are you coming?" he called over his shoulder.

With a deep breath to steady her nerves, Kathryn followed Flynt up the stairs to the wide porch that spread across the front.

Every nerve in Kathryn's body tingled and jangled as if caught and flung by a wild, corrosive power. As if glued to the surface, her feet clung to the porch and she made no motion to enter the house. Instead, she listened to the far-off sounds and watched the vaporous sights that drifted in the shadows. All of a sudden, a strong surge propelled her body through the doorway into the entrance hall of the Great House.

Her chest heaved, and she had the odd sensation of moving above the floor on roller skates.

The old house was different from the way it was two hundred years ago. The stairs, with dark wooden banister, still curved gracefully upward, but the steps and corridors were covered with a slick surface that wasn't there before. Disappointed, she saw that no candles burned in the crystal chandeliers that hung from the ceiling of the reception hall.

"Nice old building."

Flynt's voice came from somewhere, but Kathryn couldn't be bothered. The bell she'd shut out earlier could no longer be blocked. Instead, it rang and buzzed inside her head until, frustrated, she clasped her hands over her ears. And, still, it would not go away.

CHAPTER NINE

AS IF FOLLOWING a beckoning light, Kathryn glided through an open doorway into a large room. She swirled effortlessly toward a tall, arched window overlooking the porch balcony.

Around her nothing seemed real. Kathryn touched her forehead and found she was still there in solid flesh form. Satisfied, she pressed both hands across her eyelids before blinking them open to stare wide-eyed through the window into another world that wasn't there earlier.

An odd, misty haze hung over the porch, obscuring some of it from her view. The filmy fog held particles of smoke-like dust that glittered in the diminished light. Stranger yet, the sun had shifted in the sky to signal the onset of early evening twilight.

The large porch exuded elegant splendor, as the fog around it dissipated. Lavish floral arrangements proclaimed opulence and wealth, and lighted candles in the center of each table projected wispy shadows all around. Seated nearby on the flagstone piazza, a group of wispy, insubstantial musicians lifted their instruments to play a series of waltzes. Music from England, Kathryn thought absently. Not at all like the African music the slaves loved to hear. Slaves. What did she, Kathryn Jefferson Calder, know about slaves?

Around each table, groups of men and women suddenly grew visible. Their voices low, they exchanged words, gestures, and glances. Close to where Kathryn stood, a half-dozen couples got up and glided to the far end of the porch where they moved like silent shadows in rhythm to the music. The women wore long, full gowns, fashioned in pure jewel colors that in the candlelight glow created a fairyland of radiance.

Kathryn drew in her breath when she saw a young, blonde woman in a tight bodice dress dance by the window. Her tiny waist, pale skin, thin pink lips, and frail, slight frame revealed a fragile, vulnerable girl who could be no more than sixteen. But the noble set of her chin proclaimed rugged determination, and Kathryn felt a surge of admiration for her.

Peering through the window, she studied the girl's features—especially her chin. It was much like the set of her own chin. The young woman's overweight dance partner wore a high-collared, starched shirt that held him in a stiff, uncompromising posture while they waltzed. When he placed his hand on her waist at the end of the dance, the young woman pulled away as if repulsed. Her own eyes darkening, Kathryn glared at the man with the hard-lined face. Instinctively, she grew enraged as she watched him and longed to turn and flee before he could touch her.

Out on the balcony, she noticed a small dark-haired woman. Slim and fragile, she wore a silky white gown that draped softly over a crinoline undergarment. The neckline plunged low, exposing the deep, full cleavage of her bosom. A tall, lean man stood next to her, laughing at everything she said to him. When the woman strolled proudly past the window where Kathryn stood, she turned and beckoned to the young blonde woman who immediately verged on tears.

"Come here, Aimee dear." The syrupy sweetness of the woman's words thickened on her tongue. "I want you to meet my friends."

Shyly, almost fearfully, the young blonde edged toward the group of people. Her dance partner followed close behind her.

"This is my niece from England—Aimee White. She has come to live with me for a short time. Come, dear."

As the older woman's hand touched the blonde woman's arm, Kathryn felt the fingers cold as ice. Defiantly, the blonde woman pulled her arm from the brunette's grip.

The older woman's face darkened into a mask of evil; her eyes turned into black coal that smoldered with inner fire.

"Aimee. Wait. Aimee, I must talk with you." Kathryn called out, but no one looked at her. No one appeared to see her.

Aimee. Who was Aimee? Kathryn gazed down at feet she didn't

recognize, then she stared back through the window and saw a gray mass billow upward and outward, obscuring the dancers from her sight. "Wait," she called, but no one answered.

The bell rang inside her head, louder than before, so much louder. Then everything turned black.

Hands tugged at her, touched her face, felt her forehead. Through half-shuttered eyes, Kathryn glimpsed Flynt, his face contorted with worry. His strong arms braced her shoulders and held her close.

What had happened? Flynt was with her, but his presence hadn't protected her from the strangeness of this house—from the peculiar heaviness that hung in the air. She shivered. Had she glimpsed some past time at Rose Hall? If she had, she'd felt a part of it, especially when she saw the sweet, pathetic young girl.

Aimee White. Kathryn tried to pull away. She had to talk with Aimee.

"What's the matter, Kathryn? Didn't you hear when I spoke to you?" Flynt leaned toward her face and rubbed the smooth rounded ends of his fingers over her cheeks, bringing back a surge of warmth.

"No..."

"I called, but you didn't even look at me." His china blue eyes had changed to dingy gray. Much like the porch's foggy mist, she thought.

"I'm sorry," Kathryn said, but she didn't take the small chance of trying to look at him.

She couldn't—wouldn't tell him about the strange scene. How could she expect him to understand when she didn't? Turning back, she stared past him down the entire length of the porch. She saw nothing except the lovely bright sunlight, streaking and reflecting on pale, bare surfaces. The beautiful ladies in elegant gowns had disappeared, and all the tables and candles were gone, leaving the porch ghost-like and empty.

"Thank you, Flynt," she said absently, marveling at a shadow that wouldn't disappear. Glad to have Flynt near, she took hold of his hand and pulled to a standing position. "Let's go outside."

Something had drawn her back to the Great House at Rose Hall. But that something was far too strong for her to handle alone, and it was far beyond her understanding. It wasn't something she could fix. Not yet.

Silently, Flynt picked Kathryn up and carried her outside, down the steps into the garden. He placed her on a bench and sat beside her, letting her head rest against his shoulder.

All the while, Kathryn remained locked in her thoughts. What she had seen was like a waking dream, and Aimee White was the center of that dream. The name had come to her again and again, at both Rose Hall and in the Blue Mountains. And in the dreams she had in New York.

She shivered, feeling herself standing near the end of a deep tunnel, from which there was no retreat. She was in the tunnel, but she wasn't Kathryn.

She was ... No ... No ... her mind screamed and wouldn't let her see ... Wouldn't let her say the name...

If only she could hear it.

"You look like you've seen a ghost." Flynt smoothed aside the hair that had fallen over her cheeks.

"Ghosts? Do I look that bad?" She combed her fingers through her hair.

Were his words truer than Flynt knew? Had she actually seen a ghost? Lots of ghosts? Kathryn wondered. That she'd seen something no one else noticed distressed her the most and left the biggest question. Why hadn't someone else seen the things she had?

"Let's get you something to eat. Or, better yet, let's get some Jamaican rum punch." Without giving her a chance to decline, Flynt guided Kathryn directly to the bright red car.

She paused by the hood and ran her hands over its surface. The car was real and substantial, and she loved the color, red.

"Get in. We're going to drive up the beach to Montego Bay."

Montego Bay—for Kathryn the name had always conjured up visions of serene beaches and lavish landscapes. While many resorts were like that, run-down shacks lined the streets. Goats and other animals ran loose all over.

By the time they'd passed through the streets of the town, some of the color filtered back to Kathryn's face. Perhaps only her imagination had caught fire in Rose Hall; perhaps she'd mistaken a vivid dream for reality, she thought, and hoped it could be as simple as that.

❈ ❈ ❈

"What a wonderful idea," Kathryn said moments later as she sipped from a generous glass of golden rum punch. The liquid warmed her body and mellowed her mind. "I could use one of these whenever the computer develops a mind of its own." She chuckled.

"It's what both of us needed. We're letting the problems of the people here weigh too heavily on us, Kathryn." His face hardened into the firm set lines of a boxer ready for the ring. "I think you've let your emotions get too caught up with the people you're working with, like Oswald and his mother. That's why you're having some problems." He tipped his glass against hers. "We're both going to learn to relax."

"I suppose you're right, but they needed us. Colette Smith would have spent the other night hung up in the wall if we hadn't gone out looking for her." Kathryn giggled, realizing she was light-headed. "One of these will be enough." She pushed the nearly empty glass to one side. The real Jamaican people had needed her, but what about the others? What was the pull that drew her to see things she'd rather forget? Forget. How can you forget what you've never known?

"And our friend with the stuffed lion wouldn't have gotten a chance to arm wrestle me."

"I've thought a lot about what happened on the beach. I think that strange man with the dreadlocks saw me at the Obeah meeting. Maybe he misunderstood my intentions and wanted to warn me to stay away." She shuddered. "Such a scary man."

"What did you do with it?"

"What did I do with what?"

"You know. Don't play games."

Kathryn laughed. "I hid it."

"You what?"

"I hid the lion because it made me think of the fight. Besides, there's something ominous about that animal and the reason the man had it. Perhaps I should burn it."

"Kathryn, you need to be careful. The things you've gotten involved with here are more dangerous than you realize."

"Why are you so serious, Flynt?" Frowning, she leaned toward him.

"I did some reading in the library when I went to Kingston yesterday."

"And?"

"I learned a lot more about Obeah. It's not something you go into merely to learn about it. Other forces are involved."

"Such as?"

"Well, from what I read, much of Obeah is one-on-one hiring of an Obeahman—or woman—to exert a negative spell on someone or something. Some of the Obeah practitioners receive rather sizable payments for their services. At least, according to the literature."

"Hmmm." Kathryn combed her fingers through the ends of her hair, pulling it straight. "I guess I thought Obeah was something like a church service for African people."

"Not at all. One book said it was made illegal back in the days of plantation slavery. Then, and now, most practitioners keep their identities secret, so they won't get into trouble." Flynt took a sip of his second rum punch. "After what I read, I'm surprised Carole Brown took you with her to that event in the mountains."

"Hmmm," she said again. Maybe that was why she had felt out of place and unwelcome.

"If what I read is accurate, the practitioners want to maintain an air of secrecy to enhance the suggestion of special powers. Certainly, they wouldn't want all kinds of people showing up out of curiosity."

Turning her glass uneasily, Kathryn stared at Flynt.

"There are many items they consider 'stock in trade.'"

"Stock in trade? What does that mean?"

"They're things they use in their sorcery." Flynt's eyes shone steely gray.

"Did you learn what some of them are?"

"Yes, I did." He paused, then went on. "Very strange items like parrot's beaks, dog's teeth, cat bones. Then there are more things like balls of clay with hair, feathers and other oddities tied in."

Kathryn sat up straight. "Clay balls? They had one in a circle at the meeting on Friday. Feathers, too, lots of feathers."

"I don't know what to think of it, Kathryn. For these people, Obeah has a great and mysterious meaning, and it's important to some of my students."

"What about Oswald? I don't know what to think of him and his relationship with Colette."

"Oswald's trying to be a good son. He doesn't know which way to go with his mother. His job at Hibiscus Hall is one of the best Jamaica has to offer, with plenty of opportunity for advancement. Poor Oswald's walking on a crate of eggs."

So am I, Kathryn thought. Before Bradford Huntington asked her to take the assignment in Jamaica, her life had been arranged neatly. There were no loose ends, no confusing visions she couldn't explain, no interest in sorcery, and no Flynt Kincade. She had been on her way up in the corporate world and that was what she wanted, wasn't it?

Maybe not. She frowned. For the first time in her life, she was questioning her goals.

CHAPTER TEN

BACK AT HER hotel later that day, Kathryn headed to her room thinking a shower and nap were in order. As soon as she entered the corridor, she saw a man dash out of her room and run the other way. His long, black dreadlocks swept back and forth like striking snakes until he vanished from sight.

Stunned, she tried to call after him to tell him to stop, but her voice hung in her throat.

A thousand terrifying images danced through her mind, including the possibility someone else was lingering in her room, ready to strike once she opened the door.

What was the stranger doing there? Was he the same man who attacked Flynt on the beach? His hair looked the same. Taking a deep breath, Kathryn hesitated, then edged down the hall toward her unit.

Of course, her room was easy enough to enter. The balcony to the second floor wasn't far above the ground. Because of a rise in the lawn below, her balcony was probably closer to the ground than most, and the door lock was flimsy at best.

More angry than afraid, Kathryn pulled the key from the pocket of her dress and hurried to unlock the door. With a hollow thud, it swung backward and hit the wall.

For a moment, Kathryn stood still in the entrance and looked around, glad the late afternoon sunlight illuminated most of the room. She uttered a relieved sigh, for at first glance, everything appeared to be exactly as she'd left it. Heading to the bathroom, she saw nothing out of place there either.

Then, Kathryn turned to look in the closet for the piece of luggage where she'd hidden the stuffed lion. Pulling the zipper around on the wardrobe case, she jerked the top up and discovered the lion with its glassy green eyes staring back at her. Frowning, she wondered if it might have been better to find the strange creature gone.

What did the man want, if not the lion? Checking the sliding glass door to the balcony, Kathryn found it partially open. Then she noticed one of her shirts in a heap on the floor near the drapes. The man must have climbed over the balcony.

When she knelt to pick up the shirt, she espied an object lying on the floor beneath her bamboo bed. It was an odd-looking glass vial that lay on its side just beyond her reach.

Kathryn flattened her body to the floor and slid into the narrow space under the mattress frame.

She gulped. The bottle held a cloudy liquid. Did she dare touch it?

No. She pulled back. I'd better bring Mara or Carole Brown to take a look, she decided.

Kathryn went to the balcony where she discovered what easy access any intruder would have. A metal support braced the second-floor porch and contained cross bars, simplifying the climb up for most anyone willing to try. It was nearly as good as a ladder. With that fact in mind, she closed the glass door, pressed on the lock, and inserted a heavy rod to block the slide track. She was certain no one would enter her room that way again.

Before leaving the room, she attached the "do not disturb" sign to the outside of the door and turned on her radio. Hopefully, the sign and noise would discourage any other would-be intruder from entering.

Moments later, when she reached Mara's office, she noticed a light glowing beneath the door. Kathryn took a deep breath and knocked. Nervous, she shifted her weight from side to side. Why was it taking Mara so long to undo the chain and open her door?

"Oh, Kathryn. Come on in." Mara's eyes lacked their usual sparkle, and her voice didn't bubble.

Perhaps she was tired, Kathryn thought.

"What is it I can do for you?" A faint smile touched the German woman's lips.

"Mara, do you have a moment to come with me? I want to show you something in my room." Kathryn felt her face flush as she rushed her words.

"Something is not right? Of course. I will go with you happily." Mara squeezed Kathryn's hand and pulled her from the cramped office into the lobby. "Now tell me what is wrong."

As they hurried toward her room, Kathryn described the man with dreadlocks who ran out of her doorway when she entered the hallway.

"Come. Look at this." As soon as she opened her door, Kathryn headed toward the bed and immediately dropped to the floor beside it. "See what I found."

Already, as the sun dipped toward the western horizon, the natural light faded into dusk, making it difficult to see the object that lay enclosed by the shadows beneath the bed. To compensate for the darkness, Mara pulled a small, powerful flashlight from her pocket and directed the beam onto the vial. For several minutes both women lay stretched out on the floor considering the bottle and its murky contents with the pinkish cast.

Finally, Mara whispered. "Kathryn, I do not want to say to you what will cause you upset, but I must tell you—what is here could be the work of an Obeahman."

A spell by an Obeahman! Of course. From some far-away place came a vision of a small, dark cabin—the same cabin she'd seen before she collapsed that day in the Blue Mountains with Carole Brown.

"Not that I believe harm can be caused by such things, because I know they should not make trouble. Still, I do not wish for you to take the chance." Mara's silver-blue eyes dulled to gray. "We cannot bring Colette Smith into the hotel, although she is the best. We will go now and find Carole Brown. Come. That is what we must do." She stood and motioned for Kathryn to follow her.

Transfixed, Kathryn stared vacantly and made no effort to move. "I'll wait for you here." Her hollow voice echoed in her own head. In vain, she tried to recall the things Flynt had mentioned from his library readings on Obeah.

"No. I insist. We will go together or not at all."

When they left the room, it was as if Kathryn had passed from sleep to wakefulness. "Do you know much about Obeah?" she asked, suddenly curious about the psychic interests of the normally happy-go-lucky

German woman. How much did Mara actually know about the bizarre events she'd encountered during the past several days? She apparently knew that Colette Smith was some sort of expert in goodness-knows-what. And she knew Carole Brown well. What else did she know?

"I know very little," Mara said, her voice flat.

"But you want to know more?" Kathryn prodded.

"Yes. Of course. I am interested in too many things." Mara's laugh held a caustic ring. "That is what Fritz says."

"Have you ever had..." Kathryn paused, debating how to phrase her question. "Have you ever had any ... any unusual experiences?" She hurried through the last two words as though she would not get them out if she slowed down.

"Unusual experiences? What do you mean?" They paused in the corridor.

For a long moment, Kathryn stood silent. Then she cast her gaze downward to the floor. How could she explain to anyone the things that had happened since she arrived in Jamaica? And even before she'd left— in New York? None of it made sense. She'd never been interested in the paranormal—had never before heard of Obeah. How could she explain?

"I don't know what I mean," Kathryn whispered truthfully.

Mara's sharp features softened, and dimples formed in the hollows of her cheeks. "From the time I was little, I would go places with my parents and would know that place. Yet, I had not been there before. How you say it— 'deja vu?' So much of that I have always had that now I read much on the subject. There are many who have told of such experiences. Even your General Patton..."

The unexpected revelation resounded like a bell in Kathryn's head. Perhaps she could confide in Mara after all. Still, she hesitated. "Let's get Carole." They resumed walking. "After that, I'd like to tell you something else." Kathryn thought that perhaps by then she would be able to figure out what to say.

One eyebrow raised, Mara quickened her pace but said nothing. Eventually, after looking all over Hibiscus Hall, they found Carole Brown finishing dinner at Bamboo By The Sea. To Kathryn's surprise, all the chairs in the quaint little restaurant, financed by "tour" money, were filled with chattering customers. A waiting line stretched out onto the beach.

"I will be happy to come with you." Carole Brown motioned for the check. "You have a problem maybe. I am not surprised. Many strange faces in the Blue Mountains on Friday, I had not seen. I will not go back soon, for trouble is in the wind. It is not safe to go into the mountains with strangers." Carole's eyes shone like round onyx marbles in the low light. "I am sorry to have taken you there, Miss Kathryn."

When they left, Mara and Kathryn slowed their gait to match Carole's graceful, deliberate stride.

Her erect posture was more difficult to mirror.

"Do not mention this to others," Carole cautioned when the three women reached Hibiscus Hall.

Kathryn and Mara looked at each other then. Their faces somber, they nodded agreement. Before leading the way to the second floor, Kathryn glanced around the lobby, almost expecting to see a man with flying dreadlocks leap from behind a lobby chair.

As soon as they reached Kathryn's room, Carole Brown went directly to the bed and knelt beside it. Then, as if stung by a bee, she bolted upward, her chest heaving.

"The bad ones. It is the work of Granville Davis. He was born with the power, evil power. This is not good." Still shaking, Carole thrust her back against the wall.

"This has to stop. I'm going to throw that thing out the window." Kathryn started to go for the vial.

"No. No. Wait, Miss Kathryn."

Halfway to the bed, Kathryn paused.

"Granville Davis is a strong Obeahman. He works much bad magic. His mind is full of hatred. Many of the bad ones follow him." Carole's voice lowered into a dull monotone.

Perplexed, Kathryn stared blankly at the other two women. "This Granville Davis has nothing to do with me." She headed toward the bed. "Look. We've spent enough time talking about this silly vial. I'm going to throw it out." Bending over, she reached beneath the bed to pick up the bottle.

"Wait." Carole snapped. "Do not touch it. I will fix." Her hand closed over Kathryn's and held her arm immobilized.

"There is a way," she whispered. "It is like the myalism. That is white magic to counter the evil."

Kathryn pushed to her feet and stood wondering what could possibly happen next. What would Flynt say if he could see them now? Surely, he would think the whole matter absurd.

She watched Carole Brown's eyes roll back. Her head full of questions, Kathryn stared at Mara.

"It is all right." Mara squeezed Kathryn's shoulder. "Do not take chances even if you do not believe."

The whole situation turned more bizarre when Carole Brown pulled four long white candles from the large canvas bag she always carried. Lacking holders, she thrust one into each of the four water glasses that sat on a tray with the ice bucket. Then she started to move, chanting, around the room, placing a burning candle in each corner.

"Now, we shall wait." Carole motioned for Kathryn to sit in a chair she'd pulled to the center of the room. With considerable reservation, Kathryn followed the woman's instruction.

"It is time now," Carole declared later, when the candles appeared half-burned. She pulled an object from her bag and kept it concealed in her hand. Reaching beneath the bed, she placed something over the vial and pulled it out. "Not to worry. All the power is away now. Granville Davis has big magic. My magic is bigger. Not to worry." She smiled broadly, her teeth gleaming even in the darkness. The wide silver bracelet on her right arm glistened even more.

"Now, I will be going." Carole Brown placed the shrouded vial in her bag and disappeared through the doorway. "Keep the door locked," she called behind her.

Mara took a deep breath, opened the sliding door, and went out to the balcony to sit. "I'm glad that's over."

"Everything is happening so fast." Kathryn followed Mara and sat in the chair beside her.

"What were you going to tell me?" Mara leaned her seat back against the railing.

"Wait." Kathryn jumped up and headed back inside.

With a damp washcloth she extinguished the four candles. As if to help clear the episode from her mind, she carried them all into the bathroom and placed them in the sink before returning to the balcony.

"There." Kathryn turned her chair to face Mara. "Remember the day we drove together to Rose Hall?" Kathryn proceeded to relate the vision she'd seen of the woman, dressed in white, who stood in the portico calling, "Aimee."

"You saw someone in the portico?" Mara touched her shoulder. "Of course, that is why you seemed ill. Hmmm. I did not realize; I did not see."

"What I saw that day was minor compared to yesterday." Her eyes wide, Kathryn described the sudden shift from day to twilight, the dancers dressed in emerald green, sapphire blue, and ruby red gowns and Aimee White. "I knew her, Mara. I knew her, and I hated the man she was with. That makes what I saw even more scary."

Now, as she recalled the girl, Kathryn felt frail and vulnerable, just like Aimee White had looked. She stood and moved to the edge of the balcony. Leaning against the rail, she studied the dark ridged waters of the Caribbean Sea. Like the scattered images in her mind, light danced in pepper sprinkles over the water's surface.

A fragile breeze shifted strands of her hair. "Mara, I'm confused. I don't know what's happening to me," Kathryn confided. "I don't know what to think." She turned to face Mara, then placed her fingers over her friend's hand and squeezed it. "I needed to talk to someone. Thanks for listening."

Mara smiled. "I am but glad to listen. It is right you are concerned. About the visions, I know nothing, but there is a woman you need to meet." She paused, then continued quickly. "Her name is Rita Grey. She might be able to help you."

Kathryn returned to the railing and shook her head. "I don't know about meeting another stranger."

The suggestion aroused renewed skepticism in Kathryn's mind. After all, it was Mara who introduced her to Carole Brown. Meeting that woman and going with her to the Blue Mountains complicated Kathryn's life in ways she never dreamed existed when she was in New York. It had gotten her involved with Obeah.

Mara chuckled softly. "Rita is not like Carole. I can promise you for certain. Rita is a psychologist who knows much about the para... how you say it ... paranormal. It will be good. She is a scientist. You should talk with her."

"I don't know..." Suddenly, memories of Flynt flooded Kathryn's mind. He hadn't thought much of her going with Carole Brown. She suspected he would think even less of her contacting Rita Grey.

She wished he hadn't gone to Kingston to teach classes. How ironic, Kathryn thought. Only a few days ago, she'd been disappointed in Flynt for trading his well-paying corporate job for a low-salary teaching position. Now, she was wishing he was unemployed so he could spend more time with her.

Could Flynt bring her life back into sensible perspective? Or was she hopelessly lost in an endless string of odd visions and superstitious symbols? Her co-workers at Triple Gold would have a good laugh if they could see her burning candles in every corner and hiding a stuffed animal in her suitcase.

"Tomorrow, Rita Grey is speaking at a church social hall near Ocho Rios. I would like that you go with me."

"If it's at night, I won't be able to go," she noted with sensible concern for her job. With everything that had happened, Kathryn had gotten behind in her computer training. And she was in Jamaica on a job assignment, not for personal enlightenment, if she could call what was happening enlightening.

"You will have time. The meeting is at four o'clock." Mara's blue eyes brightened hopefully. "We will leave the hotel at about three."

"Do you think Rita Grey will talk about something that might help me?"

"It is that she is a psychologist, not a psychic." Mara patted the hand Kathryn had wrapped across the porch rail. "It will be fine. You will see. Rita Grey will help you. I have a good feeling about what she will do."

But Kathryn did not feel so certain.

CHAPTER ELEVEN

AS KATHRYN REACHED for the door knob to leave for her evening at work, the telephone rang. She jumped, dropping the two books she was carrying and her purse as well. The break-in and Carole Brown's candlelight vigil had her nerves teetering as if she were walking on the edge of a canyon wall.

"Kathryn."

The strong, steady voice caught her by surprise.

"Flynt?"

"Who else?" He laughed.

The pleasant sound of his voice had a wonderful calming effect on her frayed nerves. To her surprise, Kathryn realized she had never spoken with Flynt on the telephone.

"How are things going there?" she asked. A different kind of excitement put an edge on Kathryn's nerves and sent her blood surging, like fire burning a trail of gun powder.

"Fine. I have five new students in my afternoon class." He chuckled. "Oswald has been recommending me."

"I should hope so." She laughed, too. Merely hearing the calm, reassuring warmth of Flynt's voice made her feel happier.

"I really called to check on you, Kathryn," Flynt admitted. "Are you all right?"

"I'm fine," she responded quickly, automatically.

Aren't we taught to pretend we're fine whether it's true? So, it wasn't a real lie, she reasoned.

Besides, now that she was talking to Flynt, she could almost see his magic china blue eyes.

"Are you certain you're all right?" The concern in Flynt's voice was unexpected. "So much happened over the weekend, I wasn't sure how you might feel." He paused. "It's not much like New York down here, you know."

"I know," she murmured, wishing he hadn't mentioned the big city. It made her think that Triple Gold would be calling her back to New York soon, and she wasn't sure she was ready to go just yet.

"Also, Kathryn, I wanted to invite you to join me for a late dinner tomorrow evening."

"Tomorrow? You'll be back tomorrow?" Kathryn hadn't expected Flynt back before the weekend. The prospect sent a parade of joyous tingles dancing up her spine.

"That's right. My Wednesday classes are cancelled for this week, so I don't need to be back in Kingston until late morning on Thursday." He paused. "So, how about dinner?"

"All right," she agreed, wondering if there'd be any problem getting back from Rita Grey's talk in time for dinner. There shouldn't be, but she'd certainly have to work extra hard tonight if she wanted to shorten her hours tomorrow night.

"Flynt?"

"Yes."

"Uh... Nothing." Kathryn started to mention Rita Grey and the program to Flynt, then thought better of it. She was certain he would disapprove, and since she'd already agreed to go with Mara, she saw no reason to invite a negative response. "I'll look forward to tomorrow night."

"Good. See you at eight o'clock in the lobby. Maybe we'll try Bamboo By The Sea for a real meal." He chuckled. "But only if we can count on Colette Smith not being there."

Long after she hung up the telephone, Kathryn thought about Flynt. In the short time since they'd met, she'd developed a compulsive desire to see more, and still more, of him.

Never mind he didn't have the big job. Never mind her resolve for her own professional glory. She had only to think of his handsome face, strong jaw and haunting eyes, and she was captivated.

Since the day he loaned her his handkerchief in the museum, he had not seemed like a stranger. Perhaps that was because he resembled someone she knew or had known. But she could not figure out who that someone else was.

Kathryn gathered her things and started out of the room. Preoccupied with both personal and business thoughts, Kathryn found the corridors of the hotel unusually quiet this evening. These days, empty hallways made her uneasy. She quickened her pace.

Nearly a dozen day clerks were scheduled to work with her tonight. Their first assignment would be to learn the basic functions of the computers and then understand how to tie in Hibiscus Hall's reservation system with those of other Caribbean resorts. The commands and programs seemed simple enough, but most of the employees lacked the educational background and skills to get started.

Kathryn glanced at her watch and found she needed to hurry. She was worried that someone managed to get into the office and had sabotaged at least one vital program. The Jamaicans were bright and willing and caught on quickly, but they were ill-prepared to recognize criminal activity within the computer system. She wanted to teach them everything they needed to know as quickly as possible before more damage could be done.

For the first time, Kathryn was apprehensive about walking across the grounds alone. Pulse racing, she paused at her building's exit door and looked around. The moon had vanished behind a thick bank of clouds, and not one of the three outside garden lamps was burning. Her heart thumped. The grounds stood dark and lonely, and it was impossible to see the path across to the hotel lobby where she was heading. Kathryn looked warily to either side. Never had the lights been out when she crossed over after dark.

Clutching her purse tightly, she hurried through the darkness. Far across the garden, the lobby loomed quiet, without the usual evening overflow of guests spilling onto the walkway. No sounds of chatter and laughter carried through the air. Instead, a damp breeze blew into Kathryn's face, bringing with it a distasteful mustiness. The afternoon break-in had changed her views of Hibiscus Hall as a protected tourist haven.

A flicker of light tore her gaze to the left. A shadow moved behind the hibiscus plants, mimicking her motions. She slowed to peer more closely and found it was only a large banana plant flailing in the wind. Even so, Kathryn increased her pace. Her heart pumped faster, sending the sound of blood thundering in her ears.

There was another shadow—one she hadn't seen but only sensed. In a sudden sweep, a black specter fell over her. Rough hands, with a grip of steel, followed, clamping her slender arms in a harsh hold. No sound was uttered, but from the shadow came the swinging rush of a hundred snakelike locks.

Kathryn's voice hung in her throat. As if frozen in time, she could not cry out. Then, a cold, damp sphere was thrust into the palm of her right hand. In her other hand, a sticky bit of flora clung like a limp rag to her fingers.

At last, a small guttural sound came from Kathryn's throat, a sound she didn't recognize. Wriggling her body, she struggled to open her hands and throw away the foreign objects. But she could do neither. The attacker held her with an iron grip.

Then, as suddenly as he had trapped her, Kathryn's captor released her arms, and like a shadow, the man vanished soundlessly into the night. She gasped and twisted to see where he'd gone, but the only visible sign of his retreat was the soft rustle of fluttering hibiscus foliage.

Sweat beading on her forehead, Kathryn shuddered and ran toward the lobby door, only a few feet away. Pushing inside, she collapsed onto the nearest bench. No one noticed her.

With quick, shallow gulps of air, she tried to force away the panic. But any hope of calm vanished when she looked down and saw the strange objects in her hands.

In her right hand, she clutched a rancid-smelling ball of gray clay. Its pungent odor stung her nostrils, and when she looked closer, deep chills rocked her body. Disgusted, she turned her head away. A random pattern of blue and green bird feathers accented the surface of the murky ball. And a gold parrot's beak protruded like an evil icon above the feathers. Kathryn felt sick at her stomach.

Her fingers trembled. Did she dare put down the clay object, so like the ones she'd seen that day when she went with Carole Brown to the Blue Mountains? She knew she had to do something with it, so she tried to place it on a nearby table. But the gooey mess clung to her fingers.

Kathryn leaned back in her seat and drew in a long, deep breath. As her eyelids fluttered half-closed, a cloud-like mist descended on the lobby, blurring away its features and the scattering of people assembled there. Eerily, Kathryn felt herself floating, becoming part of a dark dream world, caught between reality and fantasy. In the distance, the sound of a sharp ringing bell cut through the fog.

Two women rode on horseback through the night. Kathryn recognized the scene. It was the one she had encountered over and over in her dreams.

"I will show you the ways of voodoo," Aunt Annie said.

Aimee tightened her hands on the reins of her horse. She resolved to get away. She knew she must. She would never be like Aunt Annie. She would never learn voodoo. She would rather die.

Kathryn knew Aimee's thoughts.

How could that be?

CHAPTER TWELVE

AIMEE WHITE. THE name grew out of the night and stood out in glowing letters on the edge of the mist.

Bells clanged and clamored making Kathryn's ears burn with the sound. The noise grew louder and louder until she hunched over in hopes of escaping the pounding vibrations. But instead of escaping, she found cool sensations rushed through her veins. The flow of blood surged deep into her heart, freezing it in time, turning it crystalline, like a block of ice.

Her shoulders shook, and so did her torso. How cold her body felt! So cold, it grew difficult to move even a finger.

Aimee White. The name remained written before her eyes. Pale blonde and very slight, the young woman had grown unforgettable in her mind. So unforgettable, she seemed a part of her own psyche. Kathryn shivered again.

Struggling, Kathryn flopped forward as though a lead weight clung to her chest and pulled her down. She'd fallen into a dream state or had some waking vision, hadn't she? Even now, she wasn't inclined to wake up.

Straining hard, Kathryn tried again to open her eyes, but, like a stuck window shade, they remained shut... until she heard a frenzied voice call out.

"Miss Kathryn. Miss Kathryn. What have you got there? Wake up."

At the cry, her eyes fluttered open, but the sudden brightness immediately made her close them. More cautiously, she squinted until she saw she still sat on the bench in the Hibiscus Hall lobby, and she still held the weird clay ball in her right hand.

"Miss Kathryn. Get rid of that thing," one of the office workers whispered.

In response to the frantic command, Kathryn tried to push the clay away, but the cool, sticky goo held tight to her fingers. Had the clay ball propelled her into unconsciousness? Had it sent her spinning into the past to see something she wanted to remember, but couldn't? "Oh, sorry. You must have caught me napping." Kathryn slipped her right hand, holding the clay ball, beneath the folds of her skirt.

"Let me see that, Miss Kathryn." The girl reached for her left hand.

Kathryn felt relieved when she realized the girl hadn't noticed the ball of earth and feathers after all.

"That is no good, Miss." Arlene took the white hibiscus blossom with red streaks from Kathryn's hand. "Look, you must break off the center part before you touch it."

Kathryn frowned. "Why?"

"There is poison in this piece." She pointed to the golden yellow stamen and, without touching it, broke it away from the narrow stalk. "If you touch this to your eye, it can blind you," she warned. "It is dangerous to sleep with one in your hand."

Kathryn dropped the flower on the side table. Had the man with dreadlocks intended to do harm in more than one way?

"I didn't know about the hibiscus blossoms. Thank you for telling me."

She wondered if what the woman said was truth or superstition. The past few days she'd found the line between the two was faint. But she recalled the stamen on the hibiscus blossom Flynt had given her was broken off.

"Are you feeling all right, Miss Kathryn?"

"Yes, I'm fine. Is everyone in the office, ready for tonight's lesson?" But when Kathryn started to stand, she found her legs were too rubbery.

"Ten of us are there waiting," the girl reported.

"Good. A box of computer manuals came in today. You'll find them under the window in the office. Please give them out and ask everyone to read the first chapter while I run a quick errand." Despite her confused state of mind, Kathryn gave directions in her most business-like manner.

"New books? We'll like that. Thanks." The girl smiled and headed back to the office.

After she left, Kathryn managed to stand up. She stifled a groan. Not only were her legs stiff, but her arms were cold. Had she really been napping? Is that what the attack had done for her? Put her to sleep?

Despite her discomfort she had to find Carole Brown and show her the clay ball. Since Mara was off, she headed to the main restaurant in search of Oswald.

"Ah, Missy Kathryn." Oswald smiled broadly and extended his hand to her. "Thank you and Mr. Kincade again for finding my mother. You were most kind to look for her."

"I'm glad we could help." Because the clay mishmash was in her right hand, hidden in her skirt folds, Kathryn shook his hand with her left.

"Mr. Kincade's class today was very good. Already I have learned more than in many weeks before."

He grinned. "He is a fine teacher."

"I'm glad." She glanced around nervously.

"Oswald, have you seen Carole Brown? I need to find her right away."

"Ah yes. She is in the kitchen with the new food manager. Wait here, and I will get her." Oswald bowed, then hurried away.

Moments later, Carole Brown, standing straight and tall, strolled into the restaurant. "Is there more trouble?" No emotion showed on the dark woman's face.

"Yes, there is." Kathryn shifted her gaze to look behind and to both sides of them. "I don't want to talk here." Even now, the shadows that surrounded the open-air restaurant gave her the uneasy sense she was under surveillance by unknown eyes.

"That is fine. We will go to my office." Carole took hold of Kathryn's left arm and guided her with a firm grip to a small room hidden near the kitchen. Kathryn had not noticed the plain, unmarked doorway before.

"Now tell me what has happened." Carole's dark eyes glistened like black crystal beads in the lamplight.

"A man who looked like a Rastafarian attacked me," Kathryn said.

"Attacked you? Where?"

"Here on the grounds. He ... He slipped from the shadows outside my ... my building. He ... He didn't strike me, but he caught me from behind and pinned my arms." Kathryn drew in her breath. "And ... And he thrust this into my hand." Warily, she lifted her right hand, revealing the clay ball, stuck tight to her palm and fingers.

"Oh my, Miss Kathryn. There is someone who does not much like you." For a fleeting moment, Carole lost her poise, but almost immediately recovered it.

"Is this something like the vial placed under my bed?" Kathryn asked uneasily.

Her eyes focused on the clay ball, the woman nodded.

"Do ... Do you think it's because I went with you?"

"I do not know, but I will now fix this for you." Carole Brown checked all four corners of the small room. "Do not move," she cautioned. "Wait here."

Tensely, Kathryn leaned on the back of a straight chair until Carole Brown returned. Fearing more ringing bells and the murky fog, she didn't like being alone…

When the woman got back, she carried a large shallow bowl of water. "Here," she said. "This should work quite well."

Chanting indistinguishable words over the bowl, Carole reached for the clay ball. Kathryn allowed the woman to pull it loose from her hand.

The woman doused the ominous object in the water, continued her mantra, then, throwing a towel over it, took everything outside. When she returned, the lines in Carole's forehead seemed less deep and her eyes held more sparkle.

"All is fine now," she assured Kathryn, but she didn't mention where she'd taken the strange ensemble of objects and Kathryn didn't ask.

"I am going to lend you my bracelet for a few days," Carole announced. With a smile, she slid the wide silver band from her arm and held it up in front of her as if casting a blessing over it.

"Are you sure you want to lend it?" Kathryn asked. "I've never seen you without it."

"For now, you need this more than I do."

She pressed the cool metal object over Kathryn's thin wrist and pushed it far up her right forearm until it clung tight. As it moved over her skin, Kathryn could feel the roughness of deeply etched indentations in the silver.

"Do not remove this until I tell you," Carole warned.

Although Carole didn't say so, Kathryn sensed the woman believed the bracelet had a protective charm from harmful elements of Obeah.

Kathryn didn't question the bracelet's power, for she was learning the ways of Jamaica were different from home. Even though silver bracelets had made her uneasy in the past, she accepted what Carole Brown told her.

"I won't remove it," Kathryn promised.

With Carole Brown's silver bracelet shining on her arm, Kathryn walked to the main hotel office where a room full of bright-eyed Jamaican men and women awaited her instruction.

❋ ❋ ❋

Sweat beading on her forehead, Kathryn sat up in bed. Her head was screaming. She knew the man in her dream.

She'd had long, complicated dreams before, but never one so vivid or so real—more real than anything in her waking life.

Climbing out of bed, Kathryn gathered her bathrobe around her shoulders and glided to the sliding glass door to look out. She'd seen a tall man with wavy brown hair in her dream. He spoke and moved much like Flynt Kincade except for the broad-brimmed hat and long jacket that he wore.

And there was something she would not forget. The man brought her a beautiful gift—a dew-coated bouquet of fresh yellow roses. Even in her dream, she could smell their sweet fragrance. And even in her dream, the gift brought a flow of tears that left her pillow damp.

But the man's manners and speech were different from Flynt's. Still, when Kathryn awakened, she felt certain she had dreamed of Flynt.

Groggy with sleep, Kathryn gazed out across the dark lawn where bits of moonlight flickered through the trees. In another part of her dream, she wandered in a field grown high with cane —sugarcane. As she moved deeper into the vegetation, the sharp crack of whips shocked the air. Then came terrible, forlorn cries of men and women in pain. Slaves.

Without warning, flames shot up from the fields until all around her, everywhere, fires raged. The smoke grew so thick she could no longer breathe. She needed to run, but she was trapped, all hope was gone. Far off, she saw a gray building above the smoke. Rose Hall, she thought, and then she awoke.

❋ ❋ ❋

Almost in a fog, Flynt climbed the steps into the National Gallery of Jamaica in Kingston. Funny he would want to wander through the museum collection now, when he had not been a regular visitor to the New York museums while he lived there. Perhaps placing his painting on loan to one helped change his mind. Obviously meeting Kathryn in the gallery made him see museums in a different light.

Wandering through a corridor, he glanced at a special exhibition of Haitian art. For some obscure reason, it gave him the willies, so he rocked on his heel and strode back outside to the street.

Jamaica had been hard on Kathryn, had shaken her confidence. The moment the two of them set foot on the grounds at Rose Hall, she'd become a different woman—fragile and vulnerable. Flynt smiled as he turned up the street and headed toward a small, private gallery.

For some reason, the more approachable Kathryn became, the more she appealed to him. Was that because he harbored too many memories of the strong, selfish woman who had scarred his life? Because of his ex-wife, Flynt learned to be cautious around every attractive woman he met, like Kathryn.

During the years since his divorce, he hadn't avoided relationships, but he'd managed to keep them casual, always making it clear from the outset that he wasn't interested in commitment. His mind on Kathryn, Flynt strolled up a cement walkway to the gallery, nodding to the clerk as he passed through the doorway.

Once inside, he paused in front of the portrait of a woman who reminded him of Kathryn. The painted image indulged his memory of Kathryn's delicate features and pale skin that felt like velvet beneath his fingers. Her silky tumble of lustrous blonde hair smelled of strawberries and cream. He liked the way her gray eyes brightened when she laughed and the way her fingers grew warm beneath his touch. Even her long, quick stride that almost matched his own fascinated him.

Because of Kathryn he had no regrets about coming to Jamaica. The small salary didn't matter. He had plenty of money stashed away. Six years of frugal living since his divorce had given him that. And four years of night classes had given him the advanced degree he needed to teach—his lifelong dream. Flynt Kincade, corporate executive, was now Dr. Flynt Kincade, visiting professor of economics in Kingston, Jamaica.

Flynt smiled ruefully. In the long run, money meant nothing to him. It certainly had never brought him happiness in the past. He had always wanted to teach. Right now, teaching and being near Kathryn were the two things he wanted most in his life.

Kathryn. When he thought his need for a woman had atrophied, along came Kathryn, and his desire was back, stronger than before.

A painting on the wall in the corner grabbed his attention. When he looked at it, he felt the blood drain from his face. It was a painting of Rose Hall as it must have looked when it thrived as a sugar plantation.

He studied the painting for a very long time—until he heard the clerk moving about.

"Is this painting for sale?" Flynt asked the man.

"I do not know, but I will find out. Please check back with me later this week."

Flynt stared at the image a moment longer. Rose Hall. He had to let Kathryn know about this painting. His gut told him it would be important for her to know... But he didn't know why.

❋ ❋ ❋

When Flynt telephoned her late in the morning, Kathryn was caught on the edge of two worlds. In one, she wanted to tell him everything that had happened since he'd left; in the other, she needed to hide her secrets because she didn't dare admit her weaknesses to him, of all people.

"I thought about you all last night," Flynt told her in a husky voice.

"Did you?"

"Yes. In fact, I thought about you so much that this morning I went to the National Gallery of Jamaica. It's right here in the city. Guess you got me hooked the day we met in the museum in New York.

"That seems forever ago," she whispered.

"Kathryn, I found something else." His voice dropped lower than before. "There's a small private gallery nearby, so I stopped in on my way back to the university."

"Is that why you called?"

"I miss you, Kathryn," he said. Then he laughed. "But I did call to tell you about the gallery. I think it's important for you to know this ..." Flynt paused.

"When I entered the gallery, a painting, hidden in one corner caught my attention. It's a painting of Rose Hall as it must have looked soon after it was built.

"Rose Hall?"

"That's right. A 200-year-old painting of Rose Hall. You've been so taken by that old restored building, I immediately thought you'd like to see the painting."

"Yes. I would love to see it."

"Tonight, we'll make plans for you to see it." He paused. "Our date's still on, isn't it?"

"Of course. Eight o'clock in the lobby."

After replacing the telephone in its cradle, it took Kathryn a long time to get her mind on her work at the hotel. She had begun to worry that she wouldn't get back by eight o'clock to keep her date, but she hadn't told Flynt her plans. He wouldn't approve, and, besides that, she wasn't sure she did either. Going to a church to hear a psychologist discuss phenomena she didn't understand at all seemed a bit outrageous. But her life had been outrageous for several weeks now.

❅ ❅ ❅

It was almost four o'clock when Kathryn and Mara slipped quietly into the church social hall. Although it was close to time to start, only a half dozen seats were occupied.

The barren white walls of the dark wooden structure reflected late afternoon sunlight and modest means. Except for a group of about two dozen folding metal chairs and one worn old table, no other furniture was evident in the room.

"Are you sure we have the right day?" Kathryn whispered. In a nervous gesture, she swept her left hand up and down her right arm, moving with it the silver bracelet Carole Brown had insisted she wear for protection.

When Mara failed to notice the bracelet, Kathryn decided not to mention it, or the man who'd accosted her the previous evening. As much trouble as she'd had since her arrival, Mara would be certain she was hopelessly problem-prone.

"Yes. It is this day." Mara said. "I am certain."

"But, there're not many people here."

The smile on Mara's lips reached to her eyes, giving them a pleasant twinkle. "It would be much of a big surprise to me for many people to be here. Sometimes in Jamaica, there is not so much interest in the psychology and meditation as there is in the—how you say it—superstitious."

"Of course, you're right."

From her own recent experiences, Kathryn knew the strength of superstition. But the improbable thing was that she, too, had gotten caught up in it. What—other than superstition—could you call burning candles all about a room and pouring water over clay?

Kathryn spread the skirt of her green cotton dress beneath her and sat down to wait. Mara took the seat beside her.

At a few minutes after four, a short, thin woman with tightly permed brown curls entered the room. She was young and quite normal looking, not at all like the older woman Kathryn had envisioned.

"Is that Rita Grey?" Kathryn asked nervously.

"Yes. That is Rita. She comes here twice a year from Saint Martin." Mara smiled and waved toward the young woman who nodded acknowledgment but failed to smile in return.

Trying not to stare, Kathryn studied Rita Grey's pale face and noted that she had the same serious expression and upright, starched carriage as Carole Brown.

Rita unlatched a cumbersome briefcase she brought with her and pulled from it a portable tape player. Soon, strains of new age music with bells and flutes filled the air. Kathryn sat back and let the sounds calm and sooth away some of the reservations she had about attending the program.

To begin her presentation, Rita read a short positive affirmation that was much like the beginning words of a traditional church service. "Let light in abundance shine through our lives. Let life in its radiance fulfill our dreams."

Life ... fulfill dreams ... Her dreams had become puzzles that confused her. If only Rita Grey would say something to unravel the puzzle and lift the veil that hung above her dreams.

In a soft, well-trained voice, Rita Grey began her talk. "Light. Dreams. All of us have dreams, but too often we fail to follow our star. We fail to look for that bright light that will help us understand those dreams."

The woman paused and cast her gaze around the room. When she made eye contact with Kathryn, Kathryn stiffened in her chair.

Rita Grey kept her sharp, blue eyes trained on Kathryn as she continued her talk. "Often what happens in this lifetime is rooted in a past life experience.

"Think about your childhood interests. Did you have a country that especially appealed to you? If you did, that could be a past-life clue." For a moment, Rita looked away from Kathryn to make eye contact with the rest of the small audience.

"Did you have certain people you liked immediately? Others, who for no reason, made you angry or upset? That could be another clue. Pay attention. You can learn from all these things." Her eyes were back on Kathryn, riveted as though she were in a trance.

Kathryn wriggled in her seat. Rita Grey spoke of past lives—a subject she didn't believe in.

And what would Flynt think? Thank goodness she had used her better judgment and hadn't told him. Mara had said Rita's talk would be on meditation and guided reverie. She'd made no mention of reincarnation.

"Pay attention to your dreams," Rita said, and her gaze never left Kathryn. It was as if no one else sat in the room.

Dreams. Kathryn straightened her back and slid to the front edge of the uncomfortable metal chair.

"If you find yourself attracted to a particular culture, something in that culture lived in your past." Rita looked at no one else, and Kathryn fidgeted even more. "Pay attention to your dreams," Rita directed Kathryn in a clear voice.

When Kathryn had awakened this morning, she recalled a vivid dream that surrounded her, bigger than life. If she believed in past life, she would have thought the people in her dream were from that time.

"Things that were special in your life when you were a child. Concentrate on these things, using your dreams to piece together the clues you find." Rita Grey smiled at Kathryn and suddenly looked rather pretty.

"Sit straight in your chairs." Once more directing her attention to the others in the room, Rita began her instructions. "This is called 'guided reverie.' You may find this useful, or, for you, it may be meaningless."

Without pausing in her talk, Rita changed the tape in her machine. More background music, this time with low-toned bells, came from the tape player, and Rita's voice grew deeper, more hypnotic.

"Please, close your eyes now ..."

The sounds of bells and violins intermingled.

"See yourself strolling through the grass, a breeze blowing through your hair.

"Breathe deeply, very deeply.

"Everything around you is pleasant and calm. You are happy, carefree, like a child.

"Breathe deeply, more deeply than before. Smell the air, light and sweet.

"Breathe in happiness from that air. Fill your body with perfume and joy.

"Now you are walking up and up to the crest of the hill. Let fresh air fill your lungs.

"You are there at the top of the hill. Stand still and look down far below. See the people. Listen to what they say ..."

Kathryn's shoulders slumped, and Rita Grey's voice faded away into nothingness. She was spinning, turning like a top, into a dark void.

CHAPTER THIRTEEN

BLACK WOMEN, COTTON headwraps tied over their hair, appeared in the field in front of Kathryn. Some of them were crying. Distressed wails tugged at Kathryn's heart. A single tear slid down her cheek. She loved these people who had always been kind to her and could not bear to watch their mistreatment. Yet, as a girl with no wealth of her own, she was helpless.

Except for using the whip, Annie Palmer was as hateful to her as she was to the slaves. The thought vibrated through Kathryn's mind. Since she'd first arrived on the boat from England, Annie had resented her. Belittled and ridiculed her as well. She was very much afraid of her aunt.

More screams echoed from behind the stalks of cane. "Missy, please take us to the mountains." A slave, blood seeping from wounds on his shoulder, staggered from the grass toward her. "Please help ..." He fell to the ground in front of her.

Kathryn settled into a shroud of thick, dark fog, and the sound of a low voice came out of the air.

"Come back now and climb down the hill. Leave the quiet, pleasant place you've found and walk through the grass on the other side.

"Walk more quickly.

"Count to five, and on the count of five, open your eyes. You will remember all you have seen.

"One, two, three, four, five. You are awake and alert."

At the count of five, Kathryn twitched, and a grating buzz hammered against her ears.

"Remember the pleasant scene you left," Rita directed, then, abruptly, she cut off the tape.

"The scene was unhappy, not pleasant," Kathryn said.

"I am sorry," she heard Mara say, but she didn't open her eyes to look at her.

Moments later when she lifted her heavy eyelids, she saw Rita nearby, passing out pencils and paper. She paused next to Kathryn and studied her face, then she handed her a small white pad and short pencil.

"Write down exactly what you saw."

Obediently, Kathryn followed instructions. In front of the room, Rita put on a new tape of forest sounds, bubbling water and falling rain.

As she wrote, Kathryn felt tears fill her eyes then overflow, rolling down her cheeks. There was nothing pleasant in her vision. She had experienced the unhappiness of the slaves, as if she were one of them, as if she were living with and breathing the same air of those long-ago slaves.

Even while her pencil moved over the paper, she saw them—men, women, and even small children—laboring in the fields, sweat pouring from their foreheads. Leather riding whips snapped high in the air and threatened them from every side. The one bare-backed man bore grim reminders of a recent flogging— bloody stripes across his dark, naked flesh. She could not see the faces of those who wielded the whips, but there could be no doubt that Annie was behind them.

"Keep these papers," Rita instructed. Her gaze settled on Kathryn. "Tonight, when you lie down to sleep, ask for a dream that has meaning from a past life."

Rita paused and looked about the room toward the back where more people had filed in recently. She motioned for them to be seated.

"Dreams, regressions, and reveries are ways your unconscious mind gives you past-life information. Another source is waking or meditation visions."

When she heard that, Kathryn came close to falling off her seat. Waking visions. Perhaps what she had experienced wasn't as freakish as she had suspected. At least, one other person, Rita Grey, was aware of such things.

"Put together all the clues, and you will remember much that has been lost in time." Her sharp blue gaze gripped Kathryn. "You must work with urgency." With a sudden snap, Rita closed her notebook and cut off the tape player.

"Come on." Mara grabbed Kathryn by the arm and led her to the podium for an introduction to Rita Grey.

"I am so happy to meet you." Rita looked up at Kathryn with solemn blue eyes.

As they chatted, Kathryn's attention shifted. From the corner of her eye, she glimpsed three men slipping out the entrance door. Her heart slowed and almost stopped, for their hair hung down in long dreadlocks.

Kathryn's pulse quickened when she realized they were the people who had entered late. Were they also the same men who intimidated her that day in the Blue Mountains? From the back, they looked the same.

"What is the matter, Kathryn?" Mara studied her with suspicious eyes.

"N ... nothing," Kathryn stuttered.

"Yesterday, I would believe; today, I do not." Mara, whose face nearly always wore a smile, now looked deadly serious.

"All right," Kathryn conceded. "Those men—the three who just left—I ... I think they're the ones I saw at the Obeah gathering I attended with Carole Brown."

"That would not be unusual. Many times, Rastafarians work in Obeah. They should not frighten you, Kathryn."

Kathryn shrugged. She didn't wish to go into all the details of why seeing the men disturbed her. She didn't intend to tell Mara about the man with dreadlocks who for a few moments had held her captive in the garden. She had decided not to share the violation she'd felt when three men with dreadlocks stared down at her in the car. That she suspected they were following her was something else Kathryn didn't want to tell anyone.

A cool hand touched her wrist, pulling her aside. "You have troubling thoughts. I am able to see that." Rita Grey, petite and trim, regarded Kathryn for a moment. "In the reverie, you saw that which you do not understand. Am I not correct?" Kathryn nodded.

"Very well then. Please try the dream suggestion. It can be of great help to you."

"Yes. I plan to do that tonight."

"There is something else. I can sense it, but you do not wish to talk." Kathryn raised a questioning eyebrow. "Yes. That's true."

"Perhaps, soon you will wish to speak." Rita smiled and squeezed

Kathryn's hand with a strong, assured grip. "If I can be of help to you, please call me." She pulled a business card from her purse and handed it to Kathryn. "Any time, day or night, I will be glad to listen."

"Thank you." With considerable care, Kathryn slipped the card in the side of her purse and zipped together the closure.

By the time she and Mara gathered up their things and left the building, the sky had darkened. Kathryn tilted her watch to the remaining light and saw that it was nearly seven o'clock. The guided reverie must have taken quite a long time, she decided.

Mara laughed. "The time went by quickly, did it not?"

"Yes. I suppose that's because Rita Grey is quite a good speaker. That subject—guided reverie. I want to ..."

Kathryn halted in mid-sentence. A flash of motion on her left side caught her attention and she turned to look.

Was she becoming paranoid, or were the shadows really moving? Kathryn whirled to stare in the other direction, but she saw nothing except waving palm fronds and bright hibiscus blossoms closing their petals in the darkness.

"Let's hurry." Kathryn nudged Mara. She increased her gait and lengthened her steps. To keep up, Mara had to run.

When Kathryn scrambled inside the red BMW, she pressed down the lock immediately and slid low in the seat. It was as if she wanted to hide, yet she didn't know why.

"What is it?" Breathless, as if a wild dog had chased her, Mara collapsed on the car seat and locked her door as well.

"I'm not sure. Probably nothing at all."

Keeping her head down, Kathryn scrutinized the area all around the car, trying to pick out something definite in the shadows. But she saw nothing except the same tropical foliage. She heard nothing except the rapid thumping of her heart. "Maybe I'm worried about being late for my date with Flynt."

"So, you have a date with Flynt. That is good." Mara took a deep breath, started the engine, then checked her lock to be certain it was down. "In case a persistent higgler comes along to try and sell us something," she said with a short laugh. "This bright car attracts them." She shook her head in exasperation. "I asked Fritz to get another color, but he would not listen."

Kathryn said nothing. From the moment they left the church, a car had followed close behind. Its headlights were set on high beam and glared obtrusively in the car's side mirrors.

Mara waved her arm to signal the driver to lower his lights, but he paid no attention to her. Instead, the vehicle drew so close it was almost on their bumper.

"This I do not like," Mara rasped under her breath and at the same time pressed harder on the accelerator.

Kathryn turned around in her seat to get a better look and discovered not a car, but a large truck lumbering behind them. Through the windshield, she could make out the shadows of three heads.

She took a deep breath. Beads of water dampened her forehead and her palms. She blinked hard, closed her eyes and reopened them to make sure. Yes. All of them appeared to have snake-like braids swinging at random in every direction—the horrid dreadlocks.

"Hurry." Kathryn's heart thumped like a pebble caught up and hurled by hurricane winds. "Please hurry."

"I am." Mara increased the speed to racecar power. The rough, curving road bumped beneath them, and the heavier truck fell behind.

"Look out. Something's in the road." Hoping to see better, Kathryn brushed her hand across the windshield. "It's an animal ... crossing in front of us!"

"It's a cow. Crossing the road. That is good." With a quick maneuver, Mara swerved the agile, red car to the side of the lumbering animal and passed it with only inches to spare. Almost immediately, the cow lazed to a halt and plopped down in the center of the highway.

With smiling satisfaction, Mara watched in the rearview mirror. "Good. Now, they will have much trouble passing."

From behind them came the loud grinding screech of brakes. Kathryn stared back in the twilight darkness and saw all three men tumble out of the truck and, with sticks, attempt to prod the stubborn cow out of the road.

In record time, Mara covered the distance from the obstinate animal to Hibiscus Hall. When the little car pulled into the parking lot, both women sat for a moment and let their breathing slow back to normal.

"Why?" Mara sank her shoulders forward and placed her weight on the steering wheel.

"I don't know." Kathryn spoke through dry, pursed lips. And she really didn't. She could only guess. "Thank goodness for the cow." They both started laughing.

When Kathryn and Mara entered the hotel, Flynt was standing alone, his back to the door. Silhouetted against a floral wall design, his towering body dominated the lobby.

The moment Kathryn saw him, her heart quivered. Pausing, she tried to rub color into her cheeks, paled by the sudden escape flight down the highway. "I'm glad to see you." She spoke in an even voice that surprised her with its steadiness.

Flynt turned and immediately took her hand and held it tight between both of his. All the while, his incredible china blue eyes immobilized her. More than the first time she saw him, Kathryn felt the impact of their remarkable attraction.

"Has it only been two days?" he whispered, drawing her against his chest.

The cool, roughness of his shirt brushed her face, and the thunderous pounding of his heart echoed in her ear. Kathryn closed her eyes and let the feel and scent of him overcome the caustic memory of the three men who chased them in the truck.

"You're a little late." Flynt pulled her tighter still. "I was beginning to worry."

"You were?"

That he should be worried about her held an appeal for Kathryn. Perhaps that was unfair, but she needed his interest, actually longed for it. Especially now, when the world seemed to be falling apart around her.

"Mara?" Remembering her friend, Kathryn pulled away from Flynt, but Mara, who had followed her inside, was nowhere in sight. Except for the two of them and a desk clerk, the lobby was empty.

"What happened to Mara?" she asked.

Flynt regarded her with an impish grin. "She pretended not to see me and slipped away without a word." Holding Kathryn at arm's length, he fixed his gaze on her. "I think she wanted us to be alone."

"I think you're right." Kathryn chuckled softly. "She was delighted when I mentioned our dinner date."

Secretly, she was pleased her friend had left without mentioning where they'd been or what happened on the way back. Since she didn't know how to explain things to Flynt, she wanted to put off talking about it. She didn't understand why the men might be after her, but she had begun to believe they were connected with the front-desk computer problems.

"Come on." Flynt guided her through the doorway in the direction of the beach. "Where have you been?" he asked.

"Into town." She halted just outside the entrance and surveyed the walkway and the lamplight blending into the adjacent shadows. "The Jamaicans always have something for sale in their roadside markets." Without actually saying it, Kathryn implied they'd been shopping—which was a bit true. On their way to the church, she and Mara had stopped by to inspect a sculpture set up by an artist on the street. She planned to purchase a piece of art before leaving Jamaica, but she wanted high quality work and doubted she would find it along a roadside.

"Shopping?" Flynt lifted an eyebrow. "But you didn't buy anything?"

"I couldn't find what I wanted."

His eyes serious, Flynt studied Kathryn. "I was afraid you'd gone looking for some Obeah charm out on the beach."

"Flynt, you're being cynical," she said.

"Not cynical. In the last few days, I've learned how many superstitions are left over from slavery times." He tightened his hand on her arm. "For all I knew, you were chasing down an artifact left over from the Arawak Indians."

"The Arawaks?" Kathryn shivered. "You'll have to fill me in on their history."

"Not tonight," he said.

She paused before turning on to the cement walkway that wound parallel to the beach. "I have the evening off." Her voice was quiet.

Flynt's eyes brightened. "That's good news. You need time away from the crazy schedule you've set up." His long, rounded fingers traced the surface of her cheeks. "You've been working too hard, far too hard." Although his words held laughter, Flynt's face was serious.

"This installation is important to Triple Gold," Kathryn said. "It's my job to see that it goes well." For a moment, Flynt stood still as a statue. Then he ran his fingers through her hair. She expected him to kiss her. In fact, her body tingled with anticipation. But he didn't, and she felt a twinge of disappointment thrust upward from the depths of her stomach.

The breeze that ruffled Kathryn's hair carried with it the pungent aroma of palm trees. With the sudden stir of air came a flurry of tiny sand granules that stuck to the bare skin of her legs. Her full cotton skirt swayed, then wrapped like tights against her thighs.

Leaning toward her, Flynt cupped his fingers beneath her chin and tilted her face upward. "Your eyes shine like silver in the moonlight," he said in a low, husky voice. His own eyes sparkled with subtle reflections of lamplight glitter.

Kathryn shuddered as his touch brought a wash of pure desire. How she longed to have his lips come closer, his breath blend with hers. How perfect this night in Jamaica would be if she could put aside her memories of the awful men with swinging snake hair. She needed to forget them and to feel his kiss instead. Her lips parted, she waited expectantly.

But he spoke to her instead. "So, has Jamaica failed to live up to your expectations?" His gaze held hers, but he didn't bend to kiss her.

"No, that's not it at all. I'm just puzzled by some of the things that have happened since I arrived here."

Her nerves taut as a rubber band, she still awaited his kiss. Toes curling anxiously in her shoes, she held her breath, but he pulled his hand away.

Why didn't he kiss her? she wondered. Disappointed, she felt the night air cool her chin where his hand had been moments earlier.

"Are you hungry?" Flynt asked.

"Yes." She was hungry, but not for food.

"We'll walk along the beach after dinner," he promised. "Bamboo By The Sea is close by."

"Tell me about yourself," Kathryn said as they walked. "Is teaching here everything you wanted, or does it fall short?"

Flynt paused on the beach and turned to admire the sea. "Jamaica has set me free. I've been searching all my life for a place where need and joy balance. Jamaica is that place."

"You mean that, don't you?" Desire drifted away and she watched his face with curiosity.

He chuckled, a little self-consciously. "I knew when I telephoned you this morning that everything in my life had shifted. In the past, when I've picked up the telephone, it's been because I had to. But today, I called you on impulse, because I wanted to hear your voice." He reached for her hand and took it. "I know it's just a little thing, but for me it was a giant step."

"Thank you for calling," she said. "For me, it wasn't a little thing."

Kathryn let her hand rest inside the warm, comfortable grip of Flynt's and disregarded the unusual twinge of desire that persisted. Holding hands, they walked toward the restaurant's circle of light, a few hundred yards up the beach.

A noisy barrage of chatter greeted them long before they reached the quaint beachside bar. Unlike their first visit, the outdoor dining room was crowded with customers.

In order to seat them, the manager pulled a small table and two chairs from his office and squeezed them near the outside railing. "This is my special place for lovers," the man whispered to Kathryn, then retreated into the crowd of diners.

She smiled after him. Did they look like lovers?

❊ ❊ ❊

Flynt's smile brightened the corner nook dredged out for them at Bamboo By The Sea. Thoughtfully, he propped his elbows on the table, clasped his fingers together and flattened them beneath his chin to study her face.

What was it about Kathryn Calder that tugged at him so hard? Wasn't he the same Flynt Kincade who spurned commitment as if it were a communicable disease?

Yes, he was. Yet he found himself looking at Kathryn in a different way from any other woman.

His smile vanished.

"Do you want to go back to New York?" His question came on impulse, as if from someone else's lips. More impulsive behavior. Flynt, the uncommitted, would never ask that question.

Not when it was immersed with hope she might decide to stay in Jamaica.

"Of course." Kathryn responded quickly, but her eyelids fluttered, and she didn't look at him directly. Folding her napkin in her lap, she asked, "Wouldn't you like to go back?"

"Never." Damn it. What was wrong with him tonight? Let the woman be a few minutes late, and his thinking got all mixed up. Like an overgrown kid, he was testing her resolve.

"That's too bad," she said simply.

Admitting to himself that this week had changed him, Flynt continued to watch her. "Teaching is where I belong. Now that I know what it's like, I wish I'd made the move sooner. In truth, Kathryn, I could never go back to the city."

"Have you always been so intense?" she asked, her gaze burning into his.

A waiter dropped off two menus, and Flynt picked his up, but she didn't touch hers.

"You like teaching? Someone I knew a long time ago was passionate about changing his job and becoming a teacher." Kathryn frowned. "I wish I could remember who that was."

"You don't much like the teaching profession."

"Perhaps I don't."

"Have you decided what you'd like for dinner?" Flynt abruptly shifted the subject. "You haven't opened your menu."

"No." Kathryn picked up the menu and glanced over it.

Flynt shrugged. "All the seafood sounds good."

"Mara says the lobster's best."

"That's what I'll have then. And some of that golden rum punch to start. How about that?"

Across two menus, their gazes met and locked.

"Yes. I'll have the same."

Soon, full glasses of golden yellow liquid overflowed onto the waiter's tray as he delivered them to the table. "This is our special recipe," the man declared, drying the bottom of each glass with a towel before setting them down. He placed a pitcher of punch on the table as well.

"You said we would go back to the beach. If we drink all of this, someone will have to carry us there." She took a sip and giggled. "It's very good. Sugarcane and rum." Moments later, Kathryn's mood became serious. "Slaves were brought to Jamaica to raise sugarcane for the colonies. Sad, isn't it?" She lifted her glass and stared into it. "Rum, like this, meant an increase in slave trade to the West Indies."

"That's right." Flynt lifted one eyebrow. "You must have been reading a Jamaican history book."

Kathryn stared at him with a questioning expression on her face. "I ... I don't think so. Unless it was in Mara's book about Rose Hall ..."

Flynt watched Kathryn. He had never met a woman quite like her. Such wide mood swings. From the moment of their first meeting, she had him switching directions like a yo-yo just to keep up with her wild meandering. Now, she was off again.

At the thought, Flynt's face darkened into a scowl. "There's something I want to ... no, need to, tell you." He hesitated and took a fortifying gulp of punch. That wasn't enough, so he tipped his glass upward and emptied it. Reaching for the pitcher, he poured a refill.

"Do you always drink so fast?" Kathryn asked.

"No, but this isn't something I enjoy discussing."

"Oh."

"After my father died, I went to work to support Mom and me. With Mom's help, I managed to save enough money to go to college."

Flynt twisted in his chair and took yet another gulp of punch. After so many years, why was the subject of his failed marriage still so painful.

"After I got into college, I found odd jobs that fitted around my class schedule. My best part-time job was as a photographer's assistant in a local studio. That's when I met the woman I married."

CHAPTER FOURTEEN

WHY DID THE mention of another woman in Flynt's life make her spirits fall? The palms of Kathryn's hands grew clammy and her stomach tightened. All thoughts of Obeah, the Rastafarians, and Rose Hall diminished.

"I met her when I was in college." Flynt looked into the night. He spoke as if he were reciting a story to an unseen audience. "She was a small-time model who picked up bit jobs wherever she could. She would come in from time to time to check on assignments at the studio where I worked part-time."

Kathryn said nothing. She shifted her gaze away from Flynt to the fire of the burning candle.

"She came from a family with even less money than ours. Our financial struggles gave us a common bond." He rattled the ice in his empty glass, reached toward the pitcher of rum drink, then changed his mind and continued his story instead.

"The woman knew how to feed my ego. Said I was brilliant. Called me her Greek god." He chuckled. "Of course, I knew she was not always sincere. Still it was hard to resist her charm when she poured it on." The line of his lips hardened.

"Unfortunately, she was a schemer. She had big plans for me as soon as I graduated." Flynt shook his head. "In fact, she had my career planned in minute detail.

"It was a terrible mistake. All I ever wanted to do was to teach. I cared nothing for Wall Street or rising to the top making stock trades." He grabbed the pitcher of rum punch and refilled his glass.

"You wanted to teach?"

"That was the career I planned to have until..."

"She must be a very persuasive lady."

"I thought I loved her," he whispered, his eyes a cloudy blue.

Kathryn watched him more closely. Thought I loved her.

"All my friends envied me when we got married."

Kathryn took a small sip of punch. As she listened, her own thoughts spun in her head. Flynt was a married man. The notion devastated her.

"So, you are married." Kathryn stared at him. She ached inside with disappointment, hurt, and outrage. "Why didn't you tell me?"

"No. No." Flynt looked at her, startled. "I would never do that to you, Kathryn." His voice softened.

"But..."

"We've been divorced for six years now." Flynt chuckled. "That marriage was the big mistake of my youth."

Kathryn let out a sigh of relief. "What happened to her?"

"She continued on her way and ran off with a wealthy executive who made five times the money I did. In fact, she went with him before our marriage ended."

"I'm sorry," Kathryn murmured.

"It took a while, but I'm getting my life back where I wanted it to be." His gaze focused above Kathryn on a tall palm tree, standing dark and lonely on the beach. "I wanted you to know about my past."

Flynt took her hand. "I don't want any secrets between us, Kathryn. None at all."

Her heart lurched. No secrets. She had so many. Thoughts of the Rastas and Obeah poured back.

When their dinners arrived, Kathryn felt a surge of relief. The scent of the steaming lobster served with drawn butter and hot bread was enticing.

"This is a feast." Kathryn exclaimed.

"Quite amazing, and we have Mrs. Smith to thank for her recommendation."

By the time Kathryn and Flynt left Bamboo By The Sea, she was more relaxed and confident. She had needed a good meal. They both had.

Together they strolled along the beach, arms linked. Most of the tension from Flynt's revelation was swept away with dinner and the remainder of the rum punch.

They paused near the water's edge. Memories of their earlier romantic encounter rushed forward into Kathryn's thoughts. He had been married, but it was a regrettable relationship, Flynt said. Now her own feelings confused her.

When he told her about his wife, she had pangs of jealousy. That was very unlike her. But so was much that had happened in Jamaica.

Her mind far away, Kathryn pushed the silver bracelet high on her arm. She turned toward Flynt. A shaft of moonlight fell across his face.

She watched the trace of a smile begin on his lips. Then Flynt leaned toward her and took both her hands in his.

"Thanks for coming back to Ocho Rios tonight," she said.

"Thank you for being here," he whispered. He pulled her against the taut muscles of his chest.

Kathryn was closing her eyes ready to savor the warmth of his arms when a flicker of light caught her attention. She gasped. A dark, all too human form, stood in the shadows beneath the nearby palm trees.

"Someone is watching us," she whispered.

Alarmed, Flynt grasped her shoulders with his hands and looked in the direction of her frozen stare.

"I ... I didn't tell you about the men." She spoke in low tones, certain the man in the shadows was related to the afternoon events when the Rastas chased Mara's BMW.

"What men?" Flynt rasped. As if afraid she might run away, he tightened his hold on her shoulders.

"They followed us until a cow came to our rescue."

"A cow came? What cow?"

Without blinking her eyes, Kathryn continued to watch the darkness behind them. "It was a fat cow that Mara drove around almost into a ditch to avoid hitting. After we passed, the big animal lay down in the middle of the road."

"Go on."

"There were three men in an old truck chasing after us." Kathryn caught her breath. "It was way too big to get around the cow. When they couldn't get by, the men got out and tried to push the animal out of the way."

Kathryn stepped back and continued to survey every shadow in the area around them. The beach and the brush both appeared deserted now. She could pick out no movement at all in the darkness.

"Did the men get around it?"

She shrugged. "I don't know. We didn't wait to find out."

"Kathryn, I don't understand what's going on, but I don't like the idea of leaving you here alone."

"You can't be my body guard," she said. "Maybe all these things are just coincidence."

Of course, she knew they were not. Too many events were deliberate. She had seen the perpetrators and they all wore their hair in dreadlocks like the Rastafarians.

"I would like to be your body guard." Flynt smiled in the darkness. He reached to pull her close to him once more.

"I don't see anything now." Kathryn nestled to him, enjoying his warmth.

Perhaps the movement was only her imagination. Perhaps there was no human form there. After all, so much had happened in the past few days. Who could blame her for being edgy and suspicious of every motion in the shadows?

"The men in the truck had those wild snake-like braids," she confided. Frowning, she cast another prolonged stare up and down the shoreline. "What reason would those men have for following me?"

Flint stiffened his posture. "Maybe you're right. Perhaps what happened had nothing to do with you. Lots of vehicles go up and down the roads every day," he rationalized. "Maybe the men were celebrating being off from work and weren't paying attention to you or Mara. A coincidence. That's probably it."

She knew he was trying to reassure her. After all, he was the one who had warned her to be careful.

"There've been too many coincidences," she said, digging the toe of her shoe deep into the sand.

With an increased gait, they resumed their walk. Whether the men were there or not, Kathryn didn't know, but, somewhere in the darkness, she sensed the unknown presence of someone watching. A person they couldn't see, but who was ominously aware of each step they took.

"Some other things have happened," Kathryn said tentatively. Why was she telling him that? He didn't need to know.

"What things? Tell me." Flynt caught her arm in an intense grip and pulled her to an abrupt halt. He clasped her hands close to his chest, pinning Kathryn's fingers against the heavy beat of his heart. "What else has happened you haven't told me?" He stared at her with darkened eyes.

"Let's not talk here," she said.

For a moment, Kathryn pressed her forehead into the springy dark chest hair that showed in a "v" at the top of his shirt. Against her skin, the spiral shoots felt like thin, soft wire and smelled of Ivory soap. Wrapped in his protective grip, she wanted to forget the men, but that was impossible.

"Come on. Let's get away from the beach to some place with a little more light." Flynt looped his fingers around Kathryn's elbow and guided her toward Hibiscus Hall.

He was upset. She could tell by the tense muscles in his arms. Why couldn't they enjoy one starry night alone on a moonlit beach? That was why most of the couples came to Hibiscus Hall, wasn't it? They wanted the chance to be alone in the romantic tropics.

She would like the same thing. To be alone with Flynt. To make love to Flynt. Make love? Her heart beat faster.

What was happening to her? Was she falling in love with Flynt Kincade?

Matching long strides, they hurried to a circle of lampposts that lighted the walkway in the center of the hibiscus garden. Earlier in the day, the bushes surrounding a decorative water fountain blazed with crimson flowers. Now, the blossoms hung limp, their faces closed in the cooler evening air. From the fountain, a steady rush of bubbling water challenged the surge of the sea and blended into its sound.

Flynt paused by the fountain. Kathryn took a deep breath of night air and turned to face him.

Shimmers of moonlight glowed like fireflies in his hair. With a gentle hand, he lifted her chin and lightly traced the curving lines of her face.

"How lovely you are in the starlight," he said. "I'm glad you don't have to go to work tonight."

Why did her knees seem ready to collapse, like they had the first time she visited Rose Hall? And like the first time she saw him in New York.

Suddenly, Flynt pulled away from Kathryn. Startled, she opened her eyes and watched him sidle in the direction of the lawn on the other side of the hibiscus. Finger over his lips, he turned and signed for her to stay still.

On the other side of the grass, among the yellow hibiscus plants, she saw a group of shadows leap and vanish. Her stomach knotted. The shadows had the familiar projections flying from their heads. The hairstyle she had come to dread.

Kathryn stood motionless, watching Flynt's flight across the lawn to the point where she'd last seen the shadows. She saw him beat the bushes with his hands, then part them for entry into the darkest section.

Scarcely breathing, she kept her eyes fixed on the spot until Flynt's head, brown hair tousled, poked out from the bushes.

"Nothing here now," he called to her after pulling aside the last untouched group of branches.

Kathryn was trembling when Flynt returned to her. Why would anyone in Jamaica care about following her? Was it because of her job, or something else?

"We'll talk inside." Flynt's voice, like his steel grip on her arm, was "no nonsense". She didn't argue.

Leading her past the registration desk, Flynt located a white wicker sofa in a remote corner near the rear of the lobby. They settled into the wide plush cushions, covered in bright floral chintz. Normally, she would have loved the setting, but now, Kathryn felt vulnerable and exposed.

"Kathryn, I suspect you have not told me everything." Flynt spoke quietly, his somber gaze searching her face. Without looking down, he picked up her right hand and placed it on his knee.

As concisely as she could manage, Kathryn told Flynt about a man entering her room while she was out and leaving the odd vial of liquid beneath her bed. Even as she related the incident, an involuntary shiver slithered down her spine. "What was in the bottle?"

"I don't know," she said.

Flynt's face reflected deep thought. "Did you open it?"

"No, of course not." Her gray eyes narrowed. "It might have been a poison."

"Why would you think that?"

"I ... I'm not sure why, but I'm certain the little bottle was filled with poison. I know it was."

"Did you hear or read something to make you think that?"

"No ... Yes. Yes. I read about Obeah poisons in Mara's book," Kathryn said.

"It ... it was in her book that told the history of Rose Hall Plantation.

Two hundred years ago Annie Palmer poisoned some of her slaves, and they tried to poison her." She squirmed to the edge of the cushions. "Flynt, do you think they may still use poison to get rid of people in Jamaica?"

Flynt frowned, but did not give Kathryn a direct answer. "What did you do with the bottle?" he asked.

Kathryn hesitated. "I ... I wasn't sure what to do, so I went to Carole Brown, and she took care of it for me." Because she sensed Flynt's growing disapproval, Kathryn didn't mention Carole's burning white candles in the corners of her room.

Flynt made no comment.

"That's not all," she said.

"No? What else has happened?"

As Kathryn described her frightening attack on the hotel walkway, Flynt stood up and paced back and forth, hands in his pockets. "I was holding a clay ball, with blue and green feathers and a golden beak in my hand," she said.

"Hmmm. Why would someone want to 'set a fix' on you?" Flynt thrust his hands deeper into his pockets and paced more rapidly. "It doesn't make much sense."

"Set a fix?" Kathryn slid so near the edge of the sofa, she almost fell off. "What do you mean by that?"

"I've been reading about Obeah, too," he explained. "The things you're describing might be used by an Obeah practitioner to cast a spell on someone ... but, why someone would want to do that to you doesn't make sense."

"Carole said it was the work of an Obeahman by the name of Granville Davis. She called him one of the bad ones."

Flynt leaned against a dark wooden support column. "What did you do with the clay?"

"I took it to Carole Brown, and she dumped it in a bowl of water and chanted something over it. Then, she took off her bracelet, put it on my arm and warned me not to take it off." Kathryn slid the wide silver band down to her wrist and held it out for Flynt to see.

Taking her hand, Flynt studied the surface of the gleaming bracelet. He said nothing.

More forceful than before, Kathryn remembered her vision and her dreams. With great effort she tried to force away the image of two women on horseback. But she couldn't push the memories from her mind, nor could she dismiss the face of the sad-eyed blonde woman. Without speaking, she studied Flynt's face.

There was something about him that related to her vision. She was certain of it. But she couldn't tell him about it. Not until she understood more herself.

"I believe you need someone to keep you out of trouble."

A smile touched his lips and expanded to the corners of his eyes. It lifted her spirits.

Forget the men, she told herself. No one was in the shadows after all. I have Carole's bracelet to protect me.

Strange. Kathryn Calder never had a superstitious thought before coming to Jamaica. With the palm of her hand, she traced the hard edge of the cold, smooth silver surface.

His smile in place, Flynt pushed away from the column and strolled to where she sat. "Trouble. You've had lots of trouble in a few short weeks." His hands encircled her wrists, tugging her to her feet. "You need someone to keep you out of trouble," he teased. "Someone like me." Hands on her waist, Flynt drew her toward him. Kathryn's heart raced.

"Wait," she whispered.

Kathryn tried to pull away. The lobby was the most public place at Hibiscus Hall, and she was a professional working with a sizable portion of the hotel staff. Even on her night off, she had to be aware of her image. Still, she longed to feel his lips on hers, but not here.

In compliance with her wishes, Flynt slipped his arm from her waist and linked his hand with hers. "Come on." He guided her through the lobby and out the door.

At the entrance, Kathryn resisted. "I don't want to go back out," she whispered. The realization that she had grown to fear the dark stirred a heavy ache inside her. So much had happened to make her fear dark, lonely places, in and near the resort, but it wasn't her nature to be afraid. To admit it was especially difficult.

"Shhh. It's all right," Flynt said. "We're going to the pool where we'll find other people, mostly vacationers, not the office staff." He leaned closer and whispered in her ear, "I'll take care of you." His grip strengthened on her hand and they exited the door.

As Flynt had promised, lots of guests were at the pool. Three groups of men and women sat propped up in lounge chairs or nestled into seats around the umbrella tables. Five or six expert swimmers were doing laps in the pool. A lean young man, stop watch in hand, stood at the deepest end, timing some of his friends.

At the shallow end, four young women stood in the pool. Their backs against the blue-tiled wall, they sipped drinks from plastic cups. Everyone was too involved with their own friends to pay attention to Flynt and Kathryn who strolled unnoticed toward a cement barrier that separated the pool from the beach.

When they reached it, Kathryn took a deep breath. Even the pool held bad memories for her. It was the site for one of her strange visions and the near drowning.

"Where have all these people been? I haven't seen any of them before." Kathryn propped her elbows on top of the wall and rested her chin on cupped hands.

Flynt shrugged and smiled. "Who knows? Maybe they sleep during the day."

"Perhaps they do," she said, cherishing the happiness his closeness had brought her.

❀ ❀ ❀

Despite his smile, Flynt was worried. He, too, had seen somebody moving in the darkness, someone following them, someone trying to stay out of sight.

It disturbed him that Kathryn had unwittingly gotten involved with Obeah. Apparently, a dark variation of the ancient African practice was on the rise in Jamaica. His students liked to talk, and he had overheard their hushed conversations outside his classroom door about the new Obeahmen. Not knowing Flynt could understand, the students spoke in their native dialect. But, thanks to what he'd learned from a Jamaican friend, Flynt understood everything they said.

Flynt stood behind Kathryn now. From the back, she looked soft and feminine. Her light hair with golden streaks barely touched the tops of her shoulders; her slender waistline defined the subtle fullness of her hips.

Kathryn held an intangible quality he couldn't quite discern. She was all need and all independence, both at the same time. He didn't understand her fierce longing to know everything about Jamaica's darkest side. Whatever the elusive quality was and despite her independent nature, Flynt wanted to protect her. No, more than that, he needed to protect her. And, he needed something else. He needed to touch her in a way he'd never touched a woman before.

He needed to touch her heart.

CHAPTER FIFTEEN

TAKING A LONG breath, Flynt edged closer to Kathryn. His hands brushed the soft skin of her shoulders, and his warm breath touched her hair. When she turned, Flynt's arms surrounded her, and he lifted her against his body.

Kathryn smiled and turned her face to look into his eyes. The intensity of their locked gazes stunned him. It was as if some heated force connected them.

Flynt trailed his fingers down Kathryn's graceful neck and across her narrow shoulders. The sound of the sea pulsated in his ears and his heartbeat accelerated.

Had he known Kathryn only a few short weeks? It felt as if he'd known her forever.

"I don't care about these people," she whispered. "With you here, I'm not worried about the shadows either."

Flynt slid his hands down her shoulders, along the length of her arms, to the fullness of her hips where his fingers caressed her. Then, moving even more slowly than before, he splayed his fingers behind her hips, and pulled her toward him.

His body seemed pitched on high key, like a taut guitar string. Never had he felt such desire for a woman. It was as if some force beyond himself drove him. Some force that soared beyond the boundaries of his imagination.

❀ ❀ ❀

Kathryn ... Kathryn," Flynt murmured. His breath grew more ragged until it resounded against her hair, heavy and rushed, as compelling as the rapid beating of her heart.

The wiry hair on his chest grew wet, matted beneath the dampness of his cotton shirt. Instinct urged Kathryn to yank the buttons loose and bare his skin and the soaked, springy hair to the night air, but she didn't.

Without a word, Flynt pulled away from their embrace, caught hold of her hand and led her down the cement steps to the beach below. As soon as they reached the sand, his hands, arms and entire body seemed to close around her.

Barely breathing, Kathryn tilted her head toward his lips, which, slightly parted, invited hers. At last, when their lips touched, it was like a new fire ignited within the center of her, and she could not get enough of the taste of him.

With renewed urgency, their kisses began. Sweat-soaked clothing hampered their motions, separating them from each other in a sodden sort of way. But neither of them noticed.

Caught in a mist of humid air and seawater, Kathryn stood transfixed. Through closed eyelids, she could see Flynt standing. In a field of rosebushes. The scent hung like a mountain fog all around them. The sweetness of the aroma filled her nostrils and covered her over with perfume. The thought and the smell astonished her.

She blinked as hard as she could and forced her eyes open. Then she peered around them through the dimness. Not a single rose, not one bush grew nearby. Perhaps there were some by the pool, she thought and tried to lean near the wall to see over it, but the pressure of Flynt's lips halted her efforts.

How could she think when he kissed her like that? But, how could she kiss him with the scent of roses everywhere? She had to find the source of the scent before she'd feel free to kiss him again. She needed to understand at least one part of the puzzle. "Flynt," she whispered, reluctant to withdraw her lips from his. "Do you smell roses?"

A half-smile returned to his face. "No." He glanced around them.

"Should I?"

"I ... I ... I don't know."

She stared up at him, trying to quell the disturbance in her stomach. Would she ever be plain Kathryn Calder again? Or would this strangeness follow her forever? There had to be an explanation. "Come on," she said, straightening her drenched clothes. "Perhaps they have some rose bushes in pots by the pool."

"Why are you searching for roses now?" He followed her up the steps.

"I have to find them, Flynt." She brushed her thumb across his cheek and over his lips. "Please understand."

"I'll try." They stood at the top of the stairs and visually surveyed every plant in the entire pool garden area.

"They're not here." The sound of her words reflected the disappointment rising like a cloud to fill her throat.

Inexplicably, Kathryn choked back warm tears. Even the scent had disappeared. A vision of yellow roses filled her brain, then quickly evaporated like the flash of a camera light. If only she could find one rose bush, it might help solve the mystery.

Perplexed, she bit her bottom lip. Something was very wrong with her, she thought, and it couldn't be explained by ordinary means. She would contact Rita Grey as soon as possible. Rita had promised to help her. And she needed help like she never had before.

The moment of touching and loving had vanished for Flynt and her. Kathryn feared it might never come again until she rid herself of impromptu visions and scents. Perhaps there'd never be another chance for the two of them.

"Kathryn." Flynt pushed her at arm's length from him and held her shoulders by gripping the rounded tops with his hands. "I need to know what's going on." The golden light that had surrounded them only moments before diminished and settled into the shadows.

"Is it something about your job?" He paused, his face darkened, and his eyes blackened. "Or, has it something to do with that damned Obeah?" His body temperature had dropped several degrees. She felt the coldness in her hands.

How she hated to watch Flynt turn cold. But, how could she explain to him the unexplainable? She had to see Rita Grey or someone else who might be able to help her.

"Flynt. I'm sorry. You don't understand, and I don't understand either."

She lifted his hands from her shoulders and leaned toward him until her head rested against the bare portion of his chest.

"Perhaps, it's a little bit of everything."

Flynt stroked her hair with his fingers. "Don't worry, Kathryn. The job will get better, and so will everything else."

"Yes. They will," she replied too quickly. "When I get transferred to the New York office."

Suddenly, his hands were like ice on her hair, and his soggy chest hair turned cold against her face.

Immediately, Kathryn longed to take back the last words she'd spoken. But it was too late.

And they hadn't even discussed Kathryn going to Kingston to see the painting of Rose Hall ...

❊ ❊ ❊

"Kathryn. Kathryn Calder. Is it you are awake now?" Mara, her voice high-pitched and tense, called from outside the hotel door.

Sleepily, Kathryn pushed the rumpled bed sheet from atop her head. "Mara?" Her voice hushed and tired, she scrambled from the bed and padded barefoot to the chained entrance. "Mara. Is that you?"

"Yes. Let me in, please."

Even in her half-awake state, Kathryn recognized the tremor of anxiety in her friend's voice. "Just a minute, Mara." Pulling the chain loose, she opened the door.

As soon as she saw Mara's tear-stained face and streaked mascara, Kathryn knew something was dreadfully wrong. Mara always took special care to keep up her personal appearance. "After all," she'd once told Kathryn, "the hotel's image rests on my shoulders as the activities director."

Rushing into the room, Mara tripped over the circular straw rug before collapsing on the bed. "I am so sorry to come in this way, Kathryn. It is that I need a friend to talk to me."

Kathryn adjusted her "Make It Jamaica Again" nightshirt and sank down beside Mara on the bed. She pushed back a section of hair that flopped loosely over her eyes. A splash of water in her face would help her awaken, but she didn't want to leave Mara to go into the bathroom. If only she'd been able to go to sleep last evening, she would already be up and wide-awake by now. But she had lain awake far into the night.

"Please, tell me what's wrong." Kathryn placed a hand on Mara's arm.

"It is everything. Everything, it has fallen away and broken. Everything." Mara dropped her forehead to rest on her hands and drew in a deep breath. "It has been bad with Fritz and me. It has been bad for some days now ... Always we are fighting ... Never did we fight in Germany ... Now it is not good anything I do ... Even we argue over the little red car ... I do not like the color ... He will not change ... He is angry with me ... He wants that we should pack and go back to Germany ... I want that we should stay ... It is round and round ... "A deep sigh resounded through her chest, rocking the bed.

Kathryn smiled and shook her head. She'd noticed Mara's recent preoccupation with her own thoughts but hadn't been aware of any real difficulties. Besides, she had had so much on her own mind she hadn't paid as much attention to other things as she should have.

"Why do you think you're fighting so much?"

"I do not know. Fritz, he will not even talk. He will only go round and round and argue, argue. I am so tired of constant fight, fight." The whites of Mara's lovely silver-blue eyes were blemished by red streaks. "I am so sorry, but it is that I need much to talk."

"Of course, you do. I'll be glad to listen, but I doubt I'll be much help." How could she be? Kathryn had more confusion in her own life than Mara could probably imagine. Last night, she had practically destroyed her growing relationship with Flynt. And it all happened over a phantom scent.

"That is good." Mara paused. "Yesterday, when we got back from Rita Grey's talk, it was bad with Fritz. He was angry and would not speak at all. He got out suitcases and said he would pack if I did not. Every time when I go out alone, he is like that." She looked up at Kathryn. "Why is that?"

Kathryn chuckled. "Do you and Fritz go out together sometimes?"

Mara thought a moment. "Not for a very long time." She frowned. "Not since we come to Jamaica. I have been so busy."

"Maybe that's it," Kathryn suggested. "Maybe Fritz is looking for attention. You go out with the guests, don't you?"

"Yes. But that is my job, to do activities with the guests."

"Of course, it is." Kathryn said. "But Fritz needs some attention, too."

"Hmmm."

"Could you both take a day off and go somewhere alone? Somewhere away from the tourists. A drive? Or rafting? Mara, you should know some place really wonderful, and romantic, to go with Fritz." Kathryn's smile sparkled. "After all, you send resort guests on intimate excursions every day, don't you?"

As if mulling through a file of ideas, Mara tilted her head to one side. "Yes. Yes. We should both have the time off. And one of the boat owners invited us to go out on a sail any day we can go. It is good. It is a good thing."

Mara rose from the bed and strutted to the door with renewed conviction. "Thank you, Kathryn Calder. You are a good friend. Thank you much." With a saluting wave of her hand, Mara departed a far different woman from the one who had entered moments earlier.

Kathryn twisted onto her stomach and gazed through the wide sliding glass door overlooking the Caribbean Sea. In the distance, sun-speckled waves advanced toward the shining white beach.

Couples strolled together along the shoreline, lingering occasionally to take a photograph, then trudging on through the sand. She watched them laughing together and winced. How she longed to be on that beach with Flynt, but it was too late. He'd already boarded the bus for Kingston and was probably in his classroom filled with students.

How nice it would have been to climb aboard that bus with him. How interesting to sit in the back of his classroom and listen to him teach. Kathryn frowned. To consider following a man was a new concept for her, and the idea of relinquishing control in her life was completely foreign.

Recalling the previous evening, Kathryn felt a knot in the center of her chest. Why had she broken away from Flynt's arms to search for the smell of roses? And what had possessed her to mention New York at such an inappropriate moment? Kathryn could still feel the frozen air that fell between them when Flynt pulled away.

With a clenched fist, she struck the mattress with all the force she could muster. Hot tears filled her eyes. Like Fritz, Flynt was a man. A man who needed attention, too. How stupid of her to give Mara advice she had failed to heed herself.

Kathryn rolled from the bed. Hurrying to the dresser, she pulled open the stuck bottom drawer with a vigorous yank. Rummaging through a stack of shirts, then one of shorts, she shuffled them aside and impatiently slammed shut the drawer. Where was her purse?

She was halfway to the closet when she spied the beige bag right where she'd left it, with yesterday's clothes lying on the chair. With frenzied fingers, she unzipped the side pocket and pulled out a small white card. Rita Grey's card, with her telephone number. She took a deep breath and reached for the phone.

Rita Grey agreed to see her that afternoon. After unsuccessfully wishing away the nervous tremors that had settled in her stomach, Kathryn moved tentatively down the hall toward the small room that served as her own hotel office.

Last night, she'd failed to program herself to have a dream relating to a past life. It wasn't that she didn't believe in such things, but the emotional conflict of the previous evening had been difficult to dismiss.

More than she wanted to admit, her lack of sensitivity last night with Flynt had disturbed her and still did. If only she could move back the hours, shift back the clocks, she would do things differently.

Fingering her new necklace of brightly painted parrots connected by yellow beads, Kathryn stood at the window overlooking the garden. The necklace was supposed to brighten her spirits. But it did not.

Hibiscus blossoms lifted their colorful faces toward the sunshine. Distracted, she watched the brilliant light play dancing games across every petal. Red ... Peach ... Yellow ... Pink ... White. So much color. So much beauty in Jamaica.

Reincarnation. What did she believe about the subject?

Back in her church school in Baltimore, there'd been quite an uproar when a teacher mentioned reincarnation once had been part of the Bible. Since then, because of that negative experience, Kathryn had shied away from the subject.

Now, a tie of sorts from the past tugged at her heart, joggled her memory, teased her brain. Pieces of visions, like parts of a flower, were coming together and she'd been unable to figure out the puzzle.

Kathryn plopped into her desk chair and fumbled to uncover an empty notebook. Keep a journal she'd been told. Why hadn't she done this before? Now, there was so much to write.

Kathryn flattened the cushioned volume open on her desk and picked up a pen. Beneath the fingers of her right hand, the pen fairly flew over the paper. Thirty minutes later, fragments from her visions and dreams filled a dozen pages.

Flowers from the hibiscus garden had gotten her going. They glimmered like colorful crystalline dew, emerging from the canvas on the museum wall that afternoon in New York. That day, when she watched the painting change before her eyes and smelled rose blossoms in the gallery, was the beginning of her waking visions. Her first experience, but she hadn't recognized it as such.

Yesterday, Rita Grey helped her understand a little of it. She hoped Rita would offer even more insight when she arrived for her appointment in a few minutes.

"Women in long skirts strolling, and one lone man," Kathryn wrote about the pool episode. And there'd been so much crying, she noted.

Kathryn turned another page. There, she'd scrawled notes about the dark-haired woman in the long white dress, calling "Aimee." That had happened at Rose Hall, but she'd heard Aimee's name called again while she was at the Obeah service in the Blue Mountains. She'd had a vision there of a small group of men with shadowy features who passed a container of blood among them. Kathryn shuddered.

On the next page, she'd jotted sentences about the strongest vision of all. And the most perplexing. It was as if she'd stepped through a barrier, backward into another century.

What she saw in the Great House at Rose Hall, she'd seen before. What she heard, she already knew. She recognized that as she wrote. Somehow, she knew Aimee White, knew her well. And the wretched, dark-haired woman with the evil temper—she'd known her, too. It was as if she'd traveled back in time.

On her pad, Kathryn wrote about the long, full dresses and couples dancing on the terrace. She felt as if she had been there, had been part of the group assembled on the porch. In bold, even handwriting, she described the tables with the candles and the dark-haired woman's introduction of Aimee White as her niece visiting from England. Kathryn noted her own feeling of repulsion toward a heavy-set man who danced with Aimee. That day, she had experienced a heated response that made her want to flee.

Agitated even now, she flipped a page to where she'd written of another vision—two women riding horseback at night through Montego Bay into the woods where Aimee's aunt promised she'd show her some of the voodoo she'd learned in Haiti. The wicked aunt took a bloody cat's skull, a clay ball with feathers and broken glass, as well as the doll figure of a man from her pockets.

"Sam will regret the moment he chose to defy me," Kathryn had written in the journal. Who was Sam? Was he one of the slaves the dark-haired woman mistreated?

Aimee White hated her aunt for the dreadful things she did to the black workers. That was one reason Aimee had decided to marry Richard, a man she didn't love. But, as the owner of Gordon Gardens, he could take her away from Rose Hall where she was forced to watch the hurt done to slaves whom she was powerless to help. How could she know that?

Rereading the entry, Kathryn shivered and drew her hands up to cover her shoulders that were suddenly prickly with chill bumps. She reached into the bottom desk drawer and pulled out a white cardigan she kept for cooler days.

Wrapping the sweater around her arms, she stood up, notebook in hand, and picked out several passages relating to her experiences with the scent of roses. Kathryn thought it a bit odd that all those episodes occurred when she was with Flynt. Twice she'd had visualizations of being in a field of rose bushes. And when she smelled their fragrant perfume, she had the distinct impression the blossoms were yellow.

She grimaced at the words scrawled in both printed and curling cursive strokes on the lined pages. Perhaps having a notebook to consider, Kathryn's very own psychic journal, would be helpful to Rita Grey. Chuckling to herself over the term "psychic journal," Kathryn turned toward the door where she thought she heard a soft knock.

"Do forgive me for being a little late, my dear." Rita, wearing a narrow-belted, floral-print dress, smiled pleasantly at Kathryn. In her hands, she carried a book and three audio-tapes. "I brought along some materials I thought you might find helpful." She handed the book to Kathryn.

"*In Touch with the Past*. Hmmm." Unable to contain her considerable curiosity, Kathryn took a moment to leaf through the hard cover volume.

Reincarnation. The book was filled with case studies and fact-by-fact documentation. Fingering it nervously, she turned to face Rita.

"You'll find Dr. Pettersen's work most informative. He has also done considerable research into past-life regression." Rita Grey studied Kathryn with steady blue eyes.

"How did you know?" Kathryn's voice was quiet. "I never said anything."

"You have troubled eyes, young woman. Sometimes, whether I want to or not, I see things about people. I see it both in their eyes and in their auras. When that occurs, I let them know I am willing to help, but only if they ask. It is not for me to interfere in the lives of others. Only if they ask will I try to help them."

Caught in the woman's powerful scrutiny, Kathryn shuddered as a series of chills skittered up her spine. "Is that why you gave me your card?" she asked, a tremor in her voice.

"Yes." Breathing deeply, Rita Grey shifted her gaze from Kathryn to the garden below the window. "Beautiful hibiscus bushes." She turned on her heel to face Kathryn. "I can see by the colors in your aura that they mean much to you."

"No ... Yes ... I don't know." Kathryn balked at the suggestion of aura colors.

"I see a picture." Rita's eyes fluttered shut and her voice deepened. "You are strolling in a garden, a garden filled with hibiscus blossoms. Red and gold flowers are blooming everywhere. Your skirt is long; your hair is golden." When she placed her hands on her temples, her closed eyelids fluttered open. "That is all I see. Does it mean something to you, Kathryn Calder?"

Struggling with Rita's vision, Kathryn leaned across the desk. "I think it does," she said almost inaudibly.

Picking up the clothbound notebook, she thrust it toward Rita. "Here. I've started a journal about... about some experiences I've had ... experiences since I've been in Jamaica and just before ..."

Kathryn waited for a reaction from Rita. "Visions and voices. Nothing like this has happened to me before now. To tell you the truth, I'm starting to question my own sanity." As she spoke, her voice strengthened, and suddenly, she felt more alive, more aware, more in control of her destiny than she had since arriving in Jamaica.

Rita shrugged her shoulders, then patted Kathryn's hand and smiled at her. "We shall see what it is that is happening. There is a reason for everything in the universe, for things both seen and unseen." She paused, shifting the notebook in her hands. "I believe there is a purpose for every person's life. It is up to each of us to discover our own life's purpose—what it is we are seeking to learn in this lifetime."

Kathryn's mind jolted to a deadening halt. Wait, she wanted to tell Rita. She'd been hit with a lot she didn't understand, but Rita was stretching beyond the boundaries of what Kathryn could consider.

She knew her purpose in life, and it wasn't so philosophical. It was proving to the world that she, as a woman, could be the very best at her chosen profession.

She wouldn't allow herself to get sidetracked, like Flynt had done. He'd gotten sidetracked into teaching, of all things. Despite what had happened since she'd been in Jamaica, she still thought he was wrong to have become a teacher.

Last night Flynt told her he always wanted to teach. Shouldn't people follow their dreams no matter what others think of their choices?

"I'm sorry to have gone off to a different subject." Rita placed Kathryn's journal on the corner of the desk. "Next week, I will be presenting a seminar in Kingston on life's purpose, so it is much on my mind."

For the first time, Kathryn realized they were still standing. All her attention had been on Rita Grey's words and her own thoughts, not her manners. "Please. Have a seat in that chair." She motioned toward a cushioned armchair on the opposite side of the desk. Once Rita was seated, Kathryn pushed her own straight-backed chair to a spot next to the woman.

"Good," she said. Rita's kind smile forced aside Kathryn's reservations and calmed some of the confusion in her body and her mind. "We can look at your journal together."

Rita took a few moments to read through Kathryn's entries. "Hmmm. Very interesting," she murmured from time to time. At one point, she stopped reading and studied Kathryn intently.

Uneasy, Kathryn squirmed in the chair. She tried to find something in the room or the garden on which to focus her attention. What Rita sought for her to comprehend was difficult.

"I wrote all of this today," Kathryn admitted at one point. "It would have been better if I had recorded each incident immediately after it occurred, but at the time..."

"It's all right, child," Rita declared. "There are many ways to learn about ourselves. A wise old woman once told me that. Over the years, I have found that she was right."

Kathryn saw no reason to vocalize her belief and yearning that each event would be the last.

When she had finished reading, Rita pushed the notebook toward the center of the almost empty desk surface. "Tell me what you think this means, Kathryn." She sat back in the deep cushions, linked her fingers together in front of her and watched Kathryn with curiosity etched in her intelligent face.

How can I answer that? Kathryn wondered. Through her office

window, Kathryn spotted a small yellow bird flitting among the hibiscus branches. Bright and free. That's what the bird was. Dull and trapped. That's what she was.

Trapped because she didn't understand what had been happening to her. Trapped because she didn't want to admit the possibility her visions were real.

Kathryn glanced back at Rita Grey who sat quietly waiting for an answer. Unable to put her thoughts into words, Kathryn let her gaze drift. To the floor. To her feet. To her hands. Then the shining silver bracelet caught her eye, and unconsciously, she twisted the object.

"I don't know what to think." Kathryn confessed at last. "Waking dreams, or whatever they may be, are out of my field. I understand computers, numbers, concrete formulas, reality."

"Of course." Rita closed her narrow fingers over Kathryn's hand. "But don't block out the possibility of another lifetime. After all, belief in a previous existence isn't unusual among cultures of the East where millions believe in reincarnation. Even ancient philosophers like Plato and Pythagoras believed in the possibility."

Like reaching the crest of a hill and descending to the other side, her mind contemplated the possibility of another horizon. "Reincarnation. Do you think it possible?"

"I cannot say, my dear, but some evidence exists. I cannot say what is true for you." The woman stood, peering for a prolonged moment into Kathryn's eyes. "Sometimes I see the past in the eyes, but I cannot see it there for you. That is not to say it does not exist; it is to say that you must find it for yourself."

Kathryn considered the woman across from her. Rita Grey was undeniably different, an interesting, perceptive woman. But her ageless quality seemed so strange for a woman who wasn't much older than she was.

"These tapes are for you." Methodically, Rita lined the three audio cassettes along the edge of the desk.

The image of a graceful bird winging across the setting sun formed the cover of the first tape, labeled "Relaxation." The second one, called "Self-Hypnosis," featured a golden pyramid with a shaft of violet light radiating past it. A pair of hands opened to a glowing circle of blue light reached toward her from the third tape, titled "Past-Life Regression."

"Do not let the tapes distress you." Rita's voice was soothing. "These days, they are a common tool. In fact, there are psychiatrists who use past-life regression as part of their therapy sessions with patients. Much has been written on the subject. Often people with health problems have them vanish once the cause is unearthed from the past." Rita gave Kathryn's arm a comforting squeeze. "Do not worry. It will be all right. Already, I can sense that."

"I don't know what to think," Kathryn said.

"I am offering you a link with the past, but you must decide if you wish to grasp it," Rita Grey said. Then, she smiled. "Read the book first for background, then, try the tapes." Her head spinning with uncertainty, Kathryn nodded.

"I can tell you need to relax." Rita placed her left hand on the end tape. "Listen to this. It may help you." Rita picked up her bag and stepped toward the door. "And keep your journal. Write down key words, anything you think might be important." She smiled. "Even minor details that seem unimportant."

"I'll try," Kathryn promised.

The image of two women on horseback rippled through her mind and would not go away. She was going to learn all she could on the subject.

CHAPTER SIXTEEN

KATHRYN WALKED WITH Rita to the lobby door. But as she stood at the entrance watching the woman depart, she caught a fleeting glimpse of three tall, dark men with dozens of narrow, ominous braids swinging from their heads. They stood at the edge of the woods near the entrance.

Frightened, she retreated inside Hibiscus Hall. As soon as she reached the familiar safety of the lobby, Kathryn turned on her heel and hurried down the hallway and out the side door in the direction of her room.

These were the same men who followed Mara and her, she felt certain. Were they waiting for her to leave the grounds?

Running through the garden, Kathryn wondered at the sensibility of her fear. Why was she so certain they were the same men? There must be other Rastafarians in Ocho Rios besides the ones who had threatened her. After all, she'd heard the Rastas were basically good people, that it was a group of pretenders who might wish to do her harm.

But how could she tell the difference? She could not.

If only Flynt were here, he would know something sensible to do. She could not continue to flee each time she saw a man with his hair in dreadlocks.

By the time Kathryn reached the doorway to her room, beads of perspiration stood on her forehead and the cotton shirt clung to her chest like a second skin. Even the yellow birds on her new wooden necklace seemed less bright. Holding on to Rita Grey's book and tapes with one arm, she groped for the door handle with the other. Then she stopped short and stared at the knob.

There, attached by a yellow ribbon, a white envelope hung.

Her mind racing with uneasy thoughts, Kathryn untied the bow and pulled the envelope into the light where she read her name. It was written in precise block print, Flynt's printing.

Clutching the envelope to her breast, Kathryn tried to calm the erratic beating of her heart as she entered the serenity of her room. With shaky fingers, she tore open the envelope and pulled out a short note from Flynt.

Seated on her bed, she read:

> *Dear Kathryn,*
>
> *For the first time since I started my teaching job, I did not want to go to Kingston this morning. Too much between us remains unsettled. Last night it all became quite clear to me. So much so, I don't know where we can go from here.*
>
> *Frankly, I wonder if we can go anywhere. Some things between two people can never be worked out.*
>
> *However, I know we must talk. The sooner the better. I'll be in touch.*
>
> *My love,*
>
> *Flynt*

Kathryn felt the blood drain from her face. Despite last evening, the bitterness in Flynt's letter surprised her, but she couldn't blame him. He approached her with warmth, and she pulled away from him. If only... If only she could go back to last night, to the moments when his kisses had brought a glowing energy to her lips.

Kathryn struggled to make sense of her feelings. If her job was the most important thing in her life, then why did she keep thinking about Flynt? Was she only fooling herself?

Holding the single sheet of stationery and the envelope tightly against her chest, Kathryn fell into the covers. Although she fought the flow of tears, it came anyway falling in a heavy deluge and dampening the pretty floral spread that brightened her bed.

She was suddenly tired, so tired, and the hot tears insisted upon overflowing, not only from her eyes but from deep inside as well. It was like standing beneath a tropical waterfall and being a part of it.

Waterfall, she thought, dazed. There was a waterfall on the grounds at Rose Hall. Although she hadn't seen it, she felt certain it was there.

Without rising from the bed, Kathryn reached into the nearby drawer that held her lingerie. Flynt's handkerchief was still there. As her fingers curved around it, they trembled. Spreading the soft linen square across her eyes to shade them from the afternoon light, she soon fell asleep— thinking and dreaming of Flynt.

An eerie mist drifted above the beams of light that seemed to crisscross the deserted garden. The girl, with a curtain of long blonde hair hanging sleek and straight, stood alone among the flowers. A crystal-clear light spread out from the trees, turning the grounds and the house into a scene of daylight perfection. Positioned in the middle of the green lawn, the girl slowly turned in a circle, observing cascades of yellow roses draped across tree limbs, falling over the hibiscus bushes and plunging, as if from hanging baskets, over the balconies and the porticos.

The girl was alone and frightened. A single tear fell from each eye and rolled like crystal beads down her cheeks. Then, out of nowhere, a heavy rope appeared and slithered in snake form around the girl, clasping her beneath the arms. Without a sound, the heavy viperous cord transported her straight up, lifted her to the third floor of the house and deposited her there.

A wide smile broke across the girl's face, filling with sunshine the window, by which she stood. On the grass, a tall man flexed robust arm muscles and leaned over to adjust his riding boots. Then, stretching to attention, he stood still in a wide, determined stance.

With a silent motion, the man reached his arms toward the window, but no rope came to pull him up. The girl's smile softened into a blurred light. She waved to the man standing with uplifted arms, then the blonde girl faded into oblivion. "Flynt … Flynt."

Kathryn was calling his name as she awakened in the early evening darkness. Her body shook with an unnatural coldness.

A dream. It was only a dream, nothing more, she realized finally. Still, her body trembled.

"Flynt," she murmured and reached as if to touch him. Then she opened her eyes.

Sitting up, Kathryn propped herself against the headboard. Why was she calling Flynt's name? Looking at her hands, she discovered his handkerchief clutched in the left one, his letter, with the yellow ribbon still attached, in the right.

Suddenly, Kathryn felt nauseous. She realized Flynt was the man in her dream and that she was the girl with the long blonde hair. But she did not know how she had grown so certain of their identities.

Kathryn picked up her journal from the bedside table and jotted down her dream in complete detail. She had decided to approach the visions and dreams as if they were a computer glitch to be resolved, accessing her logic and problem-solving skills and her natural ability to draw sensible conclusions from the information she collected.

This way, when she and Flynt got their chance to talk, she might have discovered something meaningful for them both.

Reincarnation. Taking a deep breath, she flipped on the light switch and began reading Dr. Pettersen's book.

It was early afternoon, and Kathryn sat on the bed, a book in her lap. The previous evening, she read until time to go to work. As soon as she had some sleep, she went back to *In Touch with the Past* and had not put the book down since. Every word of Dr. Pettersen's volume intrigued her.

Kathryn took time to study most of the footnotes and jotted down the most promising references to check later when she found a city library with a large number of volumes.

As Rita Grey indicated, the book was a systematic study of case histories—the type of scientific work Kathryn respected. Dr. Pettersen's research made the concept of reincarnation more plausible to her.

Many of the cases cited dealt with young children who possessed memories of previous lifetimes. Some of the studies contained verifiable facts that, after thorough investigation by Dr. Pettersen himself, appeared to be correct. According to the research, past-life memories usually faded and were forgotten by the time children reached late childhood.

Kathryn didn't care whether what had happened to her could be checked out. That did not matter. What really mattered was that she did feel at home in Jamaica. She felt especially in touch with something at Rose Hall. If indeed, there were such a thing as reincarnation, perhaps she had once lived in the stately old mansion. Perhaps she had known Aimee White. Perhaps she had been Aimee White.

Kathryn's arms and legs rippled with minute chill bumps. Perhaps the visions she'd had were actual memories. Memories from a past existence.

The prickly sensations washed over her again and again.

If it is true that people live more than one lifetime, that they reincarnate, why don't they remember? That question especially bothered Kathryn. Dr. Pettersen answered it in his book with another question, "When we have trouble enough dealing with facts and memories of a current lifetime, how can we hope to cope with even more mind clutter left from a multitude of lives? If we need to know, we will remember," his book declared. "Sometimes that distant memory comes from spontaneous regression when we least expect it."

"Spontaneous regression." Maybe that was what had happened to her. The extraordinary visions were spontaneous, that was certain.

Thoughtfully, she picked up the tape with the picture of hands holding a circle of iridescent blue light. Work with them in sequence, she'd been warned. Kathryn got out her earphones and the tape player. Obedient to the instructions she dropped the past-life regression tape on the bed and, instead, removed the cassette from the box with the picture of a bird floating across the setting sun.

Fitting a set of earphones over her head, Kathryn dropped the relaxation cassette into the small machine and lay across the bed to listen. Eyes closed, she lifted Flynt's letter from the bedside table and held it close to her chest.

After taking her through a series of relaxation techniques, the narrator guided Kathryn to her own special place by a lake's edge—a spot where water fell in gurgling curls over moss-covered rocks, and a giant orange-red sun sank in glowing tints of magenta against a blue-gray sky. She had reached the sought-after "alpha" state.

Where she was, time went unmeasured. She floated silently, untouched by it or by any desire to come back to reality. Her mind was blank. No stray thoughts entered. Eventually, when the tape directed, Kathryn left the simple alpha state, feeling totally relaxed and at peace with herself.

For nearly two days, she practiced using the relaxation tape and the one for self-hypnosis. Flynt wasn't due back until Saturday, so she could spend all her free time with the tapes. Perhaps because she didn't know what to expect, Kathryn put off listening to the past-life regression tape. She decided to see Flynt again before experimenting with the technique.

He would be back soon, but with each passing hour, Kathryn became more nervous about what she would say when he returned to Hibiscus Hall. The tapes helped her relax but were of little value when she thought of Flynt.

That he had not contacted her since he left the note attached to her door compounded Kathryn's feelings of loneliness. The tapes, even after the best sessions, left her with a sense of isolation.

She wished he would telephone. She longed to hear his voice.

❊ ❊ ❊

The early afternoon bus from Kingston pulled through the brick-column entrance and droned up the curved pavement through the Hibiscus Hall grounds. Kathryn stood waiting outside the hotel. When she saw Flynt, it was like her heart was caught up in a storm, fluttering like a leaf in the wind.

Suitcase in hand, dressed in a casual yellow shirt and khaki trousers, he headed toward her. She wished he would kiss her, and the scent of roses would lift sparkles into the air.

Over and over she had thought of his kiss, had longed for his touch. Flynt was in her dreams and in her fantasies. But, always her visions of him intermingled with memories of that day at Rose Hall when misty figures swirled, danced, and conversed before her eyes.

Her lips burned with desire, yearned to be touched by his. But, when she looked into his darkened blue eyes, Kathryn knew immediately a kiss was out of the question. An unseen veil hung between them, and, although she longed to rip it away, she did not know how.

Flynt smiled at her—a forced, wooden smile that seemed in danger of cracking on his face.

❊ ❊ ❊

The late day sun blazed over Kathryn's stark white dress, making it difficult for Flynt to look at her at all. He wanted to kiss her, had thought about it on the long ride from Kingston but had decided he must not fall into that trap again. Last time they kissed, she leaped from his arms and raced off looking for roses. Much as he enjoyed roses, his male ego was offended by her eccentric retreat.

Kathryn was a radical, Flynt decided the day he first met her, and after their last evening together, he had no more doubts. Putting up with another radical, ambitious woman was out of the question for him. No matter how much the sight of her set his blood rumbling, his heart wasn't ready for more crazy mistakes.

Flynt Kincade had not changed his career and come to Jamaica to be hurt by a woman who he now believed could be more dangerous for him than his ex-wife ever was. More dangerous because she was more desirable to him, he realized.

"I got your letter," she said simply.

Kathryn retreated into a patch of shade that fell across the entrance door. He observed that her pale gray eyes were clear and looked more rested than when he last saw her.

Beneath a faint application of blue shadow on the upper lids, her eyes appeared brighter and even a bit wider. The white dress enhanced her lightly tanned skin, over which she wore little makeup, except for a touch of soft blush on her cheeks and a delicate coating of pink lip gloss.

Most dangerous and most desirable, he thought. Hell. The woman made his heart pound and now gave him cause to wonder if he should take another chance.

"That letter wasn't a good idea," he said in a low voice. Although he hated to admit it, he'd sent the note on impulse.

Kathryn balled her hands into fists at her side. "You said we needed to talk."

"It may be too late for talk," he said. With a thud, the suitcase dropped from his hands.

He watched Kathryn fidget with the keys in her pocket. She seemed to want to tell him something, he thought.

"It's not too late unless you want it to be," she said. Her voice was soft, quite different from a few days earlier.

"Where can we talk?" Flynt asked, his face still serious.

As Kathryn reminded him, his letter suggested they talk. As a man of his word, he was compelled to follow through, but they couldn't stand around by the front entrance discussing their personal lives. The dining room was too public, and they'd already tried the pool area, which hadn't worked out.

"People will be coming in and out of my office this afternoon, so that's out." A small frown cut shallow lines in the center of Kathryn's forehead. Then, as if struck by sunlight, her face brightened. "Let's walk along the beach."

❈ ❈ ❈

Ten minutes later, they had changed into shorts and t-shirts for their stroll. His were blue, hers white. Bare feet digging into the sand, they trudged in silence along the beach. Only a scattering of birds and a few fluffy clouds floated across the blue sky to keep them company.

Working with the relaxation and hypnosis tapes had strengthened Kathryn. Before coming down to the beach, she gave herself the hypnotic suggestion not to lapse into a vision and not to be taken in by Obeah tricks. Today, she would be the professional Kathryn Calder—straight forward, self-assured, self-reliant.

An umbrella table and two chairs sat empty along the Hibiscus Hall beachfront. With matching strides, they headed toward the quiet refuge nearly hidden beneath the palm trees.

"That day in New York, things started out better than this." Flynt caught Kathryn's fragile wrist, and, with a steel grip, turned her to face him. Although his eyes shone lighter blue than earlier, they still lacked their normal luster.

"The things that began in that museum weren't better for me." Her back unnaturally straight, her gray eyes almost black, she stared directly into his face.

His gaze appeared frozen on hers. With much deliberation, she looked far across the water. If only she could see into the past—the whole thing, not merely fragments.

"No. They weren't," he conceded. She still had the handkerchief he'd lent her to dry her tears.

Even though Kathryn knew she had said some peculiar things that day and had been tearful, he'd liked her, she was sure of it. Perhaps it was more than like. But, could such things happen so quickly? Was there really love at first sight?

"I'm glad I was there… At the same time you were, I mean." Her gaze returned to meet his, and she watched his eyes change color—to the hue of the soft blue tiles that lined the resort swimming pool.

Kathryn leaned toward him, as if drawn by a tight, invisible cord that pulled her head against his chest. An urgent spark flickered somewhere in the center of her.

Flynt's arms moved quickly, pinning her against himself. "I'm not in the mood for talking," he whispered. "Not now."

Kathryn sensed the changes in his touch. Her skin, molten as sun-warmed asphalt, melded into him. The springy hair that stuck through the open collar of his shirt stung her face, but she didn't mind. Their bare legs collided and like magnets locked together. Her breasts flattened against his unyielding ribcage. She held her breath and fought to calm the raging fire that washed through her veins.

What was it they had wanted to talk about? She could not remember.

Flynt tilted his head downward. Warmth rising from the fingertips, he turned her face toward his. His heated lips plummeted against hers, forcing, probing, circling, demanding. His breath drew from hers until it seemed to pull a part of the essence of life force from her to him.

Today she did not care that the scent of roses hovered in the air beneath the trees. For the first time, why the scent was there did not matter to Kathryn. What mattered was the need she sensed when their lips touched. It was a need left unquenched since they were last together.

In the distance, thunder rumbled. Over her shoulder, Kathryn glimpsed a ragged flash of lightning cutting through the suddenly ink-dark sky. They ignored the approaching storm, their kisses growing hungrier, more searching. Like electrical charges, sensations flowed from her body to his, along arms and legs, chests and cheeks—wherever their touches lingered.

A few drops of rain fell from the clouds, dampening her hair and his. Then, with the sudden force of a summer squall, the heavens opened and deluged them both with rushing cascades of water.

Their clothing soaked through, they ran to take shelter next to a building. There, they stood for a moment, shaking rainwater from their hair.

"We can go to my room." Kathryn pushed the heavy strands of drenched hair from across her eyes, then, concerned that her invitation was too bold, rushed to add, "I have plenty of towels there. We can dry off."

"We'll need quite a few." Flynt chuckled. He raked his fingers through her hair, squeezing out the rainwater.

The staircase was another obstacle. Fingers linked, bodies soaked, hearts racing, they clamored up the steps. The unseen force she felt when they first met had reached impossible intensity, filling Kathryn with an undeniable desire to be with Flynt.

Flynt's hand on hers, they struggled to open her room door, its knob grown unwieldy beneath wet fingers, its key jamming curiously in the lock. At last, the door swung open and they plunged into the room, two sets of wet footprints following them inside.

They paused. Kathryn smiled. Then soaked clothing clinging to his muscular body, Flynt took Kathryn's hand and led her into the shower.

With deft fingers, he loosened the top buttons of her white shirt. Breathing deeply, Flynt gazed for a moment at the outline of her breasts showing through the wet shirt.

"Beautiful," he whispered. "Beautiful."

Kathryn closed her eyes and whimpered as his fingers lightly traced the outline of her breasts. Then, so slowly it caused her to catch her breath, Flynt guided the wet shirt over her head and let it fall with a splash by her feet.

Flynt paused to study the soft curves of her breasts, still covered by a lace bra. She leaned forward, offering herself to him. He took another deep breath and separated the back fastener. When the lace fell away, Kathryn trembled.

A wash of pleasure grew inside her. Flynt leaned close to her breasts, then took the firm mounds in his hands and brought his lips to kiss them. Slowly, he suckled each nipple until her body trembled inside and out. When he pressed his face between her breasts, Kathryn arched her back to drive her body even closer.

Water fell in random streams from his saturated hair; dark waves hung in disarray over his forehead. But his eyes sparkled as he straightened to look into her face.

With a swift motion of his hand, Flynt lifted the flimsy bra from Kathryn's shoulders and let it fall into a sodden heap with her shirt on the marble shower floor. When she sighed, he slipped his hands beneath her buttocks, all the while kissing her neck and the cleavage between her breasts.

A nervous giggle became a sigh when Flynt's mouth delivered feathery kisses from her shoulder to her breast. When he again claimed her softness with his mouth, Kathryn's knees weakened. To keep from sinking to the floor, she clung to his waist.

Her head spinning, Kathryn staggered backward against the cool hard tiles on the side of the wall. Flynt moved with her. His hands followed the warm contour from her breasts to her waist where they pressed beneath the stiff band of her shorts.

As buttons separated from buttonholes, Kathryn's heart raced. Ever so slowly, his lips still teasing her breasts, Flynt eased open her shorts zipper. For a moment, his hands lingered on her hips and drifted deliberately down, urging the clingy cotton shorts lower on her thighs until, at last, they fell in the heap with the rest of her clothing. Except for a beige triangle of shimmering satin, Kathryn stood bare before Flynt.

❀ ❀ ❀

Until right now, Flynt had not realized how good it would feel to be with Kathryn. With Kathryn, everything was different. It wasn't sex he was seeking. Something unexpected had happened; something he did not understand. He wanted to make love to Kathryn far into the night. His study of her body became a caressing stare.

Color began at Kathryn's neck and rose to her cheeks where he watched the flames settle. Apparently self-conscious, she sought to turn away from him. "I've never stood naked in front of a man," she murmured. "Never."

"Then, I have a very special privilege." Flynt's voice was low and husky. "You are as lovely as I had dreamed."

Suddenly, the realization struck him like a sharp slap in the face. This was more, so much more than he had ever intended it to be. He had opened himself to Kathryn, had opened himself to hurt. The moment he removed her clothing, he knew there was no turning back.

Now a relentless throbbing had grown, and he could not stop himself. No matter how much he would like to halt and pull back into his no-commitment posture, it was far too late.

Like a swift shadow, Flynt diminished the space between them. His hands stroked her flushed cheeks to cool them. His soaked clothing, matted close to his body, pressed harshly against her tender skin.

She gulped and his hands slid down her satiny body, pausing at each curve, exploring her navel and the mound below, exploring her completely.

"Here. Let me," she said.

As if she did it every day, Kathryn removed first, Flynt's shirt, then his shorts. "I want to feel you," she whispered. I want to feel you bare against my body." She spoke in a deep, husky tone he had not heard before.

Now he stood before her wearing only a pair of silky blue under-shorts. Her eyes sparkled. He pulled her closer.

Their bodies touching, Kathryn's desire surpassed any reservations he thought she might have. The thundering tremor of her heart pounded an irregular beat against the course, wet hairs of his chest. In response, he pressed closer, willing her to feel his heart hammering in a steady, positive rhythm.

❀ ❀ ❀

Flynt was kissing her again, this time on her lips. As the scent of roses permeated the bathroom, Kathryn could see them—a bouquet of pale, yellow buds—in her mind's eye. His next kiss, long and dewy, eliminated all sense of thought, vision, or memory.

There was only the wonderful, exotic sensation of the moment. The slow, easy wonder of his touch all over her body. Nothing before in her life had been like this, nothing had been this good.

All their surroundings held the mellow sensation of sipping from a glass of white wine. Savoring this special time, she felt only this moment, only his touch. It was as if she had waited forever.

Suddenly, they stood beneath a stream of water. It came in a torrent, flowing over their arms, backs, legs, rushing against them. Her eyes closed, Kathryn succumbed to the luxuriant rhythm of the falling water.

She recalled the feel of magic from another time when she made love beneath a fall of pure, fresh water. But not in this lifetime. She shivered in Flynt's arms, and he responded by pulling her ever closer. She stared up into his face, and there was a moment of recognition she had not expected.

Flynt slipped the last garment, his blue shorts, from his thighs, then lowered the triangle of silk, the final obstacle, down her legs to the floor. All their clothing now lay in a heap near their feet.

Kathryn sighed, forgetting the moment of recognition that no longer had importance to her. She was caught up in the sliding together of their slick, lean bodies, the timeless connection she felt with Flynt.

Now, nothing separated or held them apart. Their lips met more harshly than before. Flynt's hands slithered down her sides and settled beneath her buttocks, then moved to the warm sweet center of her. At his personal, unrestrained touch, Kathryn opened her eyes wide and gazed into his face.

Her fingers groped and found him, guiding him against her, in her, with a natural flow of richness that cascaded like a dream beneath their own make-believe waterfall. The water smelled of roses—roses that had lasted for two centuries. In her heart, Kathryn was certain of that.

A child. A woman. With Flynt, at this moment, she was both. She never wanted to leave him, never wanted to pull away from their own showering cascade that had washed away time.

For a long while, they clung to each other beneath the fragrant water, allowing its soothing flow of serenity to sweep over them both like a foaming fountain. Outside, a scattering of raindrops splattered the sliding glass door and an occasional rumble of thunder broke the bleak stillness of late afternoon.

Like sleepwalkers, they stepped from their water-laden haven, rinsed and squeezed soaked clothing. With the motion of a dreamy-eyed sleepwalker, Kathryn searched until she found an oversized shirt and shorts that Flynt could wear to go to his own room for dry garments. He did not put them on.

Dry once more, he sat instead on the side of the bed and pulled her naked into his lap. Her skin was silky against the rough hair on his legs.

"Kathryn," Flynt whispered. "I haven't made love in a long time. And never like that."

Twisting, she wrapped her legs around his waist. He laughed and fell backward across the bed, pulling her atop him. His heart pounding against her breasts felt like thunder.

The expression on Kathryn's face was serious when she leaned back and stared into Flynt's eyes. "I've never known anyone like you before. Not in this lifetime," she said.

"How serious you sound," he whispered and traced the outline of her pointed chin with his fingers. Then he kissed her again. Lightly at first, then deepening.

"Can we? Again?"

Flynt laughed and she no longer smelled roses. Only the warm masculine scent of his chest, his face, his hair. How much she longed to make love to him again. Make love to him over and over until they both fell exhausted to sleep.

CHAPTER SEVENTEEN

AS THE LATE afternoon turned into evening darkness, they made love yet another time. Much later, Kathryn glanced at the clock and reluctantly pulled away from Flynt's warmth.

New feelings and new needs. Kathryn was crossing into uncharted territory. Never before had she needed a man in her life. Now she appeared to need one very much. She shivered and reached for a towel.

Flynt stirred, pushed up from the bed and gathered the dry clothing Kathryn had found. Thoughtfully he brushed his fingers over her lips.

"We still need to talk," he whispered. The words, spoken in an emotional hush, were low and guttural.

"Yes. We do."

She knew this was not the right time for that talk. Not after she had made love to him. Her head was still spinning. She held back the hand that wanted to reach out and touch him. Such a touch would spark another round of love-making, and she needed time to sort out what had already happened.

What had happened stifled her thinking power and stripped her of all reason. She needed time to put events into perspective and to consider the logical possibilities. After all, it was completely illogical for her to make love to a man unless she was in love with him.

Of course, she wasn't in love with Flynt. Everything that had happened to her in Jamaica had turned her life into a state of confusion she was at a loss to know how to handle. Now this. So unexpected, so real, so perfect, what she'd always wanted... What she'd always wanted? No. She'd always wanted a career, not a man.

But Flynt was here, standing close enough for her to feel the moisture of his breath dancing over the back of her neck. She had wanted him and still did. How could she deny that? For the first time in many weeks, her spirits were high, and she couldn't suppress the smile on her face.

Even wearing her floppy t-shirt with the slogan, "Make It Jamaica Again," Flynt looked tall and handsome. The stark whiteness of the shirt fabric contrasted well with his glowing tan.

When the look from his magic blue eyes caught hold of her, she found it impossible to regain the composure she needed. Inside her body, the trembling she'd managed to calm resumed. All her nerves quivered as Flynt pressed one hand to her side and leaned over to kiss her.

Confused thought fragments whirled like confetti through Kathryn's mind. What she'd always wanted. She had to give herself time to think. With concentrated effort, she pulled back.

"Let's talk tomorrow."

"Not tonight?" Disappointment registered in Flynt's eyes. He bent his head to kiss her forehead.

"Kathryn, beautiful Kathryn. I don't understand you, and I don't understand your obsessions with Obeah and the Rastafarians. So much about you, I don't understand, but tonight it doesn't matter."

She smiled, but a hint of bewilderment lingered in her eyes. "We'll talk tomorrow," she promised.

It was too soon for her to place everything in true perspective. Flynt was part of the big puzzle in her mind, and it was up to her to put the puzzle together.

"Do you know anything about reincarnation?" Kathryn asked Flynt on impulse just before he left.

He lifted one eyebrow. "Not much," he said.

"We'll talk about that tomorrow."

As Flynt headed down the hall, Kathryn blew him a kiss. For the first time in ages, she felt jaunty and happy.

On Sunday morning when Kathryn went down to the restaurant for breakfast, Flynt was the first person she saw. Newspaper in hand, he was standing by the hostess desk reading.

Sunlight streaked through the plate glass window to settle on his hair, lightening it to a golden hue. The yellow sports shirt and gray trousers he wore emphasized the strong body she knew very well from the night before.

The smell of cooked bacon mingled with scents of freshly baked pastries, but Kathryn had no appetite for food. Willing her heart to slow its beat, she paused before passing through the entrance door.

She had gotten little sleep during the night. The scattered fragments of dreams intermingled with glowing memories of their lovemaking. Strange, but in afterthought, Kathryn knew she had wanted Flynt to spend the night. But he had not asked, and she did not suggest it.

When he looked up and saw her, Flynt's eyes brightened. "Good morning."

He trailed his fingers over the bare skin of her arm. Her heartbeat quickened.

"Did you sleep well?" His voice was as husky as the night before.

"Not very," she admitted.

The disparity of her feelings confounded her. She wanted nothing more than to tumble into Flynt's arms and remain there. At the moment, she cared little about her job and even less about the magic rituals of Jamaica.

She cared more about the magnetic charges that careened through the air and urged her to touch him. In response to that electricity, she moved a little closer to him until her hip nudged his. Almost simultaneously, his hand slid down her side and lingered against her thigh.

Flynt kissed her suddenly, lightly. "I wanted to spend the night," he whispered. Did you?"

"Yes."

He caught her by the hand and guided her to a table at the far corner of the dining room, away from other guests. Located by a low outside wall, hibiscus bushes spread their blossoms over the table's edge. Not far away, the Caribbean Sea surged in soothing rhythm, rising and falling like a gentle warrior keeping vigil at Hibiscus Hall.

"Kathryn," Flynt began, "what would you think if I took a teaching job that would keep me here in Jamaica...permanently?" He placed his hand over hers on the table.

"Why would you do that?"

Kathryn tried to understand her disappointment. Had she harbored a hope he might change his mind, might decide to head back to the city?

To where she expected to return.

"I have an offer to stay on at the University of the West Indies once I complete my nine-week session here for the University of the South. They've offered me the position of faculty administrator with some teaching duties as well."

His fingers played across hers, but he stayed silent, letting the idea of him remaining in Jamaica hang in the air between them. Plainly, Flynt awaited her response.

"Is that what you want?" Kathryn asked, although in her heart she knew the answer to his question.

"Would you consider staying?" Flynt asked, his gaze drifting back to their hands.

Kathryn hesitated before answering. If he had asked that question three weeks ago, she would have answered "no" immediately. Now, her thoughts were less clear. Was Jamaica growing on her or was Flynt?

She shouldn't have made love to him. Yesterday's time with Flynt had added fog to the fog. Yet one fact stuck out above the mist. She somehow had unfinished business with the past, and both Flynt and Jamaica held important roles.

"Are you asking me about staying because of last night?" Kathryn tilted her head and did her best to appear nonchalant. "Don't let that bother you. Last night was wonderful, but we both know Jamaica is a land of magic that too easily seduces."

"Does it?" Flynt's shoulders drooped, and the air around him changed. With a shrug, he withdrew his hand from hers and pushed back his chair.

As if punched, Kathryn saw that her comments had hurt him, and, in a way, that surprised her. After all, he had told her early on that he wanted to steer clear of commitment. She sighed inaudibly. So did she.

But, if so, why did the withdrawal of his hand stab like an icicle through the heart? This wasn't some man across the table from her. It was Flynt.

"I'm going back to Kingston this morning," Flynt announced suddenly. "A department head is ill. Dean Thompson telephoned earlier to ask if I could come back today to prepare to teach his classes, and I told him I would."

A somber dullness replaced the lively glow in Kathryn's eyes. She would have to forget about Flynt Kincade, forget about him completely. He planned to stay in Jamaica. She would be leaving soon. The stir in her heart would go away in time; she would will it to leave her. After all, her blossoming career was the most important thing in her life, wasn't it?

"I won't be back until next Saturday. Maybe we can talk then, since I don't have time today." As he arose from his chair, Flynt's face was as serious as Kathryn had ever seen it. He brushed a kiss across her forehead on his way out.

❊ ❊ ❊

Later in the morning, one of the desk clerks found Kathryn sitting alone moodily sipping a cup of the thick black Jamaican coffee with its heavy, syrupy texture.

"Ms. Calder. You gotta come quick. See what we found. You were right."

Kathryn shot up from her chair and turned toward the girl with alarm. "I was right? What does that mean?"

The look on the clerk's face signaled trouble, and that was something she wasn't ready to handle, not this morning. Not after Flynt whizzed off in a huff.

Frowning, Kathryn followed at a fast clip. Whatever had happened, she would be there shortly to see for herself. The day that had started out bright had reversed course and was heading in a dismal direction.

"It is Felix, Ms. Calder. Felix has upset the reservation system." The girl chattered at a nervous pace that was incoherent for the remainder of the way between the dining room and the lobby.

When they reached the computer office, every employee appeared to have been called in. The space was a madhouse, alive with people searching frantically through files and putting disks into the computer drives. Two women stepped back from the doorway to permit Kathryn to enter.

Even Jonathan Pearce was evident in the crowded room. He was the resort's general manager, whom Kathryn had seen only twice since her arrival in Jamaica.

"Ms. Calder. Good. I'm glad you're here." Pearce extended his hand to her.

"What's happened?" When she left in the early morning hours Saturday, everything was going smoothly. Most of the clerks had learned their jobs well and seemed comfortable using the computers. "Congratulations, Ms. Calder. You were absolutely correct. I had heard by rumor that you were suspicious. And you were correct to be. Felix Burton has been feeding misinformation into the system whenever he could manage to get into the office alone."

"Felix?" Kathryn frowned. She suspected someone was tampering with the central files, but not the quiet, polite Jamaican with the ready smile. Her heart felt even heavier.

"We found him early today. He had an unauthorized key and was in the office by himself, busily deleting important files from some of the major reservations disks." Pearce picked up a stack of disks. "These are some that already had missing information or errors in the listings by the time that we found him."

"Are you sure?" Kathryn stared vacantly at the more than a dozen sources of valuable files.

"Yes. We called in the authorities, and they got Felix to admit his part in the plot. At least four employees of the Royal Blossom chain are involved as well.

"We found out Hibiscus Hall is only one of the resorts they intended to sabotage. There are others scattered all over Jamaica, including our sister resort in Negril." Pearce smiled down at Kathryn. "You have no need to worry about this. It has nothing to do with the excellent work you've been doing. In fact, I've already gotten in touch with Triple Gold to let them know how pleased we are. That's the least I can do for you."

"Thank you, sir."

"We'll have all of this mess straightened up before the week is out. Please go back now and enjoy the rest of your weekend."

Kathryn frowned. She'd been right about the sabotage. Now she wondered if some of the men lurking in the shadows and hanging around outside the hotel had been part of the Royal Blossom group.

Turning on her heel, she asked the hotel manager, "Did any of the men wear their hair in dreadlocks?"

Pearce scratched his head. "No. Not that I recall."

Disappointed, she turned away. Perhaps there were others then, others who had yet to be caught.

Kathryn wandered from the office, uncertain what to do with the remainder of the day now that Flynt had left unexpectedly, and Mara appeared to still be away with Fritz. She was glad the German couple was getting a chance to be together, but she missed having her friend as a confidant.

On impulse, Kathryn thrust her hands in the side pockets of her dress, fished out her keys and hurried from the lobby, across the garden and back to her room. She had thought of something she wanted to check in her journal. Picking up the notebook, she leafed through it until she found the passage she had written there last week about a waterfall at Rose Hall. She had to find out for herself if it actually existed.

Taking the journal and her shoulder bag, Kathryn went to the lobby to summon a taxi. The drive toward Montego Bay didn't seem as long as before. The chatty driver pointed out sights along the way, including Discovery Bay where Christopher Columbus first landed in Jamaica. Distracted by her own thoughts, Kathryn paid little attention to what the man told her.

The taxi deposited Kathryn across from an attractive resort hotel. A winding road led through a golf course and up the hill toward Rose Hall Great House. Before she could decide which way to go in search of a waterfall, a heavyset Jamaican man approached her, his hand extended to shake hers.

"Let me show you Johnny Cash's house," he insisted. "I can take you there. I can take you to Cinnamon Hill."

Bewildered, Kathryn retreated a step. "I'm not interested in Johnny Cash's house," she said.

She hesitated, considering that this man appeared to be a "guide" like Oswald's mother. A Rose Hall guide was exactly who she needed.

"What's your name?" she asked.

"Leonard." He beamed a bright white grin at her and for a second time extended his hand.

"I'm Kathryn." She shook his hand, then gestured her arm toward the Rose Hall grounds. "Do you know if there's a waterfall near Rose Hall?"

His grin widened. "Yes, ma'am. I will take you to the Rose Hall waterfall."

She watched him move about like a hyperactive child. "Are you certain there's one?"

"Yes, Miss Kathryn. I take people to the waterfall every day. It is on the tour."

But, his sales-directed enthusiasm rekindled her skepticism. Still, it was important for her to determine if her feeling had merit. "All right, then. Please take me to the waterfall."

After discouraging his overtures to show her the Barrett family burial grounds and the golf clubhouse, as well, Kathryn followed Leonard across a field overgrown with grass high enough to tickle her ankles and then along a well-worn golf cart path. Pausing for a moment near the gate of Cinnamon Hill, she viewed, at Leonard's insistence, the rambling house, shielded by jungle foliage.

Then, they continued on their way, being careful to move aside for the golf carts. Eventually, they reached a point where a very small waterfall was visible, cascading down amid lush green trees and bushes.

"The falls," she whispered and hurried toward the softly tumbling waters. "They are real."

What a peculiar sensation it was to find the tiny waterfall just as she remembered it. Remembered. The thought took her by surprise. She sank down in the soft grass and drank in the cool moist air. Once, this had been her place of refuge. Aimee White had gone there often—whenever she could get away from Rose Hall and the dismal beatings that took place there.

The realization of what she was thinking shook Kathryn to the core. If this was real, then much of what she'd believed in the past was not. Her fingers trembling, she stared hard at the small, unremarkable waterfall.

One morning last week, when she had used the relaxation tape, a vision of this small waterfall came out of nowhere to fill her memories. Meditation, spontaneous recall—she didn't know what had precipitated the vision, but it was hard to disbelieve something seen in the mind, then discovered to exist in reality.

In her vision, Aimee White, wearing the same flowing white dress Kathryn had seen her in at Rose Hall, was sitting in the moist green grass beside the waterfall. A man sat by her, and Aimee was stroking her fingers through his hair.

"Miss Kathryn. Come look at the sculpture. Beautiful Jamaican sculpture. They will make you a good deal." Leonard's deep voice interrupted her moment of solitude.

Glancing to the side, Kathryn saw it was indeed true. The lovely site for quiet meditation had been decimated by a group of Jamaican vendors hawking their wares.

Distressed, she turned and walked away. Kathryn had found out what she wanted to know and felt no need to stay longer.

Twisting the silver bracelet that still shone brightly on her arm, Kathryn took a last look at the green jungle oasis. The thought sang in her mind. Rose Hall did have a waterfall, one that was important in the life of

Aimee White, and in that of the mysterious man. In Kathryn's vision, he had not turned so that she could see his face. She knew only that he had dark wavy hair—much like that of Flynt Kincade.

* * *

The week passed without significant happenings. Gradually, the Hibiscus Hall office derived order from the chaos created by the underhanded activities of Felix Burton. Everyone there who knew Felix was shocked and dismayed.

Kathryn found time on her hands, and that time she used to read more of Dr. Pettersen's *In Touch with the Past.* Studying each page, she found added validity in the concept of reincarnation.

At one point, she paused in her reading and wrote down a quote from Voltaire. "It is not more surprising to be born twice than once," he had said.

What an enlightening idea that was for Kathryn. For her, it was the planting of the seed that made it possible to believe. Birth, after all, was a surprise in itself.

Further on in Dr. Pettersen's book, Kathryn read a section on the history of reincarnation. In it, she found that people of many cultures have believed it possible to choose the circumstances of their next incarnation.

What if there were such a thing as rebirth? If she had lived before in another time, what relationship—if any—did her current lifetime have with the previous one? Kathryn pressed a cool hand against her forehead. The concept was too mind-boggling to accept. She slammed the book shut.

* * *

Kathryn had never known what dreadful sounds peacocks could make. One of the two birds, owned by the resort, was preening its feathers and strutting in an ostentatious, threatening gait toward a grounds' worker.

They're as good to have around as watchdogs, she'd been told by three different workers. Perhaps she should have had a peacock nearby earlier in her stay; then maybe the wild-haired people wouldn't have dared bother her.

As she watched, the intimidated man cowered backward from the bird, then disappeared by edging through the nearby health club door. "Pretty vicious bird, I'd say."

Kathryn lurched forward and came close to tumbling out of the garden chair where she'd been sitting. Flynt. It was Flynt. She hadn't known when he would be back, nor if he would return to Hibiscus Hall at all.

He had telephoned her once during the week, but it was only to inquire about the arrest of Felix Burton. Flynt had Burton's brother as a student. Nothing of a personal nature was mentioned during the conversation. When Kathryn hung up the phone, she had collapsed in a spent heap on the bed.

The memory of Flynt's touch lingered on her skin and haunted her all week. How very much she regretted her sudden thoughtless rebuff of him on Sunday morning. Perhaps they were star-crossed.

Kathryn's eyes, mirroring the green foliage, were full of questions. "Peacocks make an awful ruckus," she said, maintaining a steady gaze directed to his face.

"I didn't know until right before I boarded the bus whether or not I would come to Hibiscus Hall today." Flynt looped his thumbs into the pockets of his navy-blue trousers and stood near her as he answered her unspoken question. He didn't try to kiss or even touch her.

Above them, clouds gathered, obscuring the sun. A breeze picked up, bringing cool air from the Caribbean Sea. Kathryn crossed her arms and shifted her back to the wind.

As if carefully forming words in his mind, Flynt studied her and their surroundings before speaking again. "This morning, I went back to that gallery. The one in Kingston I told you about, where I planned to take you." He paused. "The old painting of Rose Hall was gone ... Sold, I learned later ... Then, the strangest thing happened." Again, he paused, as if groping for words that would make sense to him.

"What?" Kathryn sat up straight to listen.

"Another painting hung in its place. A watercolor. Something about the subject made me move closer to get a better look." Flynt shook his head. "The painting was of a waterfall. Nothing spectacular like Dunn's River Falls near here. This was a small, rather ordinary waterfall." He paused. "Even so, I had the strongest sensation of deja vu I've ever experienced."

A slow smile crinkled the corners of Kathryn's lips. Flynt admitting to deja vu surprised her.

"Maybe I've seen another painting of it," he said, but that hardly seems likely. "You see, at the bottom, the artist had penciled in the title. 'Rose

Hall Waterfall,' it said."

Kathryn stared in disbelief. "Rose Hall Waterfall? Did you say Rose Hall Waterfall?"

"Yes," he said quietly. "That's why I was certain I had never seen another painting."

"Strange," Kathryn murmured. "Very strange. Last Sunday, I went to Rose Hall to see if such a waterfall actually existed." Her smile was dubious. "It does." It was her turn to pause and consider her next words. "The falls looked and felt familiar to me."

She failed to add that she had seen the image of Aimee White seated at the foot of the water. After all, she hadn't told him of seeing Aimee White dancing on the porch at Rose Hall. In fact, she had never mentioned Aimee White at all.

"It was that painting that made me decide to come back here to see you." Flynt took a long breath. "I thought you might want to add that to your research into the unusual." His left eyebrow quirked upward, but no smile came to diminish his somber expression.

A car horn honked loudly near the hotel's front entrance. Slowly the sound registered in Kathryn's brain. Mara. This morning, she had made plans to meet Mara and drive with her to Ocho Rios to shop. When she promised to go, Kathryn believed Flynt had no plans to see her. Now that he was here, she had no desire to leave.

Kathryn pushed up from her chair. "That's Mara, Flynt. We've made plans to go shopping."

While Kathryn thought Flynt's face could be no more serious, she discovered it could. It darkened until it held the intensity of an approaching storm.

"Oh," was all he said.

"I'll see you when I get back," Kathryn promised. Her heart weighted with iron anchors, she didn't turn around to wave goodbye. She couldn't, because her tear-filled eyes would have overflowed, and she couldn't let Flynt see that happen.

Rose Hall, she thought as she walked away. The man in her vision had wavy dark brown hair like Flynt Kincade.

CHAPTER EIGHTEEN

"IT IS GOOD that we go shopping together." Mara laughed. A lively sparkle shone in her eyes and mischievous dimples dented her cheeks. "That we really go shopping," she added.

"If I hadn't promised, I wouldn't be going. Not today."

Kathryn's gray eyes remained solemn. Her heart, perhaps even her soul, was back at the resort with Flynt. She hadn't wanted to leave but could think of no polite way to avoid the trip. Not when Mara was already in the car waiting.

When she told Flynt of their shopping plans, Kathryn hoped he would offer to go along with them. But he had not. That fact was disappointing enough, but not as much as Flynt's failure to kiss her.

Reflectively, she brushed her fingertips over her bare arms where his hands had touched her flesh. To Kathryn that seemed like months ago, instead of only one week. She smiled slightly. Besides his handkerchief, she had something else of his in her room—his shorts and shirt that she'd had laundered. At least, they gave her a good excuse to see him again.

"Is it that things are bad with Flynt?" Mara lifted both eyebrows causing two lines to crease her forehead.

Kathryn shrugged. "I'd rather not talk about it." Absently, she watched Mara maneuver the small red car through the narrow streets as they headed toward the Ocho Rios crafts market.

"Oh?" She waited a moment, then added, "The red car, I like better now." Mara flashed a sheepish grin in Kathryn's direction. "It is what we could agree, Fritz and me."

"I'm glad you agreed on the color." Kathryn chuckled, then her face sobered once more. "Thank you for taking me to hear Rita Grey. She was a big help. I've been reading the book she lent me and have been listening to her tapes as well."

"Yes? They have helped you?" Her eyes wide with questions, Mara twisted in her seat to look at Kathryn.

"I ... I'm not sure." Kathryn faltered. "It ... It's all so new to me." It was unclear at this point whether reincarnation and regression were the problems or the answers. Perhaps they were both. "Dr. Pettersen's book has a long section on dreams. Recurrent dreams." Mara nodded, but said nothing.

"I've been having vivid dreams since I came to Jamaica. Dreams with the same cast of characters," Kathryn explained.

"Is it that the book has helped you understand your dreams?" Mara asked, her curiosity obviously piqued.

"Not yet, but it's made me more aware of them." She pulled her clothbound journal from her pocketbook. "I'm keeping notes in here on everything, including my dreams."

"That is a good thing to do," Mara agreed. "Rita Grey told me a journal is where I should write." She sighed. "I have not yet a journal."

"Dr. Pettersen writes of previous life dreams as being unlike normal ones. He says you can tell the difference because past life dreams are more realistic and seem as natural as waking events."

"Are yours like that?"

"Yes, and they don't fade away like ordinary, disjointed dreams do."

"Well, what do you think?" Mara asked bluntly. "Do you believe you've lived this past life you've dreamed about?" She had an uncertain expression.

Kathryn sighed. "I don't know what to think, but I'm still working on it." She brushed her hand across the notebook cover. "I'm having a hard-enough time with my present life," she muttered, "without worrying about past lives."

If Mara heard what Kathryn said, she gave no indication.

Absently, Kathryn rubbed the shiny surface of the silver bracelet that she'd worn ever since Carole Brown placed it there many days earlier. She hadn't talked much about the bracelet and had skillfully sidestepped the many questions asked by the office staff and others.

"What about you and Fritz?" Kathryn shifted the conversation away from herself. "How was the sailing trip?"

"Wunderbar!" Mara's eyes shone brightly. A smile curled up the corners of her mouth as she retraced a private memory. "Wunderbar," she repeated. "Thank you again, Kathryn Calder. You are a good friend."

By the time they reached Ocho Rios and the crafts market and Mara found a spot to park the car, dusk was falling. "Come along, Kathryn. I must buy a cute work dress for my sister. In a letter, she asked me to find her one to send back to Germany."

"You go ahead. I want to stay here and browse for a few minutes." Kathryn gestured toward a group of tables and booths filled with sculpture. "I promised to bring back a wood-carving for a friend in Saint Louis. Since I don't know what she might want, making a selection could take a long time."

"Stay by yourself? You are certain?" Mara frowned. "Do not forget. Before, you were not all right."

"Don't worry. I'll be fine." Kathryn flashed her brightest smile, but beneath the friendly facade she wished Mara would stop treating her in such a protective manner. She'd had some bad experiences in Jamaica, but she was a grown woman, capable of taking care of herself. Throwing her shoulders back, she turned to consider the artwork.

To be sure of the time, Mara tilted her watch to the light. "We will meet at the car then. One hour. Is that good for you?"

"That's fine."

Perhaps she should have looked at the sculpture for sale by the Rose Hall waterfall. But seeing the vendors there angered her, and she still felt her temper rise when she thought of their intrusion on the most beautiful retreat site at Rose Hall Plantation.

Strolling through the stalls, Kathryn fought an internal battle to concentrate on what she saw there. The wooden objects ranged from quickly fabricated bookends and statues to carefully executed and polished pieces of sculpture that were exacting works of art.

From time to time, she paused to make offers on promising pieces. The best quality work was far more expensive than she expected—even after bartering with the vendors. Besides, it was nearly impossible to keep her mind on shopping when her thoughts kept creeping back to Flynt.

As time passed and she still hadn't found anything, Kathryn began to wish she hadn't promised to purchase the sculpture. But she had, and because she didn't know how much longer her job would keep her in Jamaica, Kathryn thought it best to buy the art as soon as possible. Should she be called away suddenly, she wouldn't have time to handle last-minute shopping for friends.

Today, she wanted to stay with Flynt to talk things out with him. Yet she feared anything she might say would anger him as much as it had on Sunday. He wanted to stay in Jamaica. She did not. It was as simple as that.

Simple? No. It wasn't simple at all. She wanted to be with Flynt, but not in Jamaica.

Unable to give the art purchase her full attention, Kathryn eventually gave up and found herself wandering aimlessly between displays. Then to her delight, she espied an abstract rendering that appealed to her aesthetic senses. If her friend didn't want it, the sculpture would be an attractive addition to her own coffee table. As she headed toward the gracefully curving mahogany piece, an unexpected rustle sounded close behind her.

Turning to see, Kathryn detected a movement that was neither a part of the crowd nor of the displays. The dim area she passed had three broken light bulbs out of six on the string hung to illuminate the exhibit. Fear tightened in her chest.

The dark shadow moved closer, as Kathryn hurried toward a brightly lit area. But the figure rushed faster yet toward her. As if caught by giant ocean waves crashing against unprotected rocks, Kathryn stared in disbelief.

Snakelike shadows danced in the twilight darkness. Swinging dreadlocks held Kathryn welded to the spot, caught between the stalls of two vendors and out of sight of them both.

Her hands clammy and balled into fists, she felt the man glide so near, she could clearly hear his breathing in her ears. Hot, repulsive breath.

"Stay away from us," the shadow man hissed in a rough, clipped voice. "If you don't stay away, you will be the one to get hurt." His rasping words grazed her ears like abrasive sandpaper. Then, the tall man lurched against Kathryn, caught the crook of her left arm in a tight grip and dragged her kicking and flailing toward a thicket behind the market.

"Gimme that bracelet!" the man demanded, reaching for the broad silver band that Carole Brown had placed on Kathryn's arm to protect her from Obeah spells.

"No." Propelled by a surge of anger and determined to save her friend's possession, Kathryn found her voice. "No. It's not mine. You can't have it." She yanked her arm from the man and felt the cold metal cut her flesh.

Her forceful movement caught the man off guard, and he fell forward. By the time he regained his footing, Kathryn had rushed terrified into the light.

"Hello, Missy. Can we help you?" Four heavyset Jamaican women, all with hair tucked beneath bright bandanas waddled toward her like a bizarre parade from heaven.

A uniformed policeman, holding his cap tightly against his scalp, ran behind the women. Her hair damp, palms sweating, Kathryn watched while the officer grabbed hold of the gangly man with furiously swinging dreadlocks and wrestled him to the ground. With a hefty grunt, the law officer gripped the attacker securely from the back and pinned his hands together.

Then, with the man's arms locked in handcuffs, the policeman yanked him from the dirt and herded him toward Kathryn. "Miss, please come with me to the office."

Kathryn glanced at her watch. "Is it far?"

"No. It is there." He pointed to a small nearby wooden building she hadn't noticed earlier. Eyeing her attacker suspiciously, she followed the officer.

Moments later, Kathryn sat at a desk across from the tall, dark man who kept his eyes downcast. Like limp clotheslines, his dreadlocks drooped over his slumped shoulders. Instead of threatening, the man looked docile and confused as a lost child.

Kathryn drew in a long, deep breath. He was one of the men who had come to Carole Brown's car during the Obeah meeting. Although he appeared much younger than before, he was the same man who shook the stuffed lion at her while she lay crouched alone in the front seat.

As Kathryn listened to the questioning, her heart slowed its frantic pace. Finally, the man admitted to the policeman that he belonged to a small Rastafarian cult.

"Radicals. Radicals," the policeman muttered.

"She is a danger woman. We have an oath to get the danger women." With a wild-eyed stare, the man glared from Kathryn to the window and

190 - Mary Montague Sikes

back again. His eyes gleamed and flashed as though fired by an irrational inner turmoil.

"They warned us about them women." In disgust, he flailed his hands toward Kathryn; then, with sudden calm, cast a sullen gaze at the floor. "When we saw that woman at our meeting, we knew she was a danger woman."

"Danger woman. What's that?" Kathryn's gray eyes darkened in wonder and confusion.

"Spy. She's a spy, man." Speaking through clinched teeth, the Rastafarian continued to stare at the floor.

"What kind of spy?" The policeman looked at Kathryn when he asked the question.

"A sneakin' spy for the Locksmen."

"What's that?" Incredulous, Kathryn studied both men.

"The Locksmen are a rival group of Rastas." The officer said. The handcuffed man appeared not to hear.

"I don't know anything about them," Kathryn declared.

Flynt had warned her not to be so curious. He'd warned her not to go to the Obeah meeting, but she'd thought it would be perfectly safe. Apparently, Flynt had been right. Even with Carole Brown, she had not been safe. That one trip had haunted Kathryn's entire stay in Jamaica.

"We been watching the danger woman. We watch her with the big man; we leave the spirit potion in her room. The danger woman no bother us."

She shouldn't be intimidated by the man in custody, but she was.

The man started mumbling incoherently. The policeman leaned forward, cupping his ear to hear.

"Something about a cow," the officer reported to Kathryn. "And, a clay ball that didn't work."

Putting aside her fear, Kathryn listened with escalating interest. The man and his companions had been behind all the strange things that had happened to her. Like the clay ball being forced into her hand and the disgusting vial being placed beneath her bed. They had followed her and moved in and out of the shadows making her afraid to cross the grounds alone. Thank goodness that mystery had been cleared away.

"When he saw the silver bracelet on your arm, he was positive you were from the other group," the policeman explained. He pointed to the bracelet. An Obeahwoman sometimes wears a wide-band bracelet with magic inscriptions engraved on the inside."

Kathryn nodded. Many times, she had felt the roughly etched inscriptions rubbing against her skin, but she'd followed Carole's instructions and never removed the bracelet to look.

Studying the Rasta's face in detail, Kathryn realized, to her surprise, he was no older than a teenager. In the lamplight, his appearance had shifted to a ragged and shaken boy.

"I feel sorry for him," Kathryn told the policeman in a low voice. "Why does he believe these things?"

The officer spread his arms wide. "I do not know, Miss."

"He's only a boy," she said. "Will you put him in jail?"

"Yes, ma'am. He's a boy, but already, the cult is part of his life. Usually the Rastas do no harm. This splinter group is more radical than most. I am sorry they have bothered you."

"Can you explain to him that I know nothing of the cults— his or the rival one? Please tell him, I'm not a danger woman." Her gray eyes grew even more solemn in the dimly lit room.

"Not a danger woman," the man mumbled, followed by a string of indecipherable words. He stretched his long legs beneath the table.

"He knows that now, says he is sorry he mistook you for a spy and promises not to bother you or your friends, again."

"Good." Kathryn breathed a deep sigh. How did she know he would really leave her alone? All the peculiar Obeah omens had lent a sharp steel edge to her stay in Jamaica. Like Flynt said, she should never have gone to the Blue Mountains with Carole Brown. If she hadn't, things would have been different, except for the visions...

"Do you wish to press charges?" the policeman asked.

Kathryn weighed the question in her mind. Jail would keep him away from her during the remainder of her time in Jamaica. But there were other Rastas from his cult. She wanted him to get the message to them.

Besides, he was merely a boy. No more than fourteen, she thought, as she studied his youthful features. If she didn't press charges, would he stay out of trouble?

"Miss. Do you want to press charges?" The officer raised his voice to a higher pitch when he repeated the question. "I need to know."

Shaking her head, Kathryn studied the young Rasta. "Not if he intends to keep his promise and will get his friends to do the same." She was thinking more clearly now.

A frown deepening on her forehead, Kathryn turned to the young Rasta. "Please look at me."

Hesitantly, the youth raised his head but kept his eyes focused away from her.

"I know nothing of your group nor of the Locksmen, and I have no interest in Obeah. Not anymore." Her voice rang with assertiveness. "Do you understand what I'm saying?"

"Yes, Missy. I am sorry to have bothered you. I no more will do that, but I cannot tell my friends. I will not see them until the next Nine Night. Then I will tell them."

His eyes flashed darkly and for a fleeting moment settled on hers. She saw in that instant the raw wildness of an untamed animal.

"When will that be?" she asked.

"I do not know but maybe soon," he said.

"All right. Please let him go." Kathryn spoke softly, wondering if she'd made the correct decision, hoping what she saw in his eyes wasn't savagery.

An unexpected thought struck her. Jail time couldn't tame him. It would take someone who cared. A minister, or a teacher. A teacher like Flynt. Her mind raced with its own wildness. Jamaica needed good teachers.

Kathryn left the police station relieved from her Obeah worries, yet sorry for the young man. Before going out the door, she'd asked the authorities to check on getting the boy into some type of school that would offer guidance. Later, she would check educational possibilities with resort personnel.

When she reached Mara's car, Kathryn found her friend pacing on the sidewalk. She glanced at her watch. No wonder Mara had grown concerned. She was nearly a half-hour late.

"Where have you been?" The somber look on Mara's face expressed her misgivings more than any words could have.

"I'm sorry. It wasn't something I could help."

Kathryn told Mara what had happened. "Actually, I'm very glad to have all that behind me. Recently, I've spent too much time peering into shadows and watching for strangers." She took in a long breath. "Now all that should be over."

When she reached the resort, the first thing Kathryn did was look for Carole Brown. "I won't be needing this anymore," she said. After she told the woman what had happened, she pulled off the shining silver bracelet and handed it to her. "Thank you for being so kind to me."

"You were protected, you know," Carole told her.

"Yes. Yes. I was."

"You were protected by the water."

"Water?" Kathryn echoed.

Carole tilted the bracelet in the light for Kathryn to see. "Read the inscription," the woman directed.

"Water is the breeding ground of all living things." Kathryn felt a memory stir. She'd heard the phrase "breeding ground of all living things" before. Frowning, she tried to remember...

"That is the motto of my Obeah friends. We all have the same words in our bracelets."

"Oh? Oh." From far away, the words drifted toward her until she saw them imprinted in her mind. She'd heard the phrase that day when she fainted in the pool, but the words came from another place, too. From far off. If only she could put her finger on where...

"The purity of water will ward off all evil. It is a good omen, Missy." Carole rubbed her fingertips over the inscription before placing the bracelet on her arm. "Our motto goes back to Africa. It protected the captured ones from their masters." The captured ones.

Something about those words sparked an "almost memory." But she could not dredge it up into her thoughts. Like a forgotten dream, it lay hidden from her memory.

"Thank you, Carole." Kathryn hugged the woman and left to look for Flynt.

❋ ❋ ❋

Later that evening, Kathryn sat with Flynt in a small lounge area situated off the lobby at Hibiscus Hall. Her thoughts rambled from Obeah to Rastas to Flynt. She sipped from a light fruit drink and tried to calm her mind.

Flynt was not talkative. He stirred the ice in his drink and absently watched people coming into the small bar area overlooking the sea.

He had not noticed that the silver bracelet was missing from Kathryn's arm. She ran her hand across the bare skin. Carole said that while wearing the bracelet she was protected by the water.

Now she was on her own, vulnerable as before.

"How's your drink?" Kathryn asked. "Oswald insisted you try his new creation."

"Good." Flynt smiled. "I like the report he gave us on his mother, that since she is earning money 'giving tours' through that new resort, she is staying out of trouble."

"Our search on the beach for Mrs. Smith worked out," Kathryn smiled. "Perhaps it even saved Oswald's job."

Flynt put aside his plastic cup. "Are you ready to talk, Kathryn?" The smile slipped from Flynt's face. Kathryn hesitated.

"Are you?"

❈ ❈ ❈

Had it been only last week that he had made love to Kathryn? For the first time since his marriage fell apart, making love had mattered. But as he watched Kathryn tonight, he found her far different from the woman with him in the shower.

Tonight, she was stiff and unapproachable. Once again Kathryn was a controlled businesswoman.

Disappointed, Flynt studied her face. He had found himself falling in love with a vulnerable Kathryn, only to be confronted now by untouchable Kathryn.

All week long, he had pondered their relationship. He could not get it off his mind. It could not work, he decided finally. Not unless Kathryn were willing to compromise. He could not, would not go back to live in New York.

"So much has happened since we came to Jamaica." Kathryn broke into his thoughts.

"Are you sorry about what happened last week?"

She smiled. "You mean in my room?" Her face softened. "I could never be sorry about that. It was wonderful."

He could feel the heat rising between them.

"For some strange reason, Flynt, I felt that we had been together before, that it wasn't the first time we'd made love."

"You did?" Flynt looked at her in surprise.

"Yes. It was like we belonged together at Rose Hall." Her eyes sparkled. "It was as if we were there at the Rose Hall waterfall. Did you feel it, too?"

Flynt was uncertain how to respond. He tightened his hand around hers. He loved Jamaica and he loved Kathryn. As he watched her tonight, he knew that for certain. Both the island and Kathryn were like lost pieces of his life.

He needed her love. But he could not force her to stay, although with all his heart he wanted her.

"You didn't answer my question, Flynt." Kathryn studied him. "Did you have a sense of deja vu when we made love? I need to know."

"Why?"

"I'm searching for answers, Flynt." She appeared puzzled and confused. "I don't think I can tackle the present when I don't understand the past."

"Go on," Flynt said. Still watching her, he traced his fingers over her hand.

"All of this goes back to the first day I saw you, Flynt. In the museum in New York, I started having visions. That day and since then, I've had visions that relate to Rose Hall and the people I keep seeing there."

Kathryn took a deep breath and let it out slowly. "I ... I have to ask you this ... Do you ... Do you believe reincarnation is possible?" The fact that he had admitted the deja vu experience with the painting of the Rose Hall waterfall gave her courage to ask him.

"Reincarnation? I've never given it much thought."

"Do you think it's possible? To live more than one life, I mean?" He watched her grow tense as though savage butterflies had invaded from all directions.

"Kathryn, I'm too involved living this life to worry about other lives already over. What's past is past. That's the way things are."

"But..." Disappointment cut into Kathryn's voice. "But you had a feeling of deja vu when you saw the painting of the waterfall, didn't you?"

Flynt weighed his response. "Yes, I did," he said. "I have to admit I sometimes have deja vu experiences, but that's far different from believing in reincarnation."

❊ ❊ ❊

Kathryn struggled to remain calm. How could she tell Flynt about her beliefs on a subject he thought implausible? Since she'd been in Jamaica, visions and other psychic phenomena had become an important part of her thinking. How could she feel close to Flynt if he dismissed the subject she had to know more about?

But she wanted to feel close to Flynt. A few weeks ago, she had not even known him. Now he had become an intricate part of her life. A part she'd surely miss once she left Jamaica.

Miss a man. She never had before. Just as her visions had done, Flynt had changed her way of thinking. Somehow, she suspected Flynt had changed her life forever.

"I have a question for you." He paused and his face grew more serious than before. "I've decided to take the job here in Jamaica. You said you wouldn't stay. Any chance you've changed your mind since last week?"

Flynt's hope was plain on his face. Kathryn wanted to turn away. What was it that made her determined to keep her career?

And now there was something else. She had found it in Jamaica. A subtle fragrance drifted around her. All of a sudden in her mind's eye, she could see the bouquet ... A vibrant cluster of yellow roses ... Flynt ... Dear Father, it was coming back to her in a rush ... So many memories ... Tears filled Kathryn's eyes ... If only Flynt believed in the past...

"Miss Calder. Telephone." A man was standing beside her. How long had he been there?

Kathryn shook her head. "What is it?" Annoyance flecked her voice. She brushed aside the tears that wanted to fall.

"Telephone call from New York. Man said it's important." The dark-skinned man thrust the receiver into Kathryn's hand.

She didn't want to answer it. She was on the brink of something important. Something unexpected. Now, she had lost hold of it. Lost it like a dream that lay just below the threshold of consciousness.

"Yes. Yes. I'll take it."

Kathryn grasped the phone and held it against her breast as she sought to regain her composure.

Perhaps her memories would return later when she was alone.

His face dark, Flynt stood and walked toward the bar.

"Hello." When she heard the official voice on the other end, a smile spread over Kathryn's face.

"That's wonderful. Yes ... Yes ... I know ... I'll finish up here, then catch a plane early next week ... Yes sir..." Her voice grew more definite. "Of course ... I'm delighted to have the opportunity. Thank you, sir."

Filled with excitement, she dropped the telephone receiver in its cradle and rushed to join Flynt at the bar. Even his dull expression failed to diminish the thrill that pitched her senses to high frequency. She had hoped and dreamed this would happen, but she'd never expected it quite so quickly.

"I can hardly believe it." She spoke breathlessly. "That was Douglas Wheeler—the personnel director with Triple Gold." Kathryn slid onto the barstool next to Flynt. "I've got the job. Sooner than I ever expected. THE Job."

"Congratulations." Flynt's tone did not match the sentiment. He fiddled with his glass. "You're leaving right away?"

"Yes. I have to. The man I'm replacing is retiring in two weeks. Triple Gold wants me to work with him until he leaves." Suddenly she was aware of Flynt's mood. A mountainous lump formed in her throat. "You don't want me to go," she murmured.

Instead of answering, Flynt ordered another drink. A double rum and tonic.

The bland, serious expression on Flynt's face reminded her of another time and place. When? Where? It was there again, something else she couldn't quite grasp.

Since arriving in Jamaica, she'd gone off on wild, impossible tangents. Maybe it was best that in a few days, she'd be putting plenty of distance between herself and this strange country that had brought unsettling events and images into her life. A land of Obeah and Rastafarians. Dreams. Reincarnation.

All at once, acid etched the lining of her stomach. Her fingers gripped the glass as she tried to marshal her thoughts.

What was wrong with her? For years this job had been her goal. She should be celebrating, yet she had lost her taste for it.

"I have to start closing things down," she whispered.

"Good luck with your life." Hurt filled Flynt's eyes. Gulping down his drink, he rose straight up from the seat and strode toward the outside door. "I have to get back to Kingston."

When Flynt pushed through the entrance, a cold rush of air fell across Kathryn's shoulders. Flynt had not said goodbye. He had not even tried to kiss her.

CHAPTER NINETEEN

AFTER SHE MADE necessary arrangements with management at Hibiscus Hall, Kathryn reserved a seat on a flight to New York on Monday. Then, she went to her room to start packing.

Somehow, she could not pull the suitcases from the closet without first going onto the balcony to look at the starlit night sky. Leaning on the railing, Kathryn inhaled the clear air, an opportunity she would no longer have once she returned to the city. A breeze filled with floral fragrances wafted across her.

Kathryn could not tell what flowers they were. It really didn't matter, because she knew she did not smell the scent of roses and probably never would again.

Beneath brilliant twinkling stars on a black velvet backdrop, she heard the surf rise and fall in hypnotic rhythm. The beat of surf against the sand seemed to hold a message for her, she realized suddenly. The rhythmic pounding reminded her of something she had started but had yet to finish—the tapes.

Kathryn could not leave Jamaica without listening to all the tapes Rita Grey had given her to try. She had to discover for herself what her lapses at Rose Hall meant, and she had to learn more about the identity of Aimee White. And she wanted to smell the roses one more time.

She hurried inside her room and went directly to the hypnotic regression tape that sat atop the pile of audio equipment on her bedside table. Although regression both intrigued and puzzled her, Kathryn had put off trying it, because the thought of losing control intimidated her.

But when she focused on the plastic box, Kathryn could not drag her eyes away. Could hypnotic regression provide answers for her? Rita Grey had insisted it could help her.

Perhaps she was afraid the visions would hammer inside her head once more, and she'd be caught up in them with no one nearby to rescue her.

Kathryn picked up the plastic box and turned it over to study the cupped hands that held a glowing ball of blue light. The cover picture seemed ominous.

"I have to do this," she whispered.

Kathryn knew if she did not, the weeks spent in Jamaica would always haunt her. For the rest of her life, she would fear going back to the island. And for the rest of her life, she would wonder about the powerful feelings she had for Flynt Kincade.

Her mind made up, Kathryn removed the tape from its holder—this time without looking at the cover. Placing the small earphone set snuggly in place, she laid on her back in the middle of the bed.

To her surprise, the tape held no background music and no lead in. "Close your eyes. Listen to the sound of my voice." The man's words droned in a low-pitched monotone that soon put her in a sleepy haze.

"Inhale deeply ... through your nose ... Exhale slowly ... completely ... through your mouth ... Good ... Once more ... Breathe in very deeply..."

Kathryn balanced on the edge between sleep and wakefulness. Drowsily, she followed the directions from the tape.

"Imagine a blank piece of white paper hanging before you ... Your mind is blank and glows white like the paper ... Erase everything from your thoughts ... You see only a blank white space..."

Even in her half-conscious state, Kathryn had to struggle to put aside stray thoughts that tried to invade her mind.

"Now, you are going to relax ... Your body is light and floating ... Imagine your toes are like a cloud ... Every muscle is relaxed ... Your feet are feather light and floating ... So relaxed ... So at ease with yourself..." The voice continued the procedure from the tips of her toes to the top of her head until, through his words, each body part was relaxed and covered by a protective white light.

"So relaxed ... Now you are ready to count backward," the voice said.

"Ten, nine, eight, seven, six, five, four, three, two, one."

Her mind blank, Kathryn floated.

"Deeper, deeper ... Down deeper ... Down ..."

Enveloped in the protective white light, she continued to float aimlessly in a dark void.

"You may remove from your store of sub-conscious memories anything you wish. You are free to experience anything that has ever happened to you in any lifetime. You are free to find an event meaningful to you in your present life.

"Nothing you will experience from a past lifetime will have the power to harm you now. The glowing pure white light will surround and protect you at all times. You will remain on the outside, as if viewing your past life on a television screen.

"Take a long breath ... Allow the images to flow now ... So many images ... Deeper, deeper ... You are walking down a long, narrow hallway ... A closed door stands at the far end ... When you reach the door, you will open it ... When you open that door, you will become the person in a lifetime most meaningful to your present ... Do you see the door? ... Walk toward it ... You are ready to open that door ... Open it now..."

The doorknob was cold in Kathryn's fingers, but she squeezed hard and turned it. Effortlessly, the door swung wide. With weightless grace, Kathryn glided through the opening.

"Where are you? ... Do you see yourself? ..." the distant voice asked.

Kathryn felt an unsteady rhythmic bumping beneath her body. It wasn't like a television screen at all. She looked down and found herself seated on a saddle, riding on the back of a shiny brown horse. The sturdy, muscular animal moved beneath her with confident stride. Someone else, another woman, rode a large black steed that galloped directly in front of her. She had trouble keeping up. It was her Aunt Annie, wearing a white dress, her long, dark hair flowing loose behind her.

"What is your name?"

"Aimee ... Aimee White ..." The words came like whispers from the air.

"How old are you now?"

Sixteen, she heard herself think.

In the thick inky night, the dark-haired woman pulled her horse to a sudden halt. Reluctantly, she drew her own mount to a standstill beside the shining black horse that in nervous agitation switched its tail. The two women dismounted and walked through the meadow grass toward a cottage.

"Now, Aimee, I shall show you the ways of Haitian voodoo."

Aunt Annie laughed in a wild, frenzied pitch that made Aimee's blood go cold. Knowing she wanted nothing to do with voodoo or with her aunt's crazy rituals, she edged backward. But Annie grabbed her wrist and dragged her along, forcing her to keep pace.

When they opened the door to the cottage, a cool rush of rancid air struck their faces. Frightened, Aimee tried to pull back, but her aunt held a tight grip on her arm. "Not now, my dear."

Thick smoke clouded the room. Aimee could barely make out the forms of five men standing by a square table. On the table, there was something ... something Aimee didn't want to see. An animal. Dear God. It was a dog. It belonged to Uncle Lucci, the old slave man. The men were cutting it apart. Aimee's stomach turned inside out. She tried to go back to the door, but Annie prevented her.

"No. This will be a good lesson for you, Aimee White." The woman reached for a bowl. She took a sip from it and handed it to Aimee. The liquid was warm and red.

Smoke filled her head, and Aimee's knees collapsed beneath her. Everything around her grew dark. She could not bear to be there. Not again.

"You will go forward two years ... Your impressions now are clearer, even stronger than before ..." she heard the far-off voice tell her ...

The darkness vanished, and Aimee stood in the bright sunlight.

"Look down at yourself and look all around you."

She stared down at the pale pink dress that draped in a wide swirl to the floor. A bright red ribbon decorated her narrow waist. Young men and women, all in lavish ballroom attire, stood chatting nearby.

"How old are you?"

Through a haze, she heard the question, and she knew at once she was eighteen years old.

"Are you indoors or outside?"

On the portico, she answered in her mind. She was standing on the portico at Rose Hall in Jamaica. She dragged her fingers through the ends of her long, golden blonde hair. Even in the sunshine, she sensed an air of sadness all around.

"Aimee. I've been looking for you." The handsome man who spoke to her was tall and dark-haired. His body exuded such glowing warmth it felt good to stand near him.

With a firm grip, he pulled her aside, away from the crowd and into the shadows. "I had to see you." His hands were in her hair, stroking, tilting her chin upward. His lips met hers then his hands were beneath her buttocks, lifting her upward, against him, close into his chest.

"I love you, Aimee White. You are the woman I see when I walk through the fields here at Rose Hall. You are the woman always in my mind."

Her small, frail arms encircled his neck. She clung tightly to him, not wanting to let go.

"Come, Aimee. We will go to our place. Our place by the waterfall."

Without saying a word, she followed him, like she always did, like she had since she arrived from England. There was solace at the waterfall, their waterfall. It was their secret retreat where no one else would come to disturb them.

They had been there many times before, but, in the past, they merely sat together holding hands and talking. Aimee needed companionship, for torturous beatings and death had become part of daily life at Rose Hall Plantation.

This day was different. She knew that when she left the others to go with William. Today was safer than other days, because Aunt Annie had found a new man, one recently arrived from England. She would never notice her niece was gone.

Fire burned on both their lips as William kissed Aimee beside the waterfall. With steady fingers, he pulled loose a ribbon and pushed aside a film of silk to reveal the swelling mounds of firm young breasts. His warm mouth followed his fingers, as he slowly, methodically moved away each remnant of clothing until she stood naked in the sunlight before him.

Aimee's heart raced as she pushed and pulled against the hindering garments that covered his sleek body. Sleek as a fine stallion, she thought, when at last he stood naked with her. Her eyes bright, Aimee descended, without hesitation, when William led her beneath the small, rippling waterfall that tumbled in a soothing rush over them both.

Hair flattened against their heads, barely able to breathe, they kissed beneath the stream of water, and at once an unfamiliar surge of desire overcame Aimee.

"Please," she whispered against his cheek. "Please love me now."

Aimee knew this was their last chance to be together. Already, she had decided what she must do, and she planned to do it soon. She knew now that she and William could never marry, for, if they did, she would be held prisoner by Rose Hall forever. Or worse yet, she would be sent back to England.

His matted chest hair pressed roughly against her soft breasts, William's embrace encompassed her.

Instinctively, Aimee touched and caressed William's face, his body. "I ... I ... want you." Her breath came in halting gasps.

"Are you certain?" William's hands lightly traced the fluid curves of her body.

"Yes, yes. I am certain. Please." Water splashed over her face and into her mouth.

"I want you more than life," he whispered.

William tilted her breast to his mouth and drew her inside so deep she began to feel faint. All the while, he ran his fingers through her heavy curtain of dripping wet hair.

With one hand, he directed the water to flow down the length of her body. "I do not wish you to be sorry. Not ever."

As warmth washed deep inside her, Aimee thrust her slim hips harshly against him, forcing his decision sooner than he wished. It was too late, and he found it impossible to stop. For William, when they came together, they were bonded forever. For Aimee, it was their last chance, though he did not know it.

"Aimee, I could not love you more."

Together, they slipped from beneath the waterfall to a knoll of damp green grass. William spread a cloak on the ground, then sank down upon it and gently lowered Aimee's firm naked body on top of his. All too soon, it was over. They lay together in the grass.

"I hope you will not regret today," he said. His china blue eyes glowed in the sunlight.

"I shall never be sorry." Aimee sighed. "I shall remember this day forever."

"You love me; I cannot doubt that, Aimee." His lips moved roughly against hers. Moments later, he pulled back and gazed seriously into her eyes. "Please say you will marry me."

"More than life, I wish I could tell you that, but William, I cannot." How it hurt to tell him that this would be their only afternoon together. One afternoon to last a lifetime. "I am going to marry Richard Gordon."

Tears gathered in her eyes.

At her words, William recoiled from Aimee. "Richard Gordon." He sat up straight. "But you do not love him. We both know you do not."

She willed herself not to cry. "That does not matter."

"Love. You cannot tell me that love does not matter." Disappointment and frustration echoed all around him.

"Yes. No." Her head fell against his chest. "Richard owns Gordon Gardens, so he can take me away from Aunt Annie, away from Rose Hall."

"I could take you back to England. You would be safe from her there." His powerful hands wrapped her shoulders. "We could be together there."

"No. I shall not go back and live in poverty. I shall marry Richard Gordon. He will give me everything I want."

Hurt gleamed in William's eyes. "No. He cannot give you everything. He can give you money and clothing, but he will not give you the love you deserve. I know too much that you do not about Richard Gordon." Sadly, he turned his head and looked across the fields. "He will never make you happy."

Tears welled up in her eyes. "Oh, William. We have had one day. Some people have not even that. For me, there is no choice, because I have to leave Aunt Annie. There is no other choice; I must marry Richard."

Kathryn felt the tears burning hot in Aimee's eyes. "I cannot be happy in England. Money and clothes and a fine estate will have to be enough for me."

The tropical air cooled quickly when William Hill turned away from her. Don't go, her heart cried; don't go yet.

"Who are you with?"

From far away Kathryn heard the question and knew the answer. William Hill was the caretaker at Rose Hall. Aunt Annie had forbidden Aimee to see him because William had no money. It was Aunt Annie who had arranged for her to marry Richard Gordon.

From over the years and from another lifetime, Kathryn felt a surge of disgust and hatred for the aunt of Aimee White. The dreadful woman had beaten the slaves and tortured them, and she used bizarre forms of Obeah and voodoo to keep the slaves within her control. Besides that, she killed animals and drank their blood to cast her evil spells. Poor Uncle Lucci. Aunt Annie cast a spell on him, and he'd died.

William Hill was a kind man who cared about the poor black people.

He cared especially about the children and had even set up a school on the plantation for them. A school. Kathryn remembered all those things and could see the school as plain as day. She loved William so much that she had made love to him under the Rose Hall waterfall. But she couldn't marry him without going back to England to a life of meager means. Aimee White wanted to be rich.

"You will move ahead one month," the taped voice instructed. "What do you see now? Where are you?"

She wore a long white bridal gown. It was Aimee White's wedding day. She should be happy, but she wasn't. She was marrying Richard Gordon, a man she did not love.

A huge crowd of people ambled through the gardens at Rose Hall. They moved amidst the fragrance of hundreds of rose bushes in full bloom. She could see a man standing among the bushes. He was cutting off a blossom, a yellow bloom. As Aimee passed him, the man placed it in her hand. It was William Hill, and his eyes shone bright blue as a china cup.

"Rose blossoms and my love are all I can offer you," he whispered to Aimee. His words vibrated across two centuries, causing Kathryn to shudder.

"Now it is time to move ahead five years. Where are you? Are you happy?"

Once more, as the tape instructed her, Kathryn watched the scene shift. She was in a large room with many windows rising from floor to ceiling along one wall. Flimsy white curtains fluttered in the breeze across each opening. She lay in a very high bed, and her head ached terribly, her forehead was hot with fever. There was heaviness within her chest, as if an iron weight pressed against her ribcage.

When a tall man strode into the room, she recognized William Hill. He carried a large bouquet of yellow roses in the crook of his arm. With unexpected gentleness, he placed the flowers, one by one, in a vase on her bedside table. Tears rose in her eyes and with a feeble hand, she brushed them back.

He sat beside the bed, staring at Aimee.

"I am sorry Richard has made you unhappy," William told her as he shifted the roses a bit to perfect the arrangement. "At least, you have your little girl."

Aimee cast a wan smile at William. Her child was yet another secret she could not share. Leila had been born early in her marriage to Richard—

eight months to be exact. Richard never doubted she was his. To tell William the truth would rob Leila of her legacy from Richard. She was her only child, and Aimee would not live to see her daughter's fifth birthday. She was her only child, and she could not share her with the man she truly loved. A salty tear trickled down her cheek.

Both William's voice and his eyes revealed great sadness. "Richard cannot change his ways. Marriage has made him want even more women than before. Aimee, how much I wish things could be different. But I have only rose blossoms and my love to offer you. That love you shall have forever." William Hill bent over and kissed her tenderly on the forehead.

Like a vacant echo, the taped voice came through to Kathryn, and the scene diminished in clarity, then vanished. "Count slowly from one to five. On the count of five, you will awaken remembering all the positive details of this lifetime. The lesson you learned in this lifetime will be quite clear in your mind. That lesson will be a tool to help you in your present life.

"Count. One, two, three, four, five."

Kathryn became aware of a gray state that seemed to hang suspended between herself and reality.

"Awaken now fully refreshed and glad to be alive."

For a moment, Kathryn lay in a foggy haze, then she bolted straight up in her bed.

China blue eyes. Flynt. William Hill was Flynt. All at once, everything flashed crystal clear in her mind.

Every facet of the confusion Jamaica had brought to her life came into focus. Even the painting in the museum made sense. She had seen the fields in it—the sugarcane fields that held so much misery for the black slaves. The fields where fires burned and black people died. The Rose Hall sugarcane fields.

"Water is the breeding ground of all living things." That had been the slogan of those black slaves. It had been the rallying point that kept them together with their hopes alive. They had passed those words down over the years, generation to generation. Now, the slogan was still a part of the tradition of some Obeah practitioners such as Carole Brown, so she had it engraved on her silver bracelet.

William Hill—Flynt—cared about the uneducated slaves. She could see it all now. He had cared. Aimee had cared, too, but not enough to overcome her aunt. And, she was not strong physically or emotionally.

But Kathryn Calder was strong and capable of making wise choices, of having second chances.

Rita Grey was a wise woman, for she had given Kathryn the tools to clear away the confusing visions she was having. They were the tools to change her life.

His words came back to her and fell harshly on her ears. "That love you shall have forever." That's what William Hill promised Aimee White. In her memory, she could see him standing in a garden abundant with hibiscus bushes and roses.

Leila? She dismissed the thought. There was only so much she was ready to accept.

The taped words had instructed her to look for a lesson in the life recalled. She had found one.

Love is more important than wealth. Love is the most important thing in any lifetime. That was the lesson.

Nothing else matters, her mind screamed out. Certainly not material gain. Certainly not a job... Only love.

If you have love, any task is bearable.

A forceful tremor rocked through her body as Kathryn relived the vivid scene beneath the Rose Hall waterfall—a scene of love that Aimee knew would have to last forever.

Perhaps not. Sometimes people got second chances...

Kathryn's head reeled like an explosion had rearranged her thinking. How could she suddenly shift gears and change goals she'd had for as long as she could remember? She could, and she would. It was her life. She had a second chance. If only it was not too late.

A refreshing breeze blew in from the balcony and across Kathryn's face. A cloud lifted from her brain. She cared what Flynt thought. Only what Flynt thought.

Visions of Flynt Kincade paraded through her mind. Flynt Kincade, the teacher. Flynt Kincade, her lover. Flynt Kincade who asked her to stay in Jamaica. Flynt who was so clearly hurt by her decision to return to New York and her career.

Could it be true? Had Flynt in a life as William Hill offered her love, not wealth? Had she as Aimee White chosen wealth over love? Did it even matter? She still had time left to make a different choice in this lifetime. She had a chance to choose love, a chance for love to move across forever.

Kathryn sprang like a sprinter from the side of the bed and rushed toward Mara's room. She needed to borrow a car. She had to find Flynt before it was too late. Perhaps it already was.

As she knocked on the door, she knew nothing was more important in her life than gaining and keeping Flynt's love. If only it wasn't too late to have another chance.

CHAPTER TWENTY

THE DAY WAS hot, but Kathryn hardly noticed as she steered Mara's BMW toward Kingston, maneuvering expertly around the countless potholes.

Even though she had wanted to see the painting of Rose Hall Flynt had been eager to show her, until today, she had had no compelling interest in traveling to Jamaica's capital. Until today, she had been apprehensive about driving a car on the left side of the highway as was the custom in Jamaica.

But, her need to see Flynt took precedence over all else.

Memories ... Even memories from the distant past were difficult to put to rest ... Perhaps if those past mistakes could be rectified...

Kathryn stepped hard on the accelerator of the little red car. Thank goodness neither Fritz nor Mara had needed it for the weekend. Or had the desperation in her eyes caused them to cancel any plans?

"I am so happy that you will now go," Mara had told Kathryn as she handed her the keys. "It is good that you go to Flynt. He is a good man. Fritz and I, that is what we agree."

What if Flynt did not care to see her? Surely it would be a blow to any man's ego for a woman to choose a job over being with him.

When she looked in the rearview mirror, Kathryn noticed a black sedan pulling close to her. From where had the car come on the nearly deserted road, she wondered.

She sped up a bit, and the sedan did the same, maintaining only a short distance between them.

Uneasy, Kathryn tried to see what the driver looked like, but the windows of the vehicle had dark tinted glass. When she came to a small village, she deliberately cut through a side street and lost sight of the black sedan.

Back on the main road, she accelerated as much as she dared, considering the rugged road conditions. Before long, she found herself analyzing her first effort with self-hypnotic regression. Since Flynt had not reacted favorably when she asked his opinion on reincarnation, Kathryn thought she would not tell him about her regression. Not today. Perhaps never.

Even Dr. Pettersen, in his book, had pronounced his own skepticism about most regression experiences. He expressed a belief that only a few cases are valid. Kathryn couldn't help but wonder what he might think of the variety of episodes that were about to alter the course of her life.

Whatever they were, the visions in her regression had given her a valuable message. She was thankful to Rita Grey for opening the door to self-hypnosis. Whether or not anyone else believed in reincarnation mattered little to her. She had learned the lesson of a lifetime.

To reach the university campus at Mona, Kathryn had to drive through Kingston. She decided to stop and seek directions from an elderly gentleman she saw along the road. He located a map inside his own car and gave it to her.

Something in the rearview mirror attracted her attention as she pulled away from the curb, and Kathryn wondered briefly if it might be the black sedan. But since she was close to the campus, Kathryn was not too concerned.

With the map's help, she drove through the university's main entrance, past a chapel and into an area of lush vegetation. Kathryn pulled the car to a stop and looked around the unfamiliar surroundings.

Flynt had told her a little about the campus and its strange history. During World War II, wooden buildings there had housed more than a thousand Jewish refugees. The university began several years after the war ended and was operated as an affiliate of London University. Later, it became an independent college, granting its own degrees.

Today, silence hung like a leaden blanket over the university. Since it was Sunday, the grounds stood quiet, serene and vacant. How ghostly things seemed.

As she stood alone, Kathryn could imagine Annie Palmer and Aimee White, dressed in long skirts, riding horses across the green grass. And, she could imagine William Hill tending the flowers. But they had lived on another part of the island. Perhaps they had never come to Kingston.

When a shadow moved across the grass, Kathryn paid it no mind, thinking it was her imagination running free with visions of Aimee White's world.

Kathryn rubbed the back of one hand over her eyes. She had no idea where to look for Flynt. Across the lawn, she saw a building that appeared to house classrooms. It looked like a promising place to begin her search for Flynt. As she hurried across the lawn, another shadow caught her attention. But when she stopped and looked around, she saw nothing. Her imagination again.

Discovering an unlocked entrance door, Kathryn went down a hallway looking for an office that might be Flynt's, but she found none. When she started up the stairwell, she heard distinct creaks on the stairs below. She squinted to peer into the dim staircase, saw nothing, shrugged and continued up.

On the next floor, several small rooms served as offices. She checked the names on each door. Flynt's was not there.

It was not until she reached another level that Kathryn found a room that matched Flynt's description of where he taught classes. The small office space next to it had a card with his name attached to the door. Both the classroom and his office were locked.

Although she heard no sounds from the inside, Kathryn knocked on the office door hopefully. Only more silence came in answer.

An icy anxiety gripped her heart. Why had she let matters come to this? Deep inside, she had always known she did not want to leave Jamaica. Not while Flynt was still here. But she had not told him she would be willing to stay.

Then that phone call came, and she accepted the job automatically— without a second thought. No wonder Flynt rushed away. Who would blame him? She could not.

That she had not found Flynt where she hoped made her ache even more to see him. As she considered her next move, she heard creaks on the stairs, the distinct sounds of someone's approach. Hope sprang to her heart, and she hurried to the landing to look down. Before she could see, a heavy arm swung to meet her and caught her in the back. Wind knocked from her, she dropped to the floor and caught hold of the railing to keep from plunging down the steps.

Who was her attacker?

He was on her again. This time, Kathryn ducked beneath his arm and twisted to escape another blow. Heart beating wildly, she pitched down the stairs, sliding over the steps, hitting them hard one by one, bruising and battering her bottom. When she reached the ground floor, she grabbed for the door handle. But she was too late. His hand came down on hers and prevented her from opening it.

Heart in her throat, she turned to see the man with wild dreadlocks hovering over her. He was one of the three men she had seen in the Blue Mountains. Apparently, the boy had not gotten the message to him.

With a sudden spurt of force, Kathryn lifted her high-heeled shoe and hammered it down on his sandal-clad foot. While he rebounded from the blow, she yanked the door open and raced onto the open grounds. Immediately, the man ran out behind her.

She tried to scream, but no sound came out. She was almost at the car when the man caught her, wrapped his arms around her shoulders and clamped a lean, bony hand on her mouth.

Kathryn heard a dull thud and felt her captor go limp and fall away from her. Her body aching, she turned and found Flynt holding the subdued Rastafarian rebel.

Soon afterward, the grounds were buzzing with campus security and the police. Flynt took care of all the details in answering questions and seeing to the arrest of her attacker. While the boy had been too young, she thought, to be jailed, this man was in his early thirties and had a police record.

"Stay here," Flynt whispered and kissed her on the forehead.

Heart still pounding, she brushed her clothing and cleaned up a gash in her leg from her rushed tumble down the stairs.

Then, with a security guard nearby, Kathryn dropped down to sit, legs crossed on the manicured campus lawn. When she looked beyond the green at the university chapel and studied the old stone edifice, a strange feeling struck her.

This was a scene she had seen before. Could it be possible? Had Aimee White visited the University of the West Indies? That seemed quite unlikely.

Fumbling for her map, Kathryn looked on the back for descriptions of distinctive landmarks. The University of the West Indies was founded in 1948, like Flynt had told her. That wasn't anywhere near the time period in which Aimee White must have lived.

Reading on, Kathryn discovered a significant fact. The chapel had once been an old sugar warehouse located at Gales Valley estate in Trelawny. It was disassembled stone by stone and brought to Mona where it was constructed exactly as the warehouse had been built originally. Chills shot through Kathryn. Was she having yet another deja vu experience?

Dazed, she pushed up from the ground and edged closer to the building to examine it for more clues. She hoped to find a cornerstone or something else of significance. When she peered up at the top of the pediment, she saw a name and a date beneath the roof. "Edward Morant Gale 1799."

Beads of perspiration seeped from her forehead, yet her face and hands felt cold and clammy. The book about Rose Hall had led her to believe that Aimee White had lived around the turn of the nineteenth century— about two hundred years ago.

Because Trelawny parish was located next to James parish, she could have visited the Gales Valley estate. It was indeed possible that Aimee White could have seen this building.

William Hill might have seen it, too. A quiver of anticipation began in her stomach and rose into Kathryn's throat. If only Flynt would come. How she longed to see him.

She heard a car drive up behind the building and stop. She waited, listened and looked for someone walking toward her. No one came.

Frustrated, Kathryn sat and stared at the impersonal stone wall, then at the indifferent security guard. She glanced at her watch. It seemed she had been sitting in the grass for hours.

Then she saw him. Tall, with a long stride, he moved smoothly across the low-cut, manicured lawn toward his classroom building. Her heart caught in her throat.

Flynt had saved her from the Rastafarian who attacked her, but how should she approach him now? Would he accept her apology or was it too late for them?

Never too late, a tiny voice inside her head seemed to say. Not if she had loved him two hundred years before. Not if she still loved him now.

A breath became a sigh that blew like satin through her lips.

"I love Flynt."

She pressed her fingers into the grass and pushed to a standing position. Then, she was running, high heels digging into damp earth, blue skirt caressing her knees and flying like a kite behind.

"Flynt. I need to talk." Kathryn's voice caught in the air and seemed to travel in slow motion before striking Flynt's ears.

"Kathryn, what if I hadn't come along?" he asked.

His eyes wore a perplexed veil of gray over the blue, and no smile cut through the hard line of his lips. His expression was that of a disciplinarian who would stand for no foolishness in his classes.

She had never seen that look before and did not like it.

"I came to find you." Her slender fingers gripped his wrist.

"Why? There's nothing left to say." He looked down into her face. "You're leaving tomorrow."

Kathryn was unprepared for the hurt evident in the harsh line of his jaw and in the twist of his lips. How like the expression on William Hill's face. How like her vision of him then.

"I don't understand, Kathryn." Flynt caught her by the crook of her arm and guided her with him. His touch was not that of a friend or a lover. She did not like the cool aloofness she felt. Was it too late for forever?

"I came to talk," Kathryn whispered. But, how could she talk when the knot in her throat was growing bigger, and she knew no way to dissolve it?

"All right. We'll go to my office." Flynt propelled her through the door and up the stairs.

The office was quiet and very dark. Kathryn could barely make out the titles of the books on Flynt's shelves, but she noted there were histories of many of the Caribbean islands and volumes on island politics and government. Education had become his life. To be part of it, she had to accept his need to teach. She had to accept his goal—this time around.

"Please have a seat."

Flynt gestured toward a straight wooden chair on the other side of the small room. He sat in a swivel chair behind the desk.

"I didn't tell you what happened at the crafts market," she began.

"No, you didn't." His formality cut her to the bone.

"One of the Rastas approached me."

He lifted one eyebrow, and a vertical frown creased lines in his forehead above his nose.

"Part of the mystery was solved," she told him solemnly. "He thought I was a member of an opposing Rastafarian group called the Locksmen. He called me a danger woman." Kathryn chuckled softly. "He and his friends have been following me since I went to the mountains with Carole Brown.

They wanted to warn me off and were behind all the odd things that have happened since then."

"Like the beach attack and that peculiar vial."

"Yes."

"Did you have him arrested?"

"No, he was merely a boy, only fourteen. He promised not to bother me again and was going to get the word to his friends." She shrugged. "Guess he didn't.

"He's someone you can help. I know you want to work with the people. He's young enough for someone like you to make a difference."

"But you said ..."

"I was wrong. Now I have reconsidered my priorities."

"Priorities?"

"Yes. You asked if I would consider staying in Jamaica."

A light began to invade the shadow on his face. "That was before you got that damn telephone call." He stared into her eyes. "I'm sorry, but that's the way I feel about it." He kicked the pedestal of his chair.

"If it's not too late to change my mind, I'd like to stay." Kathryn's words came as a soft drawl.

"In Jamaica?" His eyes brightened until they glowed china blue once more. A grin turned up the corners of his lips.

"Jamaica ... or wherever you are."

"But, your job? The big opportunity..."

"I've thought about that." Her gaze polarized with his and would not let go. "I've already reached my goal—the job was offered. I'm going to turn it down."

"You would turn it down?" She nodded.

"But what about the city? I thought ..."

"I've learned a lot these past weeks in Jamaica," she murmured. "Things I once thought important aren't important after all."

Flynt stood and settled his hand over hers. In the dim light of his office, he was aware of the heat and the tremor. "Kathryn, Kathryn. I never thought I'd hear you say that ... Not after last night." He moved from behind the desk and lifted her to her feet, then drew her tight against him.

"I've been foolish before, but not this time," she whispered into Flynt's damp cotton shirt.

"Enough talk," he rasped. His lips traced feathers in her hair and stopped in the center of her forehead. Then, he kissed each temple before finding her lips.

"I love you." Flynt's breath was like a campfire, warm and comforting. How she had longed to hear those words from him.

"I love you, too." How glad she was to realize her true feelings while there still was time. "Rose blossoms and love are the most important things in life," she sighed.

"Rose blossoms?"

"Yes. They can last forever." Kathryn smiled. Rose blossoms from far memory, she thought.

"I don't understand what you're talking about, but that doesn't matter. Not now." While holding tightly to one hand, Flynt dropped his arm from around her and reached for a desk drawer. He pulled a white box from inside it and placed it in Kathryn's hands. "I got this for you last week," he said. "I didn't think I'd ever have the chance to give it to you."

Kathryn opened the box. A brightly polished silver bracelet lay on a blue velvet cushion. It was like the one Carole Brown had loaned her, but the outside edges were more rounded and delicately carved with hibiscus flowers.

"Read what it says inside," he directed.

"Water is the breeding ground of all living things," the etched inscription said.

Kathryn gazed at Flynt with curiosity in her eyes.

"Carole Brown told me what was inscribed in her bracelet. She said it had great meaning for you, so I thought you should have one of your own."

She thought of the slaves and of Africa. "Yes, it does. I've learned quite a lot here in Jamaica, more than I ever believed possible. Thank you."

For a moment she studied his face. Then their lips came together in another long kiss. Kathryn knew happiness lay ahead for them together no matter where they lived. Happiness they had failed to find long ago.

Perhaps one day she would tell him of her vision and their waterfall love scene. Perhaps there would even be another Leila.

"Will you marry me, Kathryn?"

For her, it was like deja vu, and every happiness she had ever dreamed circled together.

"Yes. Yes, Flynt."

Instantly, an idea jumped into her head. "Let's get married here in Jamaica, beneath the Rose Hall waterfall."

Their bodies molded together, Flynt stared into her eyes with a look that two hundred years had failed to tear away.

In that moment, everything she knew of Flynt and of William Hill blended together. A deluge of perfume surrounded them—the perfume of roses at the peak of their bloom. And in her mind's eye, Kathryn could see the flowers. This time, they were red, not yellow.

Kathryn thought, hibiscus blossoms are fleeting, but roses and their love would last forever. Their hearts had crossed forever and come together again.

Hearts Across Forever is part of *Passenger to Paradise*, a series of novels from Mary Montague Sikes which take the reader to exotic places.

Read other *Passenger to Paradise* novels....

Eagle Rising, set is Sedona, AZ,
Stranger in My Heart, set in Trinidad,
Secrets by the Sea, set in Antigua, and
Jungle Jeopardy, set in Central America.

ABOUT THE AUTHOR

Mary Montague Sikes is an award-winning author of eight non-fiction books and nine novels. Holder of a BA degree in psychology from the University of Mary Washington and an MFA in painting from Virginia Commonwealth University, Sikes also studied painting, sculpture, printmaking and more at the College of William & Mary. A freelance writer and photographer, she has authored hundreds of articles and photographs published in local, regional, and national newspapers and international magazines.

An award-winning artist, Sikes has shown her paintings in the United States, Canada, and the Caribbean. Her coffee table book, *Hotels to Remember*, was included in a Virginia Festival of the Book travel panel.

An Artful Animal Alphabet, a hardcover children's book, features her writing and paintings. Her fascination with the spiritual is evident in her book, *Spirit Visions Soul Songs*, published in 2018. *Hearts Across Forever* also delves into her spiritual interests. She calls this novel, "the book of my heart."

Sikes lives with her husband in a wooded landscape overlooking a small Virginia creek that she believes Captain John Smith once explored by shallop. Sikes and her husband have three grown daughters.

www.marymontaguesikes.com
http://marymontaguesikes.blogspot.com

OTHER BOOKS BY MARY MONTAGUE SIKES

Hearts Across Forever, Oak Tree, 2001
Hotels to Remember, Oak Tree, 2002
Published, Now $ell It, Bookwaves, 2005
Eagle Rising, Oak Tree, 2007
Night Watch, Oak Tree, 2010
Secrets by the Sea, Oak Tree, 2008
Dangerous Hearts, Red Rose Publishing, 2009
Jungle Jeopardy, Oak Tree,
A Rainbow for Christmas, Oak Tree
Daddy's Christmas Angel, Oak Tree
Evening of the Dragonfly, Oak Tree
The Jefferson Hotel, A Snapshot in Time, Oak Tree
The Homestead, A Snapshot in Time, Oak Tree
Hilltop House, A Snapshot in Time, Oak Tree
Hotel DuPont, A Snapshot in Time, Oak Tree
Williamsburg Inn, A Snapshot in Time, Oak Tree
Scenic James River, A Snapshot in Time, Oak Tree
An Artful Animal Alphabet, Aakenbaaken & Kent, 2017
Spirit Visions Soul Songs, Amazon, 2018

Anthologies

Happy Birthday, Mr. Lincoln, National League of American Pen Women, 2009
The Corner Café, 2012
Harboring Secrets, Chesapeake Bay Writers, 2013
Recipes by the Book, Oak Tree Authors, 2018 (The author's cover art in addition to recipes)